WHAT DARKNESS DOES

BOOKS BY JENNIFER GRAESER DORNBUSH

THE CORONER'S DAUGHTER MYSTERY SERIES

The Coroner

Secret Remains

Last One Alive

Frozen Lives

What Darkness Does

THE MUSIC AND MURDER MYSTERY SERIES

Hotel California (anthology)

Thriller (anthology)

STANDALONE NOVELS

God Bless the Broken Road

Hole in the Woods

NONFICTION

Forensic Speak: How to Write Realistic Crime Dramas

WHAT DARKNESS DOES

JENNIFER GRAESER DORNBUSH

Published in 2025 by Blackstone Publishing
Cover and book design by Larissa Ezell

Printed in the United States of America

First edition: 2025
ISBN 979-8-228-62961-5
Fiction / Mystery & Detective / Women Sleuths

Version 1

Blackstone Publishing
31 Mistletoe Rd.
Ashland, OR 97520

www.BlackstonePublishing.com

CHAPTER 1

Savannah shivered. Temperatures during these last nights of October had plunged below forty degrees, and all she had on was a light T-shirt and jeans. Her panicked mind couldn't focus, and fear dried her tears as she looked at the monster sitting across from her in the fishing boat.

She pleaded with the man, "Please don't kill me. I'll drop the charges. You'll be free."

"Put out your arms," he demanded.

Defiantly, Savannah pressed her arms to her sides, but he almost tore her shoulders out of their sockets as he yanked her arms behind her back and wrapped her wrists with duct tape.

He also ran a line of rope around her torso. As he bound her, he rambled unintelligible words in a nonsense stream of consciousness. He attached the rope to a cement block in the bottom of the boat.

The middle-aged man had unexpectedly shown up at Jonah's house a few hours ago. Now Jonah was dead, murdered. Jonah had always feared him but also taken pity on him, sometimes letting him hang out. He'd mentioned the guy couldn't help his past, but he'd also thought he should be sent to a nuthouse. Tonight the man had proved far more dangerous than either of them had realized.

Now, for Savannah, death seemed inevitable. But she still fought.

"Please! Let me li—!" she screamed. The word *live* was smothered as he stretched tape across her mouth, then crisscrossed it over her face to cover her eyes, leaving her nostrils uncovered. Under the adhesive, Savannah wailed her last plea.

He smacked her across the head, then grabbed the cement block and tossed it overboard into the lake. Savannah was yanked in after it and sank in the frigid water, pulled down by its weight.

No. Not like this!

Her system went into shock as her throat closed, a natural reaction of her epiglottis. He had wanted her to suffer. Her respiratory system convulsed, and she felt a terrible thirst. As the last molecules of oxygen in her brain were extinguished, a prayer rose in her mind.

May God's face shine on you and be gracious to you.

These same words had comforted her in those emotionally fraught days early in her unplanned, unwanted pregnancy. Of course, her feelings toward the baby had evolved. Now she gave the last gift a dying mother could offer as she prayed for her baby girl, hoping this blessing would reach her.

May He give you His peace, Brooklyn.

CHAPTER 2

A thin band of dawn was cracking open the horizon when Colton Chauncey returned to Jonah Hampton's trailer after his body dump at Lake Isabella. This morning, before it was light, he planned to remove Jonah's body and bury it deep in the woods behind the trailer. But as he lifted the bloated body by the ankles to drag it out of the kitchen, he was stopped by a sound from one of the back bedrooms.

Crying.

A baby's crying.

No.

He was hearing things.

The crying picked up, distinctively human and infant.

He followed the cry to the master bedroom and found the baby cradled in a laundry basket's pile of clothes at the back of the closet. After he drew the basket out, the baby settled, staring up at him in expectation.

Colton studied the infant's face—and though he'd never seen this baby before, an instant connection surged through him. Was this his daughter? He was surprised to see parts of himself in the roundness of the blue eyes, the thinness of the lips that drew up into a smile . . . at him.

The baby let out a gurgle and wriggled in her blanket cocoon. Colton had never thought much about having a baby of his own and was struck by how much this one looked like him. He'd realized some time ago that the timing lined up. His primal instinct seized him, but he shook it off. He couldn't have a kid. Not now. But he also couldn't leave the baby here. And he couldn't kill it. Even he had limits.

He tucked the infant under his arm like a football and grabbed the baby's bag from the bed, his mind in such a state of disarray that he sailed out the door, leaving dead Jonah on the kitchen floor and locking up behind him. No one was looking for this slob. Colton could finish the job later.

As he headed to his truck, the baby began crying. He set her in the back seat because he remembered that kids weren't supposed to ride in front. She flailed her little arms and let out a fierce wail that pierced his ears. He dug into the bag for a bottle or a pacifier, anything to shove into that baby's mouth to get her to shut up. The pacifier worked. He slammed the back door and got into the driver's side. By the time he started the engine, she was wailing again. He reinserted the pacifier.

Hurry. Just get outta here.

He threw the car into drive, peeled out, and heard a thunk.

Damn it.

A glance back confirmed the baby was on the floor, face red and mouth wide open in shock. The scream that emerged was deafening. He stopped the car and went around to help her. The baby seemed unhurt. The pacifier did its job again as he tucked her into a blanket and secured a seat belt around her midsection.

As he pulled out, more cautiously this time, onto the dirt

road, a thought emerged. A lot of people needed babies. He heard they paid good money for them too. He was owed something for Savannah Browdey wreaking havoc in his life and nearly sending him to prison. Colton's foot pressed harder on the gas pedal.

CHAPTER 3

The next Friday fell in early November, just a hair over six weeks since Nick had mysteriously shown up at Dr. Emily Hartford's family orchard after being pronounced dead by the FBI less than a year earlier. Today, in the midmorning hours, Emily piloted her new black Yukon along the back roads of Freeport County, Michigan, where she lived and served as medical examiner. Her destination was an hour south, a psychiatric ward in Rock River, where Nick was being released.

She should feel eager and excited that today he would be getting out and starting his new life. Instead, she was wary. Based on the last six weeks and yesterday's short phone call with him, Emily had no idea what kind of Nick would be returning to Freeport and taking up residence back at his lake house, which, fortunately for him, his mother had not sold after news of his alleged death in China.

Emily had only been able to see Nick for two brief visits since that incredible day he'd appeared before her looking like the walking dead on September 19, her thirtieth birthday. After their emotional reunion, his physical and mental recovery had taken center stage. Although neither of them stated it explicitly, they prioritized his healing process over exploring whether the two of them could pick up where they'd left off before he'd entered the FBI. His lack of communication from the hospital made it apparent that this was not the same Nick who'd left his Freeport County Sheriff's post for a larger adventure; before, he'd been a man utterly devoted to Emily.

Little was known except that, over a year ago, he'd been held at an undisclosed location in Beijing, China. When he'd shown up alive at the Hartford home forty-five days ago, he could barely string together a sentence. Rail thin, malnourished, and delirious from dehydration after a harrowing journey around the globe, Nick had collapsed in Emily's arms. She'd called 911 for an ambulance to Freeport Hospital, where he was stabilized before being transferred later that day to the larger medical facility in Rock River.

After seeing him through admittance, Emily had been summoned back to Freeport on a vehicle-fatality investigation. Bernadette, his mother, was eager to take over, having almost lost her only son. Events seemed to escape Emily's control soon after she'd phoned his supervisor, Agent Roger Roe, to let him know where his missing agent had turned up.

Agent Roe was head of the intelligence division at the Detroit FBI office. He and a team of FBI psychiatrists rushed to the Rock River Memorial Hospital from the regional FBI office in Detroit to perform an examination and debrief. Due to Nick's weakness and incoherence, it took several days to evaluate him. During that time, neither Emily nor Bernadette had been allowed to see him. Whatever intel Nick was able to disclose was confidential.

After another battery of physical and mental tests, he was transferred to an inpatient rehab facility and given twenty-four-hour security guards. Even if Nick had been up to seeing her more than twice over the last six weeks, nothing about any of their conversations would have been private.

The real cause of Emily's alienation came after his admittance to the inpatient facility, when Nick relayed to Emily through Bernadette that he wanted a few weeks on his own to recoup. He sent his mother away as well. The FBI's psychiatrist tried to comfort the two women by assuring them this behavior was not unusual for people experiencing post-traumatic stress disorder—or PTSD.

Over countless pots of coffee, Emily and Bernadette commiserated while speculating about what had happened to Nick in China as the FBI's Beijing attaché. These discussions were hardly reassuring.

Those mind-numbing days turned into a couple of weeks. Emily went back to the hospital to bring Nick clean clothes and a new phone charger, and barely any words were spoken between them. Emily had wondered when she'd ever felt more alone. It possibly seemed even worse than when she'd thought Nick was dead.

Then yesterday, unexpectedly, Nick had phoned. "Hey there."

"Nick?"

"Yeah. How are you?"

Emily stopped what she was doing, took her phone off speaker, and pressed the phone to her ear. "It's so good to hear your voice. How are you feeling?"

"Good. Yeah. What are you up to tomorrow?"

"Not much on the schedule—assuming I don't get called out on an emergency case. Why?"

"Can you make the drive down to Rock River and pick me up?" he asked, sounding like he needed a ride home from the auto mechanic. "I've been cleared for release."

Emily's heart leaped. "Really? So all's well?"

"As well as it can be."

"That's great. I'm so happy."

"More so, me. The food sucks here."

Emily laughed. "We'll stop for a bite on the way home. Start thinking about where you want to eat."

"Burger. Fries. And the biggest Coke on the menu. I haven't had one since . . . I can't remember, actually."

Emily grinned. "We can go wherever you want. What time should I get there?"

"They said I should be released around noon."

"I'll be there at eleven. Just in case." Emily felt that old flutter in her belly, like she'd had when they were teens. "I can't wait to see you."

"I've missed you," Nick said in a softer voice.

Emily choked up. "We have a lot to catch up on."

There was a long pause on Nick's end.

"Nick? You there?"

Nick exhaled. "I don't want to have to talk about it."

"It?"

"Things."

"You mean things that happened over there?"

"Yeah. The FBI psych said I should let you know that before we see each other."

Emily nodded, even though Nick couldn't see it. Then she verbalized her thoughts: "That's fine. I get it. There are plenty of other things we can talk about."

"See you tomorrow," Nick said, and clicked off.

Emily stood with the phone gripped between her sweating palms as her mind welled with questions she couldn't ask him. One step at a time. They'd get there, she hoped.

CHAPTER 4

"I want to file a missing person report," said the rumpled woman with bags under her eyes and a forehead creased with worry. After introducing herself, she took a seat across the desk from Freeport's lead detective, Ishkode Aditson, who guessed the woman's age was near sixty from the crow's-feet around her eyes and her shoulder-length salt-and-pepper hair. A petite lady, Lynne Hampton wore hot-pink athletic shoes and clothes twice the size they needed to be for her thin frame.

"Who's missing, Ms. Hampton?" the detective, who was in his early forties, asked in a controlled tone. What a way to start a Friday morning.

"My son. Jonah."

"Do you live in Freeport County?"

"Yes. On North Maple, right here in town. I used to work over at the hospital as a medical transcriptionist."

"What does your son do?"

"He doesn't work anymore. Jonah's a disabled vet."

"Does he live in Freeport County?"

"Yes. He has a double-wide trailer on some land over on County Road 57."

"He owns it or rents?"

"Owns. It's all paid for too."

"His age, physical description, and address, please?"

"Jonah is thirty-three. About five eight. Over two hundred pounds, I'd guess. He's got hazel eyes and he's bald—by choice. His address is 9821 County Road 57."

"When was the last time you saw your son?" Aditson typed Jonah Hampton's stats into his database to see if he had a criminal record.

"I saw him about two weeks ago. I picked him up, and we went out to a Chinese restaurant for dinner. I dropped him back at his place about eight thirty and went home."

"Have you talked to him since then?"

"Yes. We text or call every few days. On Monday, I texted him but he didn't respond. I called. No answer."

"Does he usually respond promptly?" Jonah's file was in the system. Aditson glanced at the details on-screen.

"Always. He's very responsible—well, usually. I thought maybe he got caught up with some friends. Since he doesn't drive, he's always got someone at his place helping him out or bringing him things."

As Aditson scrolled down the page, he saw that three years ago Jonah had been arrested and charged for possession and sale of narcotics.

Aditson noticed Ms. Hampton twisting a costume ring round and round her middle finger and sought to ease her nerves. "What branch of the military did Jonah serve?"

"Navy. Signed up for six years, but only served two before his injury and honorable discharge."

Aditson saw that his sentence had been a $2,000 fine and

community service hours. Both had been satisfied. He glanced up at the woman as she continued.

"I called him again Tuesday. No answer. That evening, I drove out there. He didn't answer the door, and there were no lights on inside. I walked around the property near the trailer, but he wasn't there."

"Could he have taken a trip with one of his friends?" Aditson suggested.

"Jonah would have told me if he were going somewhere."

"Did you reach out to any of his friends?"

"I don't have their contact information." She pressed her thumb and forefinger against her temples. "I didn't sleep at all last night."

"Ms. Hampton, was your son depressed or upset by anything recently?"

"No. He's a happy guy, despite his circumstances."

"Is he ambulatory?"

"Yes. He can walk, but not for long distances or a long time. Spinal injuries."

"Is he on any pain medications?"

"They give him whatever he needs. Last I knew he was taking Vicodin."

"Do you know if he uses it properly?" Aditson had been on far too many overdose calls related to prescription narcotics.

Ms. Hampton shrugged. "All I know is that my gut's telling me something's very off. It's not like Jonah to make me worry."

Aditson jotted down a few more notes and said, "I'll send a car over to his place to do a wellness check."

"There is one other thing." Ms. Hampton straightened in her chair and stopped twirling her ring. "He was supposed to give key witness testimony in a trial that started this last Monday."

"He was?" Talk about burying the lede. Aditson remained

calm. "A trial in Freeport County?" He kept up with all the major crime trials in the county. As he was lead investigator, he was often called on to testify. And he didn't recall any such trial scheduled this week.

"No. Rock River County Courthouse."

"Maybe that's why he hasn't reached out. Could he be staying down there for the duration of the trial?"

"He didn't mention it," said Ms. Hampton.

"Did he talk to you about the case?"

"No. Said it was better if I didn't know."

"Do you recall the name of the accused?" Aditson wanted to look the case up immediately.

"I think it was Chase . . . or Chausey . . . or Chancely . . ." Lynne let loose a desperate sigh. "I wish I had paid more attention."

"It's okay. We'll get an officer out to his place and check it out." Aditson had a sinking feeling. He knew exactly who she was talking about. She'd almost had his name right, but Aditson didn't want to correct her. The man in question had a police complaint file that stretched from Freeport to Rock River.

Aditson took Lynne Hampton's contact information, thanked her for coming in, and assured her he'd update her after the wellness check. He wasn't very subtle as he rushed her out of his office and into the hands of the front desk clerk to see her out.

The court case he was almost certain she was referring to concerned Colton Chauncey, age forty-four. He was from Freeport County, but the alleged crime of sexual assault had occurred in Rock River, a midsize city, population 750,000, located an hour south of their rural northern Michigan community known for its woods, lakes, and rivers.

Back in his office, he dispatched a car to Jonah Hampton's

residence. Then he phoned the Rock River County Courthouse to check in on the trial. He waited on hold for almost three minutes. When the clerk came back on the line, she told him the Chauncey trial had been postponed.

"Can you tell me the reason for the delay?" Aditson asked.

"The defendant didn't show up for court Monday morning."

CHAPTER 5

Every sinew in Emily's body was taut as she clipped down the hospital halls to Nick's room just before noon on Friday. Outside his door, she paused for a deep breath. She could hear him scuffling about inside, probably packing up his things.

"I know you're out there," his voice called.

Emily stepped into the doorway. "Hi."

Nick stood by the bed, shoving clothes in a duffel bag. His face was no longer gaunt or pale. Dressed in jeans and a white undershirt, his body still looked wiry and thin but not emaciated, as he'd been when he'd first shown up and collapsed in her arms. Warmth filled her.

"Need any help?" she asked.

"I have a few things in the bathroom, if you wouldn't mind."

She went into the en suite bath and found his razor, toothbrush, and deodorant.

"What are the discharge orders?"

"I don't know. Haven't gotten that far. Don't forget my toiletry bag." His brusqueness threw her off.

Returning to the room, Emily saw him reach for a dress

shirt hung from the curtain bar. His T-shirt rode up his back, and she gasped at the sight of a ragged scar at least twelve inches long under his left armpit: It curved from his ribs around to his back. Whoever had performed this operation had done a choppy, unprofessional suture job.

When Nick saw her aghast expression, he yanked down the back of his T-shirt.

She bit her lip, suppressing the powerful urge to ask more . . . but she'd promised Nick, and she had to respect his wishes, even if it was a struggle.

After his admittance to the hospital, Emily had sussed out from a chat with Agent Roe that Nick had traveled from southwestern China through Thailand, India, the Middle East, and North Africa before arriving in Spain. From there he was able to stow away on a container ship and make his way to the United States. Details of this trip were unknown to her, but the journey home had taken almost a full year, and she could only imagine what he'd suffered along the way. They'd yet to unpack the whole story.

The image of Nick's scar embedded in Emily's brain, igniting her imagination in all the worst ways.

"Can we get out of here?" he asked.

"Ready when you are." Emily handed him the toiletries. "Do you want help with anything?"

"All good. I don't need you to play mom. Or I would have just called her instead."

Emily bristled, but her voice stayed even as she asked, "You need to pick up any meds or—?"

"Got what I need, Doc."

She wanted to tell him to cut the crap but thought better of it. It didn't look like he was going to tell her, so she'd find another way around this.

"I cannot wait to devour a juicy one-pounder," he said. "Loaded fries. Large Coke."

"From where? Burger Barn? White Castle? Shake Shack?"

"Burger Barn. I thought I told you that yesterday," Nick snapped.

"You didn't." What was with the snippy tone?

A nurse with a wheelchair rolled in. "Ready, Mr. Larsen?"

"You don't really expect me to get into that thing, do you?"

"Rules are rules," the nurse told him.

"This is stupid. I finally get my strength back, and now you want to put me back in that thing?"

"There are others waiting." She impatiently tapped her finger on the back of the chair as if to point him into it.

"Then go get 'em. I'm good." Nick slung his duffel over his shoulder and strode out of the room. The nurse chased after him with the chair. As did Emily.

"Mr. Larsen, please. Let's be respectful about this."

As Nick headed toward the elevator, Emily rushed up to him. "We all know it's a ridiculous hospital policy created by lawsuit-happy attorneys. But they won't let you out of here unless you comply."

"Like hell they won't." Nick pressed the down button on the elevator panel. It wasn't like him to curse unless an event really called for it.

"Sir, please, just have a seat." The nurse was at his side with the wheelchair.

"Where's the car?" Nick asked Emily.

"I have a truck now. A black Yukon."

He glanced at her. "'Bout time, Hartford."

Emily's lip curled. Since when did he call her Hartford? She didn't like it.

After taking on the Freeport County medical examiner post

full-time, Emily had decided to upgrade from her electric Leaf to a Yukon. She could use it to haul decedents from the scenes of death and bring them to the morgue, like her father had done in his Suburban. It kept the chain of custody in her control and saved the county transportation costs. Also, with only two ambulances on duty for the whole county, Emily couldn't always count on either of them being free when she needed them.

"Where is it? I'll drive." Nick stuck out his hand for her to give him the keys.

"I don't think so."

Nick huffed. "Just give me the keys."

Emily crossed her arms and sent him a warning look. She had known him to be a good driver, but today she wasn't about to let him drive her new wheels. Not in his condition. And not with this attitude.

The elevator doors opened. Nick stepped in. So did the nurse. Emily stayed back.

"You go ahead. I'll be right down," she said. "I'm just going to take a second to say hi to an old friend from medical school who works in the OR."

"Don't be too long. I need to get out of here, and I'm starving."

Emily looked up at him, perplexed and taken aback by his rudeness. Nick refused to meet her gaze. She stared at him as the elevator doors closed, then sighed and backtracked to the nurses' station, where she found a secretary alternately snacking on a bag of cheese curls and tapping away on a keyboard with her hot-pink stiletto nails.

"Excuse me, I'm Dr. Emily Hartford. I'd like to get the discharge orders for Nick Larsen. He was just released."

"Oh, I'm aware." The secretary looked up without a greeting. "Are you family?"

"I'm one of the physicians who will be tending to Mr. Larsen's post care. I'm also the county medical examiner."

The nurse looked up at her with a disbelieving look. "I've never seen you around."

"I'm usually downstairs, hidden away in the morgue." Emily didn't mean to be snarky, but her annoyance at Nick was bleeding through. She pulled out her credentials badge for the nurse to verify.

Satisfied with what had been presented, the nurse went to the computer and brought up Nick's file. "Just the discharge orders then?"

"The whole chart, please."

The secretary sighed and tapped a few buttons with the tips of her stiletto nails, and the file printed out on a machine behind her. *How does she type with those nails?* When the last page was out, the woman handed the stack of papers to Emily, who took them with a simple "Thanks."

The secretary gave Emily a condescending smile and went back to her station. As Emily stepped away to read the file, she saw the secretary shish kebab three cheese curls with the tip of her stiletto nail and pop them into her glossy-lipped maw. Emily shook her head at the sight, then dove into the thick file, looking for information regarding a surgical procedure. Nothing was noted in Nick's report about a surgery or medical symptoms associated with one. She checked for brain scans that might indicate damage from a concussion, possibly explaining Nick's uncharacteristic behavior. But no brain scans had been ordered.

As Emily read through Nick's chart, she was drawn to the notes on Nick's behavior. On fourteen occasions, the third-shift nurses had noted Nick having night terrors and waking up screaming. Several times he had sprung from bed, ripped out his IV line, and been found trying to escape out of his hospital room's window.

Tormented. Belligerent. Impatient. This wasn't the kind, confident Nick who'd left for his FBI training two years ago.

She flipped over to his discharge orders. They indicated he should fill an oral antibiotic prescription and take it for ten days. She could swing by the pharmacy on their way home. But which one had it been called in to? Nothing had been noted in his paperwork. Emily was about to ask the secretary when her phone pinged with a text from Nick.

> I'm hungry.

CHAPTER 6

Colton had been holed up in his house for five days, and he was due to pick up his check in Rock River later this afternoon and head up to the UP early Sunday. He was doubtful he could tolerate the baby two more days.

The infant stank of piss and shit all the time. He had run out of diapers from her diaper bag three days ago and was using torn pieces of old bedsheets and towels. She went through one every couple of hours. He couldn't wash them because his machine had stopped working two years ago. Instead, he threw the dirty ones in a bathtub full of water and bleach. The smell curdled his nostrils and made his eyes water. He was creating a giant cesspool of filth. But every time he tried to clean them, by stirring the mess with a long handle of a rake, he began to gag.

He had not bathed the baby. He was too afraid she might drown—funny, considering what he'd done to her mother. Still, he was wound up by his desire to keep this one alive.

But feedings were problematic and confusing. There was one full can of baby formula in her bag, but now it was half gone. Colton had no idea how often to feed a baby, so every time she cried, he shoved that nipple in her mouth. He thought himself a hero when she started sucking. But after a moment, the bottle would fall from her mouth. Eventually he realized he had to hold it for her. Once he did, his attention span lasted about ninety seconds before he let go of the bottle. She wailed all over again, grating his nerves raw. He was in a state of perpetual migraine.

His friend WaliYona, who lived on the Ojibwe reservation up near Sault Sainte Marie, was tied up with tribal affairs in Canada but would be returning home by Sunday afternoon. He could reset there before meeting a contact in Toronto next Wednesday. His plan was to deliver the baby to his buyer, then slip away to warmer climes more than $50,000 richer.

Two days seemed like a lifetime away. Colton hadn't slept in forty-eight hours, and his head throbbed. His vision was blurry, and he couldn't keep anything in his nauseated stomach.

This baby was killing him.

Through spasms of pain, he struggled for a solution.

It came in the answer of an hourglass-shaped, charcoal-haired exotic dancer.

Sure, he'd have to offer Raven a cut of the sale, but in the short term she'd know what to do with the kid.

CHAPTER 7

High school seniors Angyl Green and Carlos Torres skipped classes on Friday to meet for an afternoon delight. When they drove into the parking lot at Lake Isabella, they were relieved to find it empty, knowing they'd have the lake to themselves.

It was more of a pond than a lake, only twenty-two acres in size, with a top depth of only four feet. Many ponds were typically dirty, mucky, as they were fed from underground, not filtered in the same way that a lake was. In contrast, Lake Isabella's waters were clean and clear, due to a crick running through it, a twiggy branch of the Grand River from the north.

Many locals didn't even know Lake Isabella existed. Those who did spoke little of it out of a desire to protect their hidden gem from weekenders and summer visitors. It was pristine fishing and turtle-hunting territory. And because it was off the beaten path, it was not a draw for families or large groups. Lake Isabella attracted local fishermen wanting a private pond to hook a freshwater catch.

It was also difficult to reach. A dirt two-track was the only road leading from the main highway to a trailhead path on the

Manistee National Forest parking lot. From there, visitors to Lake Isabella had to hike three miles in.

Carlos had three condoms in his pocket, and he carried the cooler with snacks and beer that Angyl had packed for them. They crossed the parking lot toward the trailhead and set out on the several-mile walk to the lake. Minutes into their hike, Angyl removed the sweatshirt tied around her waist and slipped into it. Overhead the sun was high and the sky was clear, but under the shady trees the air was cool and damp. As they reached the north side of the lake, Angyl thought she smelled a rotting animal.

"Maybe we should set up farther down," she said, holding a sleeve over her nose.

"Just keep walking. It's probably in the woods over there," Carlos told her.

As they approached the grassy bank of the lake, several turtles popped their heads out of the water to see who was interrupting their daily routine.

"There's an open space here," said Carlos.

But Angyl still smelled the horrible odor. She looked across the small lake to see if there was another open area along the shore where they could go. And that was when she saw a spot of red bobbing in the water. "What's that?" She pointed.

"Looks like someone lost a shirt," Carlos said. Red material floated on the surface of the water.

"Fabric sinks, dummy."

"It's shallow there. Might have washed up onshore."

They dropped their cooler and blankets and hiked the sandy shore toward the floating object. Moving closer, they made out a pair of bloated, fleshy arms outstretched from a red T-shirt. The corpse's midsection buoyed it on the water's surface.

Angyl let out a yelp and froze.

"Holy shit!" hissed Carlos.

A turtle circled, diving under the body. Fueled by morbid curiosity, Carlos stepped into the pond for a closer look. Small waves from his movement reached the body, jostling it so they could see the side of a face. It looked chewed up.

"What are you doing?" asked Angyl, her voice quavering.

"I wanna see who it is."

"Don't touch it! Haven't you ever seen *Forensic Files*?"

"I think it's a she." Carlos pointed to the dishwater-blond hair splayed out above the neck of the T-shirt.

"I wonder if she fell in," Angyl mused.

Carlos shook her head. "I think she's chained to something."

Angyl followed his gaze to a silver chain looped around the body's waist. It crisscrossed her torso, then wrapped her neck. Angyl thought of the tow chains her father insisted she keep in her truck in case she ever needed them to get out of a ditch. She got another whiff of the decaying woman and bent over, gagging. But nothing came up.

Carlos smelled it too. "I'm gonna be sick." He tried to step out of the pond but found he had sunk ankle deep in the lake floor. He gagged, trying to hold down his toast and banana from breakfast. But with the next inhale of the putrid odor, it all came up, spewing into the lake. He fell backward onto the soft bank and loosened his feet from his tennis shoes. He crawled from the pond, leaving them sunken in the swampy bottom.

Angyl was struggling to get cell service. "Damn it. No bars." Even if they ran the whole way, it would take them at least a half hour to get back to the parking lot.

Cold, wet, and muddy, Carlos drew up next to Angyl, who was ashen and shaking. They glanced back at the body rocking in the ripples.

Angyl grabbed Carlos by the arm and yanked him from shore. "We gotta get out of here. Now."

CHAPTER 8

"You seem on edge," Emily said as she accelerated her Yukon onto the highway, heading sixty miles upstate to Freeport.

"I'm tired. Didn't get a wink of sleep in that place. See how you'd feel after six weeks of sleep deprivation."

"I'm sure that's no fun."

"I'm hangry," he said, trying to smile before taking a giant bite of the burger they'd just gotten at a drive-through.

"Well, it looks like you've gained some weight in the six weeks you've been in rehab."

"Barely. But I've always had a high metabolism."

Emily thought he was still not that much more than skin and bones, but at least he was no longer the skeleton who'd shown up in her backyard. She wondered if he'd lost a lot of weight when he was in Beijing or if that had happened afterward. She knew not to ask right then, keeping her eyes on the road and her lips pressed together. Even so, her mind churned with questions. What was he escaping from? Why had he had to trek back home in such secrecy? What had he endured over there? Was he still in any danger?

As Nick made his way through his bag of fries, Emily couldn't help but speak up. "Nick, are you planning to go back to the FBI?"

"As soon as I clear psych."

Emily knew she should stop asking questions but found it hard to resist. It was how she was built. "What does that involve?"

"More tests." Nick crammed in the last bite of burger.

"When?"

"As soon as I get it scheduled."

"When will that be?"

He popped a handful of fries into his mouth. "I'm exhausted, Hartford."

What's with this "Hartford" business?

"It sounds like you'd bug out again if the FBI called."

"It's best for both of us if we focus on the right-now. Dwelling on the past has never worked well for us."

Was he really going to try to sweep this all under the rug, pretending it never happened? "You don't seem to care how I feel or that I went through hell while you were gone."

"Oh, this is all about you—what you went through?" said Nick, staring out the windshield.

Emily clenched her jaw and willed herself not to respond. Eventually, she couldn't help herself. "Here's what happened after you went radio silent," she said. "I literally got sick from worrying. Delia Andrews investigated and was told you were MIA. I flew to China and spoke to your coworker to find out for myself that you were really gone—I couldn't accept it any other way. I ended up bringing a box of your belongings back to the States . . ." She didn't mention the fact that she had also brought back Nick's grandmother's wedding ring, with which Bernadette told Emily Nick had been planning to propose to her. Not long ago, after her hope had finally run dry, Emily had returned the ring to Bernadette.

"I don't know what to say," he said. "I was just doing my job."

"Nick, I went through all the stages of grief mourning your death, and now I want to look forward. Will you request to go overseas again?"

"I don't know." His gaze turned to the passing landscape as he stirred the bottom of his cup with his straw. She marveled at this foreign creature in the truck's passenger seat, seemingly carved from stone.

"Didn't you miss Freeport?" she asked quietly.

"Of course." His voice was weak when he added, "Mostly, I missed you."

The old Nick again!

"There was a time when I didn't think I would make it without you," Emily told him, her voice cracking. "It hurt so bad."

He nodded, unable to meet her glance. "You never thought about dating after you thought I was dead?"

"I want to be honest with you, Nick, because you deserve to know." Nick's head snapped away from the window. "After I accepted your death, I restarted my relationship with Brandon."

"Are you guys together now?"

"No. It didn't work out." If he wasn't going to get into details, neither was she.

"I'm surprised you went back to him."

"You were dead."

"You sure you're over him?" Nick pinned her with a distrustful look.

"One hundred percent." She infused her words with conviction.

"We'll see about that."

"It's over, Nick. He dumped me." She glanced his way again and noticed his forehead beading with sweat. She reached over to feel his face. "You're burning up."

He tilted his head away from her. "I'm fine."

"You're supposed to be on another round of antibiotics," she told him. "Let's stop at the pharmacy in Freeport and get this filled before I take you home."

"No more meds. They're wrecking my stomach."

"You clearly have a fever. I can't believe they discharged you like this." Emily considered bringing up what she'd found in his file, but her phone buzzed with an incoming call. She wouldn't normally have interrupted their conversation but saw that it was Detective Ishkode Aditson.

"Hey there, Detective," she said, broadcasting on Bluetooth through her vehicle's speakers.

"Hope you're not too busy today," Aditson said.

"Just coming back from Rock River. You remember Nick Larsen?"

"Of course I do. He's legendary," said Aditson, who had moved from a post in the Upper Peninsula to take on Nick's position after he left for the FBI.

"He's with me right now. Freshly released back into the real world."

"That so? Welcome home, Larsen."

"Thanks, Aditson." Nick was abrupt and uninterested.

"What's up?" Emily asked, switching the conversation to her earpiece.

"Two high school students playing hooky found a floater at Lake Isabella. How soon can you meet me there?"

"Gotta drop Nick home, and then I'm on my way. An hour, tops."

"See you soon," he said, and she ended the call.

"Barely out of the hospital, and you're already rushing off," said Nick.

"I thought you wanted to rest."

"We could rest . . . together?" Nick suggested.

"Are you expecting that you and I will just pick up where we left off?" Emily said.

"This is a lot more complicated than I imagined it would be," he said.

"You got that right."

CHAPTER 9

Colton waited in the parking lot of the Silver Slipper men's lounge until he spotted Raven Kane exiting the back of the building around four on Friday afternoon. Raven worked as a dancer and waitress, and for the last five years they'd been seeing each other off and on. Tuesday through Friday, she took the day shift waitressing. Weekends, she worked nights as a dancer. Colton was always turned on by her waitressing uniform: short black leather skirt and low-cut white tank. When dancing, she wore not much more than a thong and heels. He liked it better when more was left to the imagination. This afternoon, coming out of the joint, she had on a pair of joggers, her leather jacket, and sneakers.

Raven was searching her bags for keys to unlock her cobalt-blue 2014 Rav4 when he rushed up behind her and startled her. "Hey, beautiful."

She leaped back from the door, positioned in a defensive stance. When she saw it was him, her frightened expression relaxed. "Shit. Scared the crap outta me. What are you doing here?"

"Just wanted to see you."

"I don't wanna see you. Goodbye." She took a step toward the Rav4, but he blocked her.

"Not so fast. Just wanna talk." He pressed his body against the driver's door.

"I'm tired, Colton. I wanna go home."

"I thought you said you wanted to talk. You keep calling me."

"What do you want now?" Her voice had a gravelly edge.

He got to the point. "I need you to babysit for a couple days."

"What? Hell no."

"Please. I'm . . . I don't know what to do."

"Aren't you supposed to be in Rock River at your trial?"

"A miracle. Charges were dropped."

Raven looked skeptical. "Move away from my car, please," she demanded.

"It's true," he said. "That bitch dumped her baby on me."

Raven placed her hands on her hips, eyes never leaving his. "You kidding me? You want me to take care of the kid of the girl you screwed while you and me were together?"

"I'm talking abandonment. It's not the baby's fault."

"How do you even know that baby is yours?"

"I'm not planning to keep her."

"What are you going to do with it?" Raven was rattling her keys at her side.

Colton shrugged.

"Typical. You sure you didn't kidnap the brat?"

"Shit, no. I don't wanna be no daddy."

"Then give her back." Raven inched toward her Rav4, trying to nudge him away.

"I'll make good on this. I promise."

"How?"

"Give you a cut."

"A cut of what?" Raven squinted at him, and then the penny dropped. She lowered her voice, hissing at him, "You would sell your own kid?"

"Like you said, I don't even know if she's mine."

"Maybe you should figure that out first."

"That bitch never showed up for court Monday; then she dumps this baby on me. What does that tell you?"

Colton stepped closer to Raven, his eyes tender. He could tell she was digesting it as she cocked her head.

"Didn't that pregnant friend of yours turn up with a new Escalade, a designer wardrobe, and a flat belly after her little three-month retreat to Florida?" he asked. "Why shouldn't you get in on that? The kid gets a good home. Everyone wins."

"How much of a cut?" she asked.

"Fifty-fifty."

Raven considered the offer, then added, "Plus any shit I need to buy for her."

"Of course."

Raven looked over his shoulder toward his car across the parking lot. "She's in there? Now?"

"Cute as a button."

"What's your plan?" Her voice was stiff, but her body language told him she was giving in.

"I've gotta hit a gig in Rock River to get some traveling money. After that we can take a little family trip. Visit Disneyland?"

Raven looked around to make sure there was no one else in earshot. "You sure the mama's not coming after you?"

Colton looked her square in the eyes. "Dead sure."

CHAPTER 10

Emily arrived at Lake Isabella that afternoon via a turnoff located on the main county highway that, oddly, she had never noticed before. The road bypassed the small dirt parking area where hikers could access the trailhead into the national forest. But it continued into the thick woods on a rutted, two-track dirt drive. Three bumpy miles later, she was at an unmarked public access site for the petite Lake Isabella. As she approached, she saw Detective Aditson across the lake, taking photographs of a set of footprints in the mud a few feet from shore. Luminescent yellow crime scene tape stood out in the green of nature. He'd secured the area around the body, and Emily could see the back of a person bobbing among lily pads. A breeze wafted the reek of decomp across the surface of the water toward Emily.

Aditson looked up and waved her forward. Emily trekked along the water's mushy edge, scanning the area around the lake. Directly behind them was a rickety fishing shack. It looked more like a shed than a habitat.

"Have you looked inside there yet?" she asked.

"Empty and abandoned," Aditson replied.

Emily glanced at the GPS map on her phone. On the south side of the lake was a cottage, recessed at least fifty yards from the shore.

"How 'bout that place?" she said, tapping the screen.

"It seems well cared for and lived in. But the homeowner wasn't home when I stopped by earlier."

"We can try again after we're finished here." Emily tucked her phone into her pocket. "I didn't even know this lake existed." She'd lived most of her life in Freeport County.

"It's a haven for fishing and turtle hunting," Aditson explained. "So I'm told. I've never been here before either."

"Hard to get a large boat in on that narrow two-track."

"Those who come down here have to use small vessels—canoes, kayaks, or rowboats."

Emily stepped closer to the body to get a better look but stayed outside the tape.

"I'm waiting for EMTs so they can haul her out," said Aditson. "Then you can do your initial examination on land and get her to the morgue."

"Her? Are you sure?" Emily had no desire to get into that murky water.

"Long blond hair. Painted fingernails." Aditson shrugged. "Just my guess."

They both knew that these days length of hair and nail style didn't always indicate gender.

"Have you talked to the kids who found her?" asked Emily.

"Their parents brought them into the station. Both were underage and playing hooky."

"Out here? Why?"

"Take a guess."

Emily grinned at a quick memory from her early high school

days, when one warm spring afternoon she and Nick had ditched school à la Ferris Bueller and headed off to a Lake Michigan beach.

"Did they offer up anything useful?"

"Not really. They saw the body, the guy puked, and then they ran back to their car to call 911 because there's no reception out here."

Emily glanced at her phone. The signal bars were not lit up.

"There was one thing the girl, Angyl, mentioned. She said she saw a yellow baby pacifier on the woman's finger."

Emily glanced over. Nothing was there now, but she did notice a cross tattoo on the woman's hand.

"Where's it now?" Emily asked.

"No idea. Maybe it got knocked off her finger by a turtle. There are tons of them in here," said Aditson. "But here's the kick in the gut. If this is who I think it is, she had a baby. Nine months old. A girl named Brooklyn."

Emily's heart groaned.

Aditson pulled up a document on his cell phone, and she leaned over to look at the image of a smiling young woman. "Savannah Browdey was reported missing four days ago by her father. She's just nineteen. She left the house saying she was going to visit a friend last Saturday afternoon. But she never came back home."

She had been missing almost a full week. Emily braced herself to deal with a highly decomposed body. "And the baby?"

"Browdey's father stated she took Brooklyn with her, plus a diaper bag and a change of clothes for the baby."

"Only one change of clothes. Then she was probably planning to be gone just for the day," Emily said, studying the image. Savannah had blond hair. Gray-blue eyes. The information below the picture said she was five feet, six inches tall and 130 pounds.

"She told her father she'd be back later. She didn't specify an exact time."

"From where I'm standing, it looks like this could be Savannah," said Emily.

"This seals the deal for me." Aditson scrolled down to a second image, a close-up of a tattoo on Savannah's right hand: a Saint James cross tattoo, the amateur piece of body art Emily had just seen on the floating corpse.

As Emily examined the victim more closely, she saw that her hands had been secured at the wrists with duct tape and were floating in front of her head. Her bloated arms were stretching her red short-sleeve T-shirt to its limit.

"Is she from around here?" Emily asked.

"No. Rock River."

"So where's the baby?"

Aditson pulled up the image of baby Brooklyn on his phone for Emily to see. The laughing baby had her mother's gray-blue eyes and fine blond hair, with small curls forming at the base of her neck. Her cheeks were round and full, her lips parted in a wide smile. Brooklyn was an adorable, flawless child. Emily's heart snapped.

"You don't think . . . ?" Her gaze scanned the rippling lake.

"I've got cadaver dogs and a team of divers on their way."

Emily knew he was entertaining the same thought: The seclusion of Lake Isabella made it a prime location to dump a body. Or two.

"Savannah's father, Ivan Browdey, tried reaching her and worried all day Sunday. He phoned her boyfriend. He hadn't heard from her either. Monday morning, first thing, Browdey filed a missing person report."

"No mother? Or are they divorced?"

"Her father told me Savannah's mother is no longer living. Died of cancer some years back."

"Did anyone else see Savannah and Brooklyn that day?"

"I don't know. She didn't tell her dad which friend she was visiting or where."

"She just disappeared?"

Aditson shrugged. Apparently.

Emily heard voices from across the lake and looked up to see the arrival of the recovery team. Two EMTs engaged in small talk as they donned long rubber gloves, goggles, and waders, then sloshed into the waist-deep waters. Their plan was to place a large mesh trampoline base under the body, then float her out of the weeds and across the cleaner part of the lake so they could move her onshore while keeping her as intact as possible. That no potential evidence was disturbed was key to the retrieval. They each took an arm and a leg in an attempt to slide her body onto the mesh disk. As they tried to roll her over, the body wouldn't budge.

"She's caught on something," one called out. He felt along the girl's back. "It's a chain wrapped around her." His hand moved underneath the water and around her torso. "It's attached to something down below."

"Can you see what it is?" Aditson called back.

"Water's too murky."

"What do you want us to do?" asked the other EMT.

"Anything necessary to get her out," Aditson instructed.

"But be careful not to disturb her too much," Emily added quickly, hoping they wouldn't destroy crucial evidence in the retrieval.

The EMTs grabbed the chain on either side of her, braced themselves, and began to pull. Step by slow step, they emerged from the lake. As they drew the body from the water, Emily and Aditson were able to help them drag the corpse onshore. The EMTs continued reeling in the chain with much effort.

The muddy lake bottom and the resistance of the water worked against them, but eventually a blue-painted cinder block surfaced.

Emily began a cursory examination of Savannah. Decomposition had created gases in her body, which had caused it to rise to the lake's surface. She was dressed in jean shorts and a red T-shirt with a logo for the band Paramore. The items of clothing seemed intact. On her right foot she wore a Brooks running shoe and gray footie sock. The left foot was bare. There were no bruises or cuts, from what Emily could see. Further examination at the morgue might reveal otherwise. Emily uncurled the young woman's fingers to reveal clean, unscathed palms.

"No defensive wounds," Emily pointed out to Aditson.

"She didn't—or couldn't—fight her way out of this one." Aditson sighed.

"This one?" Emily turned to him. "What do you mean?"

"Savannah Browdey was sexually assaulted by Colton Chauncey about sixteen months ago," said Aditson. "The crime happened in Rock River County. But Chauncey is a Freeport County resident, born and bred. Age forty-four."

Emily didn't recognize the name. Aditson showed her a photo of Chauncey on his phone. He had a broad face, thin lips, and a receding hairline. In the photo he looked younger than his forty-four years. Closer to his early thirties. He wore a long-sleeve green flannel button-down, jeans, and brown leather boots. He was lean and muscular with the rugged appeal of a Midwestern hunter or fisherman.

"He's six four, a hundred and ninety pounds, according to his driver's license," said Aditson. "Which expired three years ago."

"You don't think he did this, do you? Isn't he sitting in jail awaiting trial?" Emily asked.

"He was—fifteen months ago. For a hot second after he was charged with Savannah's rape."

"And then?"

"He made bail."

"And the trial was set for this past Monday?"

Aditson nodded.

"He's been out free this whole time? What protection did Savannah have?"

"Geographical distance was the main factor. She lived in Rock River with her dad, Ivan, and brother, Peyton."

It was a foolish and weak move on the part of the judicial system. Emily was sick at the thought. "Judge didn't set the bail high enough."

"That's a beef to pick with our legal system. Right now Colton Chauncey is our lead suspect, but we can't exclude other possibilities."

"The motive is so strong," Emily argued.

"It is, but as soon as we start assuming he's our only suspect, we risk losing perspective on the case, and we could overlook something."

Emily would take extra precautions to examine and preserve evidence on the body once she had the victim in the morgue.

"Did Chauncey show up for his trial?" she asked.

"He did not."

"Please tell me there is a warrant out for his arrest."

"Yes indeed."

Emily hoped he would be found quickly. But first they had to confirm their ID of Savannah Browdey with the family. Emily continued her field scan of the body. After finding no other visible wounds on the front of the corpse, she asked the EMTs, "Can you help me turn her over?"

They rolled the young woman onto her back. As her thick,

shoulder-length dishwater-blond hair peeled back from her face, Emily let out a small gasp. Her eyes and mouth had been duct-taped, but her nostrils had been left open. She would have been forced to breathe in water. Emily glanced up at Aditson, who was staring in horror, and she guessed that he, too, was imagining the terrifying scenario of this young woman's drowning. Even with the tape covering her face, Emily felt certain this was the missing Savannah Browdey. Every nerve in Emily's body went tight and hot. She was ready to play judge and jury and put a stake through the creep who'd committed this heinous act.

Instead, Emily continued to scan the victim's body for any visible wounds or bullet entrances. Nothing indicated she'd been knifed or shot. If she'd been struck or bludgeoned, Emily wouldn't be able to tell until she had her undressed on her autopsy table. Aditson said little, but Emily read the concentration in his face. No doubt he was plotting the next steps of his investigation.

After a while, Aditson said, "I'm calling out a manhunt for Colton Chauncey, and I'll get a search warrant for his home. According to county deed records, it's an old two-story about ten miles from here, which he hasn't paid taxes on for years." His voice had an uncharacteristic waver to it.

"You're shaken, aren't you?" Emily asked.

"Who allows a violent offender like him out of jail?" He shook his head.

"Like you said, that's a battle for another day. Let's get her out of here." Emily wanted to get Savannah away from this undignified environment as soon as possible.

"Whoever killed her—and possibly her baby, Brooklyn—took great care to ensure that she died a hideous death," said Aditson.

Emily signaled to the EMTs to bring the body bag. She glanced back at the duct-taped face.

Ruthless. They were dealing with a cruel predator.

CHAPTER 11

Ruby finished pulling the weeds on the first row of her farmyard garden, which was drying up and dying in the early-November warm spell. She unhunched her back and worked out the cricks along her spine. She rubbed her achy hips down to the bone as if kneading dough. So much of her ached. Her right arm, her legs. Her ribs stung when she twisted. These bones had suffered breakage. Some had been set by doctors in hospitals. Many had not. Hospital staff asked too many questions that back in the day she had not been allowed to answer.

Ruby had faced up to what she was: a seventy-two-year-old woman with more regrets about motherhood than good recollections. Maybe she'd fixated too much on her kids, but one by one, they'd peeled away. She could hardly blame them for wanting to escape her husband Thomas's reign of terror. Now they were all free of him, but she missed the comfort of being surrounded by family.

Her oldest had to be nearly forty years old now. Maybe even early forties. His birthday was in July—the latter half. That she did know. He was born in the dog days of summer. Humid.

Buggy. Not a breeze coming through the house as she sweated and toiled to birth him. Now, her life was one endless day after another. She counted only seasons and moments. Not dates. Today it was late fall—that was evident from the blanket of reds and yellows covering her property. And she was nearly out of food, which meant months had passed since her last grocery delivery from her eldest.

Only he was still in touch. Only he had tried to protect her from Thomas, at least when her husband had been home. Only he had been fathered by a man she truly loved—not her husband. Her eldest son was the offspring of an auto mechanic. Back in the day, she'd found things wrong with her car just to go see handsome, sweet Charlie. He'd fixed her brakes, rotated her tires, and buffed out dents Ruby'd created on purpose, on a regularly scheduled basis. That was forty years ago, and now Charlie was a distant memory, worn to the bone and retired to the junkyard of her mind.

She tried to forget the others. Her selfish other two sons were long gone. They never called or visited. Some Christmases they'd send cards with simple signatures. Her middle child, a daughter, might be dead, for all Ruby knew. Twenty-plus years had passed since she'd heard from her. The fifth, a girl, had died in a car accident when she was thirteen. She and Ruby were going to town for groceries and an oil change when a pickup truck ran a stop sign and rammed into the passenger side. Ruby hadn't believed in seat belts. When the vehicle slammed into their car, her daughter's body had functioned as a cushion, protecting Ruby from serious injury. Ruby never drove after that. That was when her and Charlie's long love affair had ended as well.

Her beloved oldest had Charlie's navy eyes, a fearless personality, and a high intellect that was God given, not inherited from either parent's DNA. She was proud that her son had once been the defender of weaklings. All this she'd treasured in her mother's heart until the day Thomas had figured out her son's paternity. That was when her most beloved boy became the target of her abusive husband's fury.

Under this onslaught, her eldest's navy eyes had turned black, and his tender, caring spirit grew troubled and mean. He tortured animals around the farm. He beat up boys in his class. He tormented his younger brothers, locking them in closets and the cellar. But he was never vengeful to his mother. Not once.

He still lived in the area. Ruby didn't have his address, nor had she ever seen his home. She didn't need to. He seemed to know when she was running low on groceries or needed something repaired around the house.

Yes, he'd stayed by her side when all others had forgotten her. She looked forward to only a few things now: watching her garden grow and awaiting her oldest son's visits. She liked to think that in some way, he still needed her in a world where no one else did.

Ruby was sure she heard a car engine in the distance and turned her gaze to the woods beyond her dilapidated two-story farmhouse. She thought she saw the glistening of metal and glass moving up the dirt driveway through the trees, but as she limped across the grass toward the house, a second look revealed it was the flutter of her wind chimes, throwing off the sun's reflection and sinking her hope.

CHAPTER 12

Late Friday afternoon, Emily was getting ready to leave the morgue and head home, very much looking forward to lounging on the sofa to enjoy pizza and a movie with her half sister, Anna, and two nieces. But plans abruptly changed with a text from Aditson that contained an address and the message *Looks like a 2 body day.*

As she maneuvered her Yukon down the dirt road of County Road 57, Emily's mind spun over her conversation with Nick. She had texted him from the morgue while she was working, but he hadn't responded. Maybe he was busy settling in. Or sleeping. Or maybe his mother had tasked him with chores around the house.

She turned into the dirt driveway of Jonah Hampton's residence: a double-wide trailer on an overgrown plot of land outside town. The site was typical for local residents wanting to be left alone with their thoughts and guns.

As Emily parked her truck, she saw a petite older woman in hot-pink sneakers waiting on the front steps of the trailer. Aditson had called Emily earlier to warn her that the deceased's mother, Lynne Hampton, had rushed to the scene after he'd called her with the sad news that Jonah's body had been found. A police officer was posted outside the trailer to wait with the grieving mother because she kept trying to enter the crime scene.

Emily looked at Lynne's blotchy face and bloodshot eyes with a compassionate gaze. "Mrs. Hampton, I'm Dr. Emily Hartford." She offered a handshake and held Lynne's hand for a long second to show her empathy. "I'm the doctor who will be examining your son to determine cause of death."

"I really want to see him," said Lynne, choking back tears.

"I understand that completely. But I don't think you want to see him in this state." The rank stench of human decomposition wafted from the poorly insulated trailer. "Wouldn't you feel more comfortable over there?" Emily motioned to an area in the front yard where Jonah had created a firepit and picnic area with several picnic tables.

"No. I don't want to sit down."

"Okay. You do what is most comfortable for you. I need to enter the premises and conduct my part of the investigation."

"When will I know . . . what happened?"

"I'll have an official report for you in a few days," Emily told her, hoping to get her to back away from the front steps. She recognized how anxious it might make a mother to not be able to enter her own son's residence, so she extended her sympathy. "I'm so sorry about your loss. I understand Jonah was a veteran?"

Lynne nodded again, tears rimming her eyes. "He signed up for six years, but he only did two before an injury in Afghanistan. Jonah was a kind person, and I don't know what to do—" A sob overtook her.

"If you need help making arrangements, I'd be happy to refer you to a very compassionate funeral director."

"Thank you. Jonah always said he wanted to be buried with his buddies at Arlington."

"That's a beautiful request. The funeral director can definitely facilitate that."

That put Lynne a little more at ease. "I can't imagine having him so far away from Freeport."

For several minutes Emily stood in solidarity with the grieving mother. She could hear Aditson rustling through the trailer, going through cupboards and drawers. Moving objects on coffee tables and shelves. Bedroom doors squealed open on their hinges. Bathroom cabinets creaked.

"What's he looking for?" Lynne said, hearing it too.

"Anything that might help us understand Jonah's death." Emily was purposefully vague. "Was he taking any medications?"

"Yes. He had high blood pressure."

"Run in the family?"

"No. He also had a lot of pain," said Mrs. Hampton. "They gave him Vicodin."

Emily thought he was young to be on meds for blood pressure but guessed the prescription was related to stress or a high-fat, high-salt diet. She made a mental note to look for signs of plaque in his arteries when performing his postmortem exam.

"I know he was involved with drugs," said Mrs. Hampton. "Dealing mostly. I'm not ignorant of my son's transgressions."

"Do you think he abused drugs?" Emily asked, relieved that his mother was aware.

"No. Even so, drugs aren't what got my son killed."

"What makes you think he was killed?"

"I got a funny feeling about this one guy who kept coming around."

"You think this person had it out for him?"

"Jonah had a soft heart. Always helping out the underdog. One time I was here, and a couple of friends came over to see my son. We all sat down for drinks when this guy showed up, junked out on coke."

"Had he been invited? Did Jonah know he was coming?"

"No. He just barged in. Didn't knock. Like he owned the place."

"What did he want?"

"Nothing that I could figure. Just to hang out, I guess. But it got uncomfortable fast. No one wanted him here. Jonah took him aside in the kitchen and asked him to leave. But he wouldn't. Then the woman who'd been visiting Jonah—Gina was her name—joined their conversation, hoping to use her persuasive powers to get him to leave."

"I'm guessing that didn't go well."

"He went into a rage, grabbed Gina by her long hair, and slammed her head into the floor."

Imagining the violence made Emily quiver. "Was she badly injured?"

"She had a concussion. But that was nothing compared to what he did to her boyfriend. Who, of course, came rushing in to defend her."

"How bad was that?"

"Broken leg, several cracked ribs, black eyes, and a concussion."

"What was Jonah doing while all this was going on?"

"Jonah rushed into his bedroom and got his shotgun. He ushered the guy out, but the damage was already done."

"Did anyone call the cops?"

"I started to, but Jonah grabbed the phone from me. No one wanted to press charges and go through all that."

"Why not? It was clearly assault and battery with several viable witnesses."

"We were more focused on getting Jonah's friends to the hospital."

"You didn't want to call later?" Emily asked.

"I brought it up. As Jonah pointed out to me, what good would that do? He'd already made bail several times for other offenses. Guy was like a cockroach that just kept coming back."

"Do you remember his name?"

"I told Aditson I thought it was Chasey . . . or Cauphey . . . I told that detective about him. He was the same guy Jonah was supposed to testify against this week."

At that comment, Emily was covered in goose bumps. "I'm so sorry to hear all this."

"In the end, Jonah became just another victim on the trail of this creep's rampage of violence. My baby boy . . . paid the ultimate price. How many more will? This guy has to be stopped and locked up. Forever!"

He's not the only one who's suffered from Colton Chauncey's presence, Emily wanted to tell her. But of course she wasn't at liberty to talk about Savannah Browdey's murder. Nor had it yet been proved that either death had been at the hands of Chauncey.

Rampage was a good word to describe his actions, more than Mrs. Hampton realized.

"Where do you think this guy might be right now? Any guesses?"

"Don't know. And until this moment, I didn't care. I try to stay as far from him as I can."

"Dr. Hartford?" Aditson called from a bedroom in the back of the trailer. "Could you please join me back here?"

Mrs. Hampton instinctively stepped forward, but Emily gently stuck her hand out to stop her. "Sorry—"

"I just . . . habit." Lynne stepped back.

Emily entered the trailer and followed the rustling sound

coming from its master bedroom in back. But she didn't see Aditson. "Detective?"

"In here." His voice came from the small closet with an accordion door hanging off its track.

Emily padded over to where Aditson was using gloved hands to extract a dirty baby diaper in the trash bin.

"And look at this. I think it's from a diaper bag," he said, holding up a tag with the name *Brooklyn.*

Baby Brooklyn had been there. "But was she here before or after her mother was killed?" Emily asked.

"Why would the killer want to keep her alive? I hate to say it, but we need to dredge that lake."

Emily understood his logic. But she couldn't shake the rising question in her mind: *If you're just going to kill the baby, why take the diaper bag?*

CHAPTER 13

The first two months of freshman year of high school had brought a whirlwind of emotions for Flora Johnson, Emily's niece by her half sister, Anna. Graduating from a small private junior high school to the massive public high school had, at times, been overwhelming. Being on the volleyball team helped. After tryouts, Flora had been placed on the varsity team. The older kids looked out for her and provided an instant connection. The downside was that she didn't know many of her own classmates because she was spending most of her free time with the team.

This autumn Friday afternoon after school, she was with three junior teammates and two basketball players from the boys' team who'd invited her to go hiking with them on the Serpent Trail north of Freeport County.

"Are there snakes in these woods?" Flora said as they started off from the trailhead.

"Some," replied Noah. "Why? Are you afraid of snakes?"

"I mean because of the trail's name. Are there a lot of them here?"

“The trail runs along a series of lakes that form the shape of a serpent,” Noah explained.

She felt a bit better about it after that.

“Don’t worry, Flo,” said Noah. “I got your back.”

Flo. She hated that nickname. But she was enamored of the one who gave it to her.

Noah was a junior and a basketball star: tall, lean, and muscular. He wore his auburn hair in a man bun. His skin was tanned from a summer of working out and lifeguarding at Lake Michigan. And he had chosen her. Or so she’d been told by her teammates. Of the six games the volleyball team had already played this season, he had shown up to every single one. He would meet her at her locker in the morning before their first class. He was easy to talk to. He liked to laugh, and he made her little origami figures.

“We’ll take this offshoot and see if we meet back up with you,” Noah said to the others.

Before Flora knew it, they were kissing hard, and he was drawing her toward the forest floor.

A sharp stab into her kidney made her squawk, and she jolted upright.

“You okay?”

She turned to look for the offending object. The splintered nub of a bone was sticking out of the ground.

“Ouch,” he said, then drew his face close to her to continue their make-out session.

She pulled back, her interest redirected to the nub. She used her fingers to dig around it, loosening the soil, being careful not to touch it.

“What are you doing?”

“I want to see.”

“It’s just an animal bone.”

"How do you know?" she challenged.

He shrugged. "Why do you care?"

"I'm curious."

He sat at her side and watched as she excavated a thin bone with a head. It was about six inches in length, if Flora had to make a guess. She brushed off the matted soil and held it up.

"Deer. Or fox," Noah guessed.

Flora rotated it in her hand, examining all surfaces. There was a one-inch diagonal groove in the center that gave her pause. It looked unnatural to the structure of a bone. Like someone had cut it. "I'll take it home and have my aunt Emily look at it."

"Why?"

"She's the county medical examiner."

He shrugged again.

"What if it's a human bone?" asked Flora.

"What's she gonna do about it?"

"Investigate." She unzipped her backpack, took out her sweatshirt, and wrapped the bone in it. "It could be a missing person. Or connected to a crime."

"You're a strange one."

"Is that bad?"

"No, it's good."

"Why is that?"

"Because you're not like the other girls."

But Flora desperately wanted to be like other girls. After the past couple of disheveled years—with her parents' divorce and the move from Rock River to Freeport—she'd wanted nothing more than to fit in, to find friends and maybe a boyfriend. Making the volleyball team had helped her feel part of something important. Special.

Noah tipped up her chin and went in for another kiss. Her whole body went tingly.

When they unlocked lips, she smiled up at him. "You know . . . there might be more," she said.

"More?" He raised his brow and started to lay her back down.

"More bones." She went rigid and sprang to her feet. "We should search the area."

"Um, okay. Ah . . . how do we do that?"

Above them a breeze rustled the tree branches, and off in the distance thunder rumbled.

"We need to go," he said, getting to his feet.

"It's still far off."

"The others will be looking for us, Flo."

She gave him an indignant look. "I hate that nickname, by the way."

"Sorry. I didn't—"

"My name's Flora. After my grandmother. On my mom's side."

"It's a pretty name," he said.

Lightning glowed overhead, and thunder rumbled louder.

"Whoa. Let's get outta here," he said. "Come on. Before the lightning gets closer."

"You're not scared, are you?"

"Of some old bones?"

"No. Ghosts in the forest," she teased, making her voice sound spooky. "Skinwalkers."

"What's that?"

"This is Chippewa country, right?"

"I guess so."

"In Native American culture, skinwalkers are creatures that roam the earth and torment humans."

"Maybe a skinwalker got this guy," Noah joked as he took her by the hands, touching his nose to hers. "I was wondering,

Flo-ra." He exaggerated the *ra*, and she giggled. "Will you go to Christmas Dance with me?"

She felt a few drops of rain plunk onto her forehead. "You're planning ahead." The dance was December 15, right before they went on holiday break.

"I just wanted to lock you in."

Flora gave him a questioning look.

"I mean . . . not like that. I wanted to ask you before . . . before someone else did."

Flora smiled. "I'll think about it," she told him. She had to ask her mom first but didn't want to admit that to a junior basketball star with a driver's license.

A steady rain started trickling through the tree leaves. Noah leaned over and gave her a tender kiss on the lips. "Just say yes."

"It's a definite . . . maybe." Flora grinned. First kiss. First dance invite. When she and her mom and younger sister, Fiona, had moved to Freeport from Rock River, she wasn't sure that being a teenager in a small town like Freeport would be any fun at all. But it was turning out differently than she'd expected. As she slung her backpack over her shoulders, the wind picked up and the rain pelted harder. The two of them hurried along the now-muddy path, back to the trailhead to meet the others.

CHAPTER 14

"I'm worried about you being here all alone," Nick's mother, Bernadette, told him. She'd arrived the morning after Emily had dropped Nick off and was now filling the pantry with ten bags of groceries she'd bought for him.

"I was alone here before," Nick countered.

"It's different now," she said. "After I stock the kitchen, I'll dust and vacuum."

"You don't have to do that, Mom."

"I want to help. It's a big house for one person to clean."

The four-bed, three-bath ranch-style home sat on two acres and boasted a sprawling backyard that led to a sandy beach. For the past two years it had been uninhabited and overlooked.

"Have you checked the bathrooms?" asked Bernadette. "How are they? Do they need a good cleaning?"

He realized that she wasn't just trying to help; she was looking for a reason to stick around. "It'll feel like they're smothering you at first," his therapist at the rehab facility had told him. "They just want to help, but you can set the boundaries. You *need* to set the boundaries. When the heart and mind have space to heal, the body heals better."

Nick also knew she wanted answers about the past two years. And he didn't want to talk with her about what had happened in China. That was over. He'd survived. Time to move on.

"How's Mandie?" asked Nick, referring to his younger sister.

"She and Mark are expecting a baby," Bernadette said.

"That's nice."

"You're going to be an uncle."

"You're going to be a grandmother."

"Ick. Don't say that word. Makes me feel old," Bernadette chided. She took care of her looks, worked out, and as a result looked much younger than her fifty-eight years. "You should call your sister."

"She should call me." He didn't mean to say it with an edge. Everything from his mouth had a sharp edge to it. Nick felt awful that he'd sliced up Emily with his harsh, impatient words. The tone boiled up from a place he didn't understand and that had never existed before his time in China. It wasn't him. And yet he felt incapable of curbing it.

It'll take time to adjust. Be patient with yourself. His therapist's repetitive mantra.

"Why don't you stay with me for a while?" Bernadette lived alone now that Nick's dad had passed and Mandie and Mark had relocated to Denver, chasing job opportunities and the mountains.

"Thanks, Mom. I'll be fine here."

"I could use the company."

"Get a dog." He hadn't meant to say it sharply.

"Don't be a smart-ass." Bernadette wasn't easily riled by him. "And for your information, I have a dog."

"You do? Since when?"

"Since we thought you were dead."

"What breed?"

"A black Lab. From the rescue."

"What's her name?"

"His name . . . is Nicholas."

"Mom—really?"

"Don't give me that. I was grieving."

Nick folded up the empty paper grocery bags that he knew his mother used to recycle her old magazines and junk mail.

She finished stocking the cupboards and came up next to him. "I still can't believe you're here."

Since his return, he hadn't liked to be touched, but he let her put her arm around him.

"My goodness. You're burning up, son."

"It's warm. We need some air in here."

Nick slipped from her arm to open the sliding door that led from the kitchen onto the back patio overlooking a moderately sized inland lake. Meanwhile, Bernadette searched her purse for a pill bottle. She took out two aspirin and handed them to Nick. "When was the last time you had a good night's sleep?"

"Probably before my FBI training." He popped the pills into his mouth and swallowed.

"When is your next checkup?" she asked.

"In a month." His doctors would want to make sure he was gaining weight. His physical therapist, to make sure he was increasing his strength. And his psych, to discuss the night terrors.

"I assume you'll be returning to work at some point."

"I hope so."

"When?"

"I don't know."

"Overseas again?"

"It's not up to me."

"You could always quit. Go back to the local police force."

"I like the FBI."

"Even though they left you for dead?" She raised her brow at him.

Anger burned through his brain. Indeed, someone had left him for dead. But he'd never tell her that. Hearing that story would be worse to her than him actually dying.

"It doesn't matter. I'm here now." Nick glanced out the patio door to the expansive yard and lake beyond. "You could have sold this place."

"I thought about it," Bernadette told him. "But whenever I picked up the phone to call a Realtor, I couldn't do it."

He smiled his thanks. "Stay for lunch?"

"If you're making it."

He went to the fridge, where she had just put sandwich meats and cheeses into the crisper.

"Make yourself two," she said. "You need it. I expected you to gain more weight in that facility."

"Hospital food." He brushed her off.

"What's next on your agenda?" she asked him.

His mom knew him all too well: Nick didn't let grass grow under his feet. He concentrated on making the sandwiches. "First, I'm going to sleep long and hard in my own bed. Then take the boat out. Do some fishing. Unless . . . you didn't sell that, did you?" He handed his mother a sandwich cut in half.

"I didn't touch a thing. It's in the boathouse. Just how you left it." Bernadette nibbled on her sandwich as she watched him closely. "Your friends would probably love to see you."

He scarfed down the first sandwich in three bites. "Yeah. I'm sure they're all really busy." Many of them were married with kids or had kids on the way—at least according to the small talk he and Emily had on their drive back to Freeport.

"You could throw one of your famous backyard barbecues?"

"In November?"

"Winter never stopped you from doing it before. New Year's Eve barbecues. Super Bowl. Saint Paddy's Day."

She was right. But the last thing he wanted right now was a house full of people with their thousands of questions. Nick grabbed his second sandwich.

"I can help with the food," his mom pressed.

Nick's phone buzzed from the dining room table. He dashed to see who it was, and recognizing the number, he pressed accept.

"This is Agent Larsen." He identified himself out of formality—not because the person on the other end didn't know who they were calling.

"It's Roe. I wanted to reach out to see how you're doing."

"Good. Yeah. Doing great. Nice to be out of the rehab clinic."

"I bet. Hey, the reason I'm calling is about your recent psych eval."

Nick hadn't told Emily that they had already given him two tests: one when he was first admitted to the hospital and another a few days before he was to be released.

"I'll just cut to the chase, Larsen. You failed."

"I—what?" Nick went out the sliding door off the dining room and onto the porch, where he could hide the conversation from his eavesdropping mother. "That makes no sense. I'm fine."

"Your leave has been extended."

"I want to get back to work."

"You can retest in eight weeks. In the meantime, we're sending you a list of approved therapists."

"I don't need a shrink—" He regretted the words as soon as he said them. Arguing with his superior wasn't going to change the orders or win any favors.

"No one's forcing you to go. But no one who's ever undergone circumstances as stressful as those you went through has ever passed the psych eval without a little help."

"I understand."

"It's not something you can fake. You get that, Larsen?"

"Yeah." Nick hung up and stared at the water.

"Son?"

He glanced over his shoulder to see his mother at the patio door.

"Everything okay?" asked Bernadette.

"Yeah."

"News?"

"It's work checking in."

"Hey, why don't you come back in? I made you another sandwich."

Food smothering. He didn't want another sandwich. His stomach hurt. It had shrunk to what felt like the size of a bean, and he was still getting used to Western food. He turned toward the house, which started to become fuzzy and wavy.

"There's also something I've been meaning to tell you," said Bernadette.

As he took two unstable steps toward the house, his mother's words became muffled in his ear canals.

"It's about your grandmother's wedding ring . . . Emily . . ."

Nick heard the name, then passed out.

CHAPTER 15

"Any news about the elusive Mr. Chauncey? Did you get a chance to check his home?" Emily yawned. She had crashed before 8:00 p.m., overslept her alarm, and dashed out of the house as dawn was breaking. Without coffee or a chance to check her texts. It was a tough morning, but the thought of baby Brooklyn being out here alone and alive trumped her weary state.

With each stride she stretched the stiffness out of her tired limbs. She and Aditson were traversing the perimeter of Lake Isabella, heading south. They had returned to the site again Saturday morning to look for any signs of baby Brooklyn. Search-and-rescue dogs and their handlers were also combing the lake and woods around them.

"Sent a team there last night. Searched his home and property. As expected, he wasn't there. Nor was the vehicle he has registered with the DMV. The exterior of the house was in shambles, and the interior looked like a hoarder's mansion."

"Find anything that might connect him to Savannah?"

"We did luminol tests for presence of blood. All negative.

Unfortunately, it doesn't look like he's been living there for a while. Lots of cobwebs and mice turds in the living spaces. Even his bed."

Emily winced.

"We posted a BOLO for Colton Chauncey to all Michigan, Indiana, and Illinois law enforcement agencies around midnight," said Aditson, "and we already got intel. Here. Look." He held up his phone for her. "This is security footage from Freeport's Main Street gas station taken about a week before Savannah turned up dead. One of the attendants said Chauncey came there regularly to fuel up." Aditson showed her a grainy black-and-white image. Chauncey's hair was overgrown, and a beard was taking shape. Underneath it, Chauncey's face looked gaunt, and she saw the slight protrusion of his Adam's apple from his narrow neck. He wore a gray T-shirt in the photo that read in block black lettering: *DON'T ACT LIKE YOU'RE NOT IMPRESSED.*

Narcissists were easy to spot. Emily locked his image into her memory.

"And what about Brooklyn?" she asked.

"The state cops are just now issuing an Amber Alert," said Aditson. That meant law enforcement would spread the word among themselves about the missing baby and let other state officials and broadcasters know. "I had to argue she's in imminent danger." He added, "Another tip came in—Chauncey was spotted yesterday afternoon at the Silver Slipper. A patron saw him and one of the dancers talking outside by her car."

"What time?"

"Around four, I believe."

"Did you get a name or description of the dancer he was talking to?"

"I did. Her name's Raven Kane. She's worked there several years, according to the owner."

"Did you talk to her?"

"She's on my short list."

"I've dealt with a few of the young ladies over there," said Emily, who'd once impersonated a dancer to gain intel for a case she was working on. "They're not too keen on cops. Let me know if you want company."

"I might take you up on that."

She swatted at a swarm of gnats in her path. "Are we getting close?" An aerial view of the lake revealed it was the shape of a Y, with the leg pointing north and the two arms pointing southwest and southeast. Savannah's body had been found on the bottom of the Y leg. The only structure on that side of the lake was the abandoned fishing shack situated about fifty feet from the lake's northernmost tip.

"Did we ever find out whose shack that is?" asked Emily.

"The county deed records showed it belonged to Emmett Johnson. He died thirty-seven years ago, but the property was passed down to next of kin."

Emily thought that its sagging roof, rotted side boards, and rodent infestation made a strong case that his relatives had not thought much of the place.

"And who is that exactly?" she asked. "Are they still around?"

"Emmett was Chauncey's grandfather, on his mother Ruby's side."

"I see. And that's why Chauncey would know this lake was here."

Emily and Aditson headed to the southwest Y branch, where they'd seen from the GPS a single cottage that looked to be about seven hundred square feet. It was set back thirty feet from the lakeshore and shrouded in thick pines that obscured any clear view of Lake Isabella. Why anyone would want to live in such seclusion was beyond Emily's comprehension.

When they made a turn and could no longer see the north side of the lake, Emily spotted the metal glint of a Volkswagen SUV parked next to the cottage. A good sign.

Aditson rapped the front door, and an enormous bark greeted them.

Seconds later, a Great Dane stood at the door next to his master, his lean torso as high as the man's waist. The man was in his late sixties, an inch or two over six feet, with a full head of silver hair and the build of a runner or avid hiker.

"I saw you coming up from the lake," he said. "Don't get many visitors up here."

Emily glanced up and confirmed his surveillance camera above the door. Coming to his house, she had noted that there was no way anyone from this property could have seen where Savannah's body had been found on the leg of the Y. Only from the center of the Y were all three branches visible at once.

"Detective Aditson and Dr. Hartford," Aditson announced. "Do you have a minute?"

The man stepped onto the patio with his dog and shut the front door behind him. The Great Dane clung to his master's side, all the while eyeing Emily and Aditson.

"What's your name, sir?" Aditson asked politely.

"Hank Shepherd."

"This is your residence?"

"It's my home. Yes."

"How long have you lived here?"

"I should say, it's my summer home. I've been coming up here off and on for nearly eight years."

"Oh, where do you call home?"

"Glen Ellyn, Illinois."

Emily was familiar with the western Chicago suburb. Upper

middle class. Americana. Safe and tucked away from the frays of city life. "That's a nice place to live," she commented, smiling and hoping to put Shepherd at ease. "I used to live in Chicago."

"Oh, did you? Where?"

"In the Loop."

"I worked in the Loop for thirty years."

"And now?" Aditson said, building his line of questioning while maintaining a friendly tone.

"Retired. Two years."

"Congratulations," Emily said. "I'm sure it feels good to get away from all the hustle and bustle."

"I like the quiet," Shepherd said. Emily could tell there was more behind the simple statement.

"How long have you been up here?"

"Since the beginning of May. With a few overnight trips back to Chicago for various things. Why do you ask?" Shepherd's voice had a tinge of impatience. Anyone choosing to reside this far away from civilization likely would not relish interruptions from others.

"We're investigating a potential crime that occurred on Lake Isabella," Aditson said. Emily understood his tactic. People were more apt to add information when it was given to them first.

"What kind of crime?"

Aditson dodged the question. "Have you been at your residence the last couple days?"

"Mostly."

"Have you seen anyone around the lake in that time?"

"Out here? Nah."

"Any hikers? Fishers? Turtle hunters?"

"I chose this place because it's off the beaten path."

He hadn't answered the question directly.

"Hear anybody or anything unusual?" Aditson tried again in a roundabout way.

The Great Dane shook his head as a fly buzzed his left ear.

"A couple evenings ago, Milton and I were on the patio reading." He scratched Milton on the scruff. "I heard a crying sound that went on for a few moments. Milton perked his ears and started howling."

"Do you remember which evening?" asked Emily.

"Saturday? No, maybe it was Sunday. I don't know. It was the weekend."

Aditson noted it.

"Probably just a fox," said Shepherd.

"Did you see a fox?" asked Aditson.

"I see them all the time around here. But in the moment, that's what I assumed it was, and I didn't bother getting off my patio to look." Shepherd sounded convinced.

Emily glanced at the security camera hung above the front door. "How much storage does your camera keep?"

"I don't know. Never had to go back through it more than a day or two. I use it mostly to watch the parade of wildlife traversing the property. I saw a bear and her cubs once. Right on the front patio."

"Mind if we take a look?"

"I guess not. What exactly happened out here?" Shepherd pressed.

"I'll just need to get the storage card from the device. It will be returned to you," Aditson promised.

"Should I be worried?" said Shepherd.

Neither of them wanted to answer that.

Milton watched them as Shepherd took down the camera and removed the memory card for them. "You said you were a doctor?" Shepherd turned to Emily. "What's a doctor doing out here?"

Emily glanced at Aditson.

"Has someone been found dead?"

"We are investigating a death on the other side of the lake," Aditson told him in vague language. Shepherd would find out about Savannah soon enough through local news outlets or gossip.

"Was this person killed?" Shepherd reached down for Milton and stroked the top of his head.

"We can't divulge any details," Emily said.

"Am I in danger?"

"It's always a good idea to remain vigilant."

"That offers little comfort."

"If you see or hear anything from now on, will you please reach out to me?" Aditson handed Shepherd his card.

They left the man and the dog standing on the patio, staring at the lake, their serene paradise tarnished by the dark news.

When Emily and Aditson arrived back at the death-investigation scene, the cadaver dogs had identified three areas of interest. One was where Savannah's body had been found. The other two places were to the north and south, each about five feet away from the first. The divers went in to look more closely at both locations but soon found out that under the lake's three feet of water was a soft, silty bottom that sucked them down like quicksand. In a matter of minutes, they were thigh high in the muck and abandoned the search. Nothing more could be done.

Emily sighed. It had already been a long day yesterday, and she hadn't had enough hours to start the autopsies for either Savannah Browdey or Jonah Hampton. "I'd better get to the morgue."

"I'll catch up with you later," said Aditson.

As Emily hiked out of the woods toward the main road, her cell service returned, and she saw that she had two texts. One was from Flora. A picture of what looked to be a radial bone—the lower half of an arm.

Need ur help!

The second was from Nick's mom, Bernadette. Nick was at Freeport General. He had been admitted and was alive. But unresponsive.

CHAPTER 16

Raven slept in fits and starts, as the baby now dictated her schedule. The child had woken her up at five on Saturday morning. She got out of bed, fed the baby, changed her, and, worried that the active infant might roll off the couch, created a makeshift bed for her on the living room floor. Then she had tried to go back to sleep for a few hours. Each time the baby moved or cooed, Raven jolted awake. By eight, she started phoning Colton, but she kept getting his voicemail. Texts to him went unanswered. She was beginning to think he'd been full of shit. He knew how to play on her emotions. Maybe it was his plan all along to unload this baby on her. Her friends at the club always chided her for being gullible; those who were even harsher called her a fool. Maybe they were right.

Out of pure exhaustion, Raven canceled the following night's waitressing shift and drifted back to sleep on the sofa when her cell rang.

Maxie, a dancer friend from the Slipper.

"Hey, Max," Raven said in a tired voice.

"Hey, baby doll," the sugary voice sang back. "You okay, sweetie?"

"Yeah. Why?"

"Rich just told me you canceled your shift tonight."

"Feeling under the weather," she lied.

"Oh, sorry to hear that, baby. You need anything? Bread? Soup? Cold meds?"

"You're sweet, but I'm good. See you later?" Raven was in no mood for idle chatter.

"Sweetie, wait. You sure you're okay?"

"Just need some sleep." Next to her the baby cooed.

"What was that?" Maxie said, hearing it over the line.

"Oh . . . just a big yawn," Raven let out a nervous laugh. "You caught me sleeping."

"So you haven't heard? That girl who accused Colton of rape?"

"Okay?"

"She turned up dead."

Raven shot up to a seated position in a rush of adrenaline. "What? You sure?"

"Yeah. I heard from one of the cops who comes in here to see me."

"What happened?"

"Murdered, he said, but he wouldn't tell me how. I guess her baby's missing. My cop thinks she's probably dead too."

Raven's throat went instantly dry.

"Have you seen him lately?" Maxie asked.

"Who?" Raven played dumb.

"Colton, baby doll. Your ex. Or whatever he is to you this week."

"Max, my stomach doesn't feel so good." That was the truth. "Talk to you later, 'kay?" She hung up, her skin flushed and sweaty as a real wave of nausea swelled inside her.

It was confirmed: She was a fool.

CHAPTER 17

Ruby's bare foot gently grazed the wooden slats of her front porch as she swayed back and forth on her glider. Her mind twisted itself around a memory she hadn't given thought to for nearly thirty years. Leslie Albright had been the pretty girl from her eldest boy's class that he was going to marry—or that was what he'd told Ruby the day he brought the sweet young thing home to meet her.

Truth was, that day Ruby had been sipping a little homemade hooch. She'd been on the front porch, watching the drive and waiting for her husband to show up, just like she did every late afternoon. Thomas had been up north, working a job for God knew how long. More likely, he was with his mistress. Ruby had sometimes prayed he'd stay up there for good.

But it had been her son who pulled up their dirt drive that day. He jumped out and ran around the car to open the door for his pretty girlfriend.

"Ma, this is Leslie Albright." He proudly presented her to his mother like she was a twenty-pound bass he'd just snagged from the river.

Leslie smiled uncomfortably, and later, after they'd gone inside, her eyes darted around the humble dwelling. Ruby could see the girl trying to hold back her shock.

Later, when Ruby looked around their rooms after Leslie left, she saw them how the girl must have. The nubby, worn carpet. A dusty fireplace mantel cluttered with knickknacks. Faded, ripped curtains sagging over dirty windows.

"Your name's Albright?" Ruby had asked as they entered the house. "Isn't your father a lawyer in town?"

"That's right."

"Where do you live? Do you have any brothers or sisters? What's your mother like?" Ruby had pelted her with questions, trying to make conversation.

Leslie had been brought up in a fancy two-story Victorian in town. Her mother did a lot of volunteer work, and they were members of the Freeport Country Club. She had three younger brothers. The four kids were spaced evenly in age: sixteen, fourteen, twelve, and ten. Her brothers were sometimes pests, said Leslie, but she loved them just the same. Even so, she couldn't wait to get away to college.

Ruby hoped her eldest was headed for college too. Maybe they'd go together.

"Please have a seat. Can I get you some tea?" Ruby offered.

"No, ma'am. Thank you." Leslie took a seat on the sofa, staying on the edge of the cushion, as if she didn't want to dirty her white slacks and soft pink sweater.

"That's sure a pretty sweater you got on," Ruby told her.

"It's cashmere. You have to hand-wash it."

Ruby had no idea what cashmere was or why someone would bother with an article of clothing they couldn't toss into the washing machine.

When it was time for Leslie to leave, she shook Ruby's hand

politely, saying that it was nice to meet her. Ruby knew before that girl was off the front porch that Leslie Albright would not be coming back and that her darling boy was not going to be marrying this one. He was beneath her, though the poor kid couldn't see it yet. No matter how handsome or chivalrous her son was—and he was a gentleman—this girl was not going to be part of his future.

Several weeks later, that boy was ripped to shreds when Leslie Albright broke up with him. Just three nights after, she went out with a fancy-schmancy college boy.

"He's someone's douchebag son from her pa's country club," her baby had told Ruby while hiding his bloodshot eyes behind sunglasses.

Late that night she'd found him sneaking some of her hooch. She hadn't scolded him. Instead, she led him to the kitchen table, set out two small mugs, and poured them half full. While she sipped hers, he had slammed his, then refilled the cup. Ruby allowed it. He took down a second draft. They sat in silence as she waited for him to talk, get it out.

But like her husband—he held it in.

Shortly after that, her baby boy, an A student, started skipping classes and sleeping in. The supply of hooch in the cellar under the house dwindled. He'd take her car and leave her stranded for weeks at a time. His appearance morphed from a clean-cut, clean-shaven young man who took pride in pressed shirts and clean jeans to a slovenly, long-haired, bearded vagabond. If Ruby didn't know he was her son, she'd never have recognized him as one of hers.

He left one night and returned several months later, dressed in the same clothes he'd left in. He said he'd been out West. She didn't ask for details, only if he was okay. And was he hungry?

"I'm good, Ma. Thanks for not hounding me." He handed her a grocery bag of items from the market. "Got ya some food."

She unpacked the bag and made a meal for them.

The next morning her son packed the car with his belongings and left.

Ruby watched him leave from her porch glider, a throbbing ache in her chest. His final exit crushed any hope she clung to that he might find a better position in society and take her with him.

In the following weeks, she settled into the rhythm of living on her own. She found that without the fear of losing anyone else, there was a new peace.

When the ground thawed and the threat of frost passed, she planned her garden. It started with a six-by-ten-foot plot that she dug out on the side of the house, southeast facing. Each year she expanded the garden by another sixty square feet. Eventually it took up the entire east and south yards, and it was still creeping west over the septic tank. Ruby grew mostly sunflowers around the perimeter of the farm home. Next season, she lined the driveway with them. Then she planted them along the exterior of the garden. Her happy golden family, who started the day facing east, then bowed to the glowing western sun in the evening.

On this late-fall day, their heads bent low, mournful, and their leaves curled, withering brown. Tomorrow she'd harvest the heads and dry them in the cellar for next year's planting. So they'd rise again for a new generation.

CHAPTER 18

After leaving Lake Isabella, Emily drove to Freeport Hospital to check on Nick. Before entering his room, she asked to see his chart. His first blood work results were in. There were concerns.

Outside Nick's room, Bernadette was waiting for her, her face gray with worry.

"Have you been in there?" Emily asked her.

"Not yet. I'm a little nervous."

Emily grabbed two N95 face masks from the receptacle on the wall outside Nick's room. Peeking inside, she found Nick lost in thought and standing at the window, his gaze fixed on the sky. She handed one mask to Bernadette. "Put this on, please."

Bernadette noticed Emily holding Nick's chart. "What does his blood work look like?" she asked.

"Let's just say it's a good thing he's here." Emily wasn't going to give any specific medical information away without Nick being present. When they were both masked, she asked, "Ready?"

Bernadette nodded as Emily opened the door, and they entered the room.

"Hey," Emily said softly, coming to Nick's side, unsure what version of him she was going to get today.

He turned to her, saying nothing, his face soft with a grateful smile. The old Nick.

"What happened?" Emily asked Bernadette.

"He blacked out and collapsed on his patio," Bernadette gushed, her voice trembling with worry.

"Just a little low blood sugar," Nick said, brushing it off.

"He had just eaten a sandwich," Bernadette informed Emily.

"It's definitely more than just low blood sugar," Emily told him.

"So how bad is it?" he asked.

"Your white blood cell count is over fifteen thousand. And your C-reactive protein is at a sixteen. And your hemoglobin's at an eight."

"English, please."

"Normal CRP is less than one. And your WBC is five thousand higher than it was when you were tested a week ago. The low hemoglobin indicates anemia."

"Which means?"

"You've got an infection ramping up. And frankly I'm surprised they let you out of the hospital with a WBC over ten K and no orders to get retested in a few days. The question is where this infection is stemming from. Do you feel pain anywhere?"

"Just in my side from time to time."

"Near the scar?"

"Sort of in the bottom of my rib cage."

Emily placed her stethoscope on his chest to listen to his lungs. "Have you been feeling short of breath?"

"Ever since I left China." Nick was woozy and sounding less coherent in his speech. "But I manage."

As an attending doctor at Freeport Hospital, Emily was able to order a TB test from the nurses' station on an educated hunch. With Nick's history of travel, he might have contracted the disease in any number of countries he'd passed through.

She administered the test right away, rolling Nick's arm over and inserting a needle just below the skin. She pressed the syringe. The liquid antigen made a small bulb that looked like a mosquito bite.

"Now what?" asked Nick.

"We wait twelve hours. If the injection site forms a red lump, you're positive for TB. In the meantime, Bernadette, it's best if you don't overexpose yourself to him right now."

Bernadette paused to look at her son. Emily could tell she wanted to run over and hug him. She put her hand on Bernadette's arm.

"I promise you'll see him again. But you should say your goodbyes from across the room."

Bernadette squeezed her son's arm. "Good night, son. Sleep well."

Emily followed her out of the hospital room and into the hallway.

"He's not gonna die, is he?" Nick's mom asked.

Emily didn't speak until they were well outside his earshot and down the hall. Then she said, "This isn't 1910. We can treat TB with a long-term, heavy course of antibiotics. But he'll have to be in quarantine."

"Here?"

"Initially."

"For how long?" Bernadette asked, her worry ramping up.

"A couple weeks."

"But aren't you worried you've been infected?"

"I'll be fine." But Emily did have a sprout of concern, especially since she had been in close contact with him on the ride home yesterday. And with this new homicide case on her plate, she couldn't afford time off.

"May I stop by later?" Bernadette's tone was more command than question.

"Not today. Not until we know what we're dealing with."

"What if Nick needs something from home?"

"You can drop it at the nurses' station," Emily insisted.

"You'll keep me posted?"

"Always." Emily gave her a quick hug.

Bernadette slouched off down the hospital hallway and into the elevator. Emily waited until the doors closed before she trekked back to Nick's room.

"I'm going to order you a chest x-ray to check for lesions," she said. Since he hadn't shown these symptoms or complaints during his stay at the hospital in Rock River, there was no reason they would have checked his lungs. "After that, you'll have to be admitted to a room in quarantine."

Nick sighed. "Just one more stop on an already long stretch of horrible luck."

"No wonder you can't gain weight." She eyed him. "Did you suspect you had TB?"

"Yeah, maybe."

"But you've never been treated?"

"I was on the run. How would I get treatment?" Nick bit back.

She sighed and let it go, putting on her bulletproof doctor exterior.

"Em, I know that I've been short with you and . . . I don't know . . . Being back here. I can't explain it."

Emily took a seat on the edge of his bed, relieved that he was at least aware of his behavior. Relieved that he'd confided something to her.

"I want to help," she said gently. "I want to be here for you."

"And you are." Nick reached for her hand. "I'm still sorting things out."

Emily drew his hand to her cheek and caressed it.

"What does it feel like . . . to be you right now?" she asked.

"I'm trying to figure out what's real and what's not, and if my world's going to come crashing down . . . again."

There was so much in those words that Emily wanted to dig into. Was he having a psychotic break? Dissociative problems? Nick was radiating a sense of fear and foreboding that she had never seen before. What had caused it? If he was never able to talk about it with her, no doubt it would drive a wedge between them.

"I want to help, but I don't know how," said Emily, squeezing his hand. "Can you let me in? Just a little?"

"I was . . . taken," he sputtered, the words coming out painfully.

"Taken how?"

"Imprisoned."

Emily's throat tightened at the word. The idea itself wasn't a surprise to her. He had returned bedraggled and war weary. She didn't have to draw a very long line to the idea that he had escaped from a situation so dire that it had almost killed him. She wanted to burrow her head into his chest and hold him until they both turned wrinkled and gray. And even then, it wouldn't be enough time.

"Nick, I'm so sorry." She paused to swallow the lump in her throat. The platitudes formed on her tongue. *You'll be okay. There's a reason for everything. What doesn't kill us makes us stronger.* They dissolved with a stale taste.

"It's what I signed up for, isn't it?" he said, looking up with an ironic smile.

She didn't try to talk him down because she knew he wouldn't hear it. "Where were you taken to?"

"I don't know. It was like a warehouse. It felt like a clinic. I remember rows of beds. Doctors. Nurses. Officers. Horrible smells. Urine. Shit. Rubbing alcohol. Sometimes I was aware of being there, but it was a fog. I was sedated the whole time. I couldn't talk or feed myself."

Emily felt her heart breaking. "How long were you in this place?"

"I've tried to piece together a timeline. From when I was captured until my escape . . . was a couple weeks—I think? I don't exactly know." He looked down and swallowed. "Describing it . . ." Nick couldn't go on.

"Makes it real?"

Nick nodded.

Emily reached with her free hand to feel for the scar she knew was on Nick's side. Before she even touched him, she felt the area radiating with heat that might indicate a lingering infection in the tissue.

He pulled back before she could touch him.

"I think you need a stronger antibiotic," she said. "Maybe several."

"I'm fine."

"You are most certainly not fine."

"That your official medical opinion?"

"Yes. And I'm just trying to understand what's best to do. I really am."

The door swung open, and a team of masked nurses rolled in a portable x-ray machine. Emily's hand slipped from his, and she slid off the bed to make room for them.

Time to see how much damage had been done.

CHAPTER 19

While waiting for the hospital to return with Nick's x-ray results, Emily dashed home to grab a bite to eat. After she made sure Nick was settled and receiving proper treatment, it would be another long stint at the hospital and the morgue. Emily headed to the kitchen and grabbed turkey slices, Swiss cheese, mustard, and the remains of a loaf of wheat bread. Cradling them in her arms, she plopped them onto the marble countertop and was starting to assemble her sandwich when Flora flew in.

"Did you get my text, Aunt Em?"

"I did. I've been meaning to get back to you. It's been a bit hectic."

"Mom told me. How's Nick?"

Emily shook her head, and Flora took the cue not to press further.

"You hungry? I can make you one." After Flora agreed, Emily pulled up the bone picture on her phone. "So what's this all about?"

"I found it when I was hiking in the woods with my friends."

"Well, where is it now?"

"In my room."

"Oh." Emily's tone rang with surprise.

"Did I do something wrong?"

"If you're worried it might be human, best to leave things in their places so you don't disturb any potential evidence."

"Yeah. I didn't think about that."

"But next time you will. Go get it. Let's take a look." Emily placed two sandwiches on a paper towel.

Flora rushed away, and then Emily heard her half sister's heated voice talking to someone on her cell phone. After a few moments, the ever-stylish-even-when-running-errands Anna, nearing forty and without a gray hair on her head, ducked into the kitchen.

"You're home?" she asked.

"Only for lunch," said Emily.

Flora came flying back into the room with the bone.

Anna turned to look at her eldest. "And what's on your agenda for the rest of the day?"

"Hang with Aunt Emily?"

Anna's brows went up as she checked Emily for a response.

"Fine by me. You want me to make you a sandwich?" Emily offered.

"No thanks. I've gotta drop Fiona at Premiere for her riding lesson. Are you sure you're okay with looking after Flora?"

"I'm fourteen."

"Exactly," her mother answered.

Flora put the bone on the kitchen table. "This is what I found on my hike."

Emily rolled it over in her hands. "It looks like a radial bone. Lower part of the arm. But human? Not sure. I have a friend in anthropology at the University of Michigan who can tell us."

"Do you think there might be more out there?" asked Flora.

"I'll talk to Detective Aditson and let him know what you discovered. If this is from a *Homo sapiens*, he might organize a search."

"Really? I found something important?"

"Possibly. We have to treat it like a missing person. Aditson may want to talk with you first."

"About what?"

"Where you found it. How it looked when you saw it."

Flora nodded. "I can do that."

"Could you bring us back to the location you discovered it if you had to?"

"I think so."

"We should wrap it up to protect it."

"I have a few old newspapers," Anna offered.

"Good work, Nancy Drew," Emily praised her niece.

"Who's that?"

"Seriously?" She met Flora's blank look with her incredulous one. "Only a classic mystery series featuring one of the first strong crime-solving female protagonists that literature ever created."

"Really?"

"And she's a teen."

"Where do I find these books?"

"Ever hear of a library?" Emily teased. Her niece gave her an annoyed look. "Start with *The Secret of the Old Clock*. Then we'll talk."

"Can I help you in the morgue today?" Flora asked.

"It's a pretty gruesome case, Flora."

"How am I gonna learn anything hard if I don't get my hands dirty?" Over the past year, Emily had been mentoring Flora through various cases that came across her desk. But so far, Flora's assistance had been strictly in office. She had not been out on the field.

Emily admired Flora's resolve and curiosity. Emily had been investigating cases with her father at Flora's age, and it was true he hadn't sheltered her from the tough ones. She had seen traffic fatalities, scenes of suicide by gunshot, and the aftermath of grisly house fires.

"The victim has been submerged in water for a few days," she said. "She's almost unrecognizable, and the smell—it's the worst, except for maybe charred human remains."

"How will I know unless I try?" Flora wasn't going to back down.

Emily liked that about both Flora and Fiona. They had the strong Hartford will in their DNA. "Okay. But change into your grungiest, oldest clothes. Something you don't care if you need to bleach or toss out later."

"My yard work clothes."

"Then find an old pair of sneakers and put your hair up in a bun."

Flora nodded, taking note.

"Hope you liked your sandwich, because you may end up tasting it twice," quipped Emily.

"I'm stronger than you think, Aunt Em."

"Tell that to your autonomic reflexes. They have minds of their own." Emily rose from the table, sweeping off crumbs from her sandwich onto a paper towel. "Wheels up in ten."

Flora scurried off to change, and Anna again stuck her head into the dining room. "You think she's ready for this?" she asked.

"She wouldn't be asking if she weren't ready. Trust me, I didn't ask my dad to join him in the morgue until I knew I wanted to be there," Emily said to quell her half sister's worry. "The question is, Are you?"

"More ready for this than this Noah who asked her to the school dance."

"Who is he?" asked Emily.

"A junior from school. She was certainly glowing when she got home from her hike."

"Crush glowing or first-kiss glowing?" asked Emily.

"Can you tell the difference?"

"It's all in the gradation of the cheek shading."

"That sounds so clinical."

"The pinker the cheeks, the more intimate the interaction."

"Have you read studies on this or something?"

"Professional observation," Emily stated with the voice she used when asserting her medical authority.

Anna cocked her head at her sister, unsure. "Part of me wants to believe you."

"So which was it?"

"I haven't seen the scale you refer to," Anna joked. "But if I had to guess, I'd say shades of a first kiss."

Emily grinned. "I see. And what do we know about this boy?"

"He was with her when she found that bone." Anna's glance went to the table where it lay.

"I'll see if I can do a little Nancy Drewing on Noah while we're in the morgue."

"That's exactly what I needed to hear," said Anna. "Thank you, Mildred Wirt Benson."

"Who?"

"The author of the series. Well, of the first twenty-three books."

"I thought it was Carolyn Keene."

"That was her pen name," said Anna. "And that of the other authors, both male and female, who continued the series."

Emily realized that she had never really considered Nancy

Drew as the creation of an actual person's imagination. She'd started devouring the series in third grade, finding a kindred spirit in Nancy, whose adventures she related to. Even at that young age, Emily felt she would follow in her father's footsteps as a mystery solver. She'd never thought about the masterminds behind the plots. Emily smiled to herself. She was Carolyn Keene more than Nancy Drew, an investigator following clues in her own pursuit of justice.

Her phone pinged with a text from the head radiologist at Freeport Hospital. He had spotted an unusual result on Nick's scan.

CHAPTER 20

Saturday afternoon, Emily and Flora arrived at Freeport Hospital. Emily sent Flora to the cafeteria for a snack while she rushed to the radiology department to check in again on Nick. After looking at his charts, she didn't need a TB test to tell her that Nick was positive. Also, something else deeply sinister was found in the scans.

Neither she nor the head of radiology and his team could quite believe what they were seeing.

Emily proceeded slowly to the fourth floor, where Nick had been assigned a negative-airflow ICU room. She was trying to formulate a way to tell Nick about his scans.

Pausing outside his hospital room to don her gloves, goggles, and N95 mask, she took a deep breath, cleared her head, then gave a rap on the door. "Nick, it's me," she said, her voice muffled by the face mask.

When she entered, he was sitting up in bed, scrolling on his phone. He looked up.

"Bad news first," he said, holding out his arm. A small red welt was starting to form at the antigen injection site.

"Definitely positive for TB," she said. "Which means you'll be quarantined up here for a minimum of two weeks, unless your symptoms go away."

He sighed.

Emily went to his bed. "I know. You just got your freedom back." She attempted a smile until she read Nick's grim face. Instead, she reached for his hand with her gloved one and squeezed it. Nick squeezed back. Emily didn't let go for a long moment. She had more news to share, and it wasn't good.

"I rechecked your blood work and noticed your cortisol levels are also high, which would explain why your body is having a hard time fighting off infection. It's not surprising, given the amount of stress your body has been under the past year plus."

"So what do I do about this?"

"Good news: If the antibiotics are doing their job and your blood work is back to normal, they'll release you sooner. But you'll still need to take it easy for another six to eight weeks. And you'll be on antibiotics for about a year."

"That's a long time."

"Tuberculosis is a serious disease."

"And the x-rays?"

Emily didn't know how to break the next part of her news to him. After reviewing the results, she was in shock herself. She had even spoken to the head of radiology to make sure she was looking at the correct scans, and yep—they did indeed belong to Nick. There was no denying what she'd seen.

"Your right lung shows some lesions. Maybe thirty percent. My guess is that you've had TB for quite some time and your body never fully healed. Then, with the stress you put on it with your traveling—"

"I did what I had to." Nick's lips tightened.

"And you'll recover." She paused. "But there's something else. More concerning."

"Cancer?"

"No, it's not cancer. Nor is there any other disease present that we can detect from the x-rays."

"What is it then?"

"Nick, your left lung is— I don't know how to say this. It seems so unbelievable."

"Just say it."

"A third of your lung is missing."

"What?"

"It appears as if it's been surgically removed."

Nick stared at her in disbelief. "Are you sure?"

"Do you want to see your images?"

"I sure do." Nick scooted up in his bed, and Emily placed the images on the light box mounted to the wall. She was aware that living organ donors could contribute partial lung lobes to their recipients. But Nick didn't seem to have willingly offered this gift to anyone. So how had it happened, and why didn't he know about it? She pointed to the missing area. "There is significant scar tissue here, and I suspect you're sustaining an infection just beneath the surgical site or, worse, internally."

"Am I going to be okay?"

"You survived this, but you'll always be a bit compromised." Emily watched for his reaction. "How did this happen?"

Nick's stare turned hard. He swung his legs off the bed. "I need to talk to Roe."

"Where are you going?"

He started to pace. "Where are my clothes?"

"Nick, you're in quarantine."

"I can do that at home."

"You are not well. Let them monitor you until your body can recover."

"I'll be fine. I made it across the world, didn't I?"

"Your body is breaking down. It will not sustain you forever."

"The antibiotics will kick in, and I'll be fine."

"You need to avoid stress and strenuous activity. For a good eight to twelve months."

"You gonna tell my boss that?"

"You're not even approved to be back to work." Emily's voice rose, and she planted herself in front of the door.

"I'm not gonna stay locked up in this place."

"Quarantine is not optional."

"You can't arrest me," he said, finding his shirt and slipping his arms into the sleeves. "And this isn't a prison."

At the mention, Emily began to worry that being cooped up in a hospital room might be a trigger for Nick. "I know you, Nick. You think you're okay, but you're not."

He stopped dressing and glared at her. "I know what you're implying."

"Your emotional health is just as important as your physical health."

"I don't need more therapy."

"If you don't want to talk to me about it, okay, I get it. But you need to talk to *someone* about what happened to you over there."

"And there it is, the pity." Nick sighed, slapping his arms against his sides.

"That's not what— I'm just trying to help—"

"Then treat me like a normal human being."

Emily held her hands up. "Listen, tough guy, you're not breaking quarantine on my watch," she said, blocking the doorway to the hall.

Nick backed down and plopped onto the two-seater visitor sofa in the corner of his private hospital room.

"What can I do? Can I bring you anything?" Emily softened her voice once she saw Nick was being compliant.

Nick sighed and placed his head against the headrest. "Just stay here with me a bit longer. Please."

Emily made sure the door was sealed closed. She took a seat next to him. His sunken eyes studied her tired ones.

"You look exhausted," he said.

"It was a two-body day, and I still have to do the exams."

"Wanna talk about it?"

She wasn't sure how much she should be saying. But she so desperately wanted to connect with him.

"I know. I know. Confidentiality and all that. My lips are sealed," he said, and brushed his hand against hers, hooking their pinkie fingers together.

She started from the moment she'd first arrived at Lake Isabella.

CHAPTER 21

Colton arrived at his friend Terrell's fifth-floor apartment in Rock River late Friday night and jimmied the locked door. Once inside, he expected to find the place looking as it had two months ago, when he'd visited: the worn clay-colored couch, thinning sandstone carpet, and aluminum foil over the windows. Terrell hadn't been a clean or organized person. Colton expected to see stacks of junk mail, books, and piles of old newspapers leaning against the smoke-stained custard-colored walls. He expected to crunch across a sea of fast-food wrappers that used to litter the floor from living room to kitchen. He expected to smell the overflowing kitchen garbage can. But it was different today.

The living room was barren of the hoarder's collections, as was the bedroom of the Section 8 housing. Its couch and carpet were the same, but the windows were draped with thick green velvet curtains that blocked outside light and provided color to the otherwise bland room. They were hung precisely and securely from the window trim. The kitchen had been cleaned up; the garbage can was only half full. The cupboards were lined with clean dishes, glasses, and serving ware. The small pantry to the left of the fridge contained various dry goods: crackers, canned soup, rice, sugar. None of the junk food Terrell always had lying around. The old fridge was wiped clean inside and out and held a half gallon of milk, cheese, vegetables in plastic wrap, and a bag of apples.

Colton continued to the single bedroom. Terrell's belongings were neatly stacked in the oversize closet. Notably his prize saxophone case was in front, standing like a soldier to guard his things. Terrell's queen-size bed was made and covered by a simple cotton comforter. Only a digital plug-in alarm clock, drinking glass, and ink pen sat on the garage sale wooden nightstand.

In the bathroom, Colton found one black bath towel hanging over the shower curtain rod. One toothbrush sat in a cup on the sink countertop. And one set of hand towels hung on a bar under the bathroom window.

Terrell didn't have any relatives that Colton knew of. Who was living here now? And when had they moved in?

Colton began unpacking the bedroom closet to find the box he'd come for. He pulled out Terrell's valuables: antique war relics, his great-grandmother's jewelry collection, various other musical instruments. The saxophone had been Terrell's baby, his companion, his soulmate. Over the past year, Colton had turned the valuables into cash when he needed extra reserves.

But the box was gone.

After tearing apart the closet, Colton searched the entire apartment, which, now that it had been cleaned up, took little time. Frustration fueling him, he stacked the stuff in the closet back in place, setting the sax where it had stood guard. Colton was fuming, sweating profusely as he paced the place four times over in a futile effort to find the damn thing. Whoever was living here now, clearly squatting, most certainly knew about the box

Colton was looking for. Maybe they'd even pawned it. He'd have to hide out for a few days to survey the place and confront the loafer. Give him a shakedown.

But where to stay? Had to be close by so he could keep watch.

He slipped from the apartment, relocking the simple door handle lock that provided little true security to the place. He descended three flights of stairs, then crouched under the staircase between the first and second floor. He remained motionless as he waited for his opportunity. An hour went by before a woman in her twenties wearing a medical uniform entered the building at ten past eleven. She must be coming off a second shift, Colton surmised. He observed as she checked her mailbox in the lobby, then shuffled tiredly to her first-floor apartment at the back of the building. He unfolded himself from his hiding place.

The dim hallway was made even dimmer by a burnt-out set of bulbs in a fluorescent light fixture overhead. As she was digging for her key at the bottom of a very large purse, Colton tiptoed up behind her. She was completely unaware of his hulking presence as she unlocked her door. As soon as it cracked open, Colton smothered her mouth with his oversize hand and pushed her inside. They both disappeared without a sound into the apartment, lock latching seconds later.

CHAPTER 22

"What's the VapoRub for?" asked Flora as Emily wiped a small amount of menthol gel on Flora's upper lip.

"Second line of defense." Emily secured her face mask, and her eyes met her niece's. "Breathe only through your mouth."

They entered the morgue in the Freeport Hospital basement; the heavy metal door slammed shut behind them, sealing them into the chamber. Under a thin sheet, Savannah Browdey's body was on the metal autopsy table in the middle of the cooled room. The acrid odor of decomp accosted them.

Flora, out of habit, drew in air with her nose and started to gag.

"Pucker and use your mouth." Emily showed her how to take little sips of air along the bottom of her throat.

"That actually helps," said Flora after small puffs of breath billowed her face mask in and out. "I can still smell it."

"After a few minutes, you won't notice the stench. Our olfactory bulb takes only ninety seconds to get used to a strong odor. That's why after a short time you don't smell burnt toast. Or that heavy dose of perfume your classmate is wearing."

Emily went to her workstation to collect tools necessary for the exam. Flora stood back near the door, eyes locked on the victim draped under the sheet.

"Gloves and apron are in the drawer next to the sink. After you put them on, would you mind removing the sheet?"

Flora shuffled to the sink.

"First, we'll photograph the body and then undress her and draw a blood sample. After that, I'll open her up, and we'll take a look at her organs. You can help me weigh and measure them. Okay?"

She nodded. Her silence and wide-eyed look indicated to Emily that her niece was taking it all in. Flora removed the sheet but averted her eyes, not looking at the body. She backed away and stood there, embracing the crumpled sheet and awaiting further instruction.

"You can fold it and place it on the countertop."

Emily worked her way around Savannah's decomposed corpse, doing a cursory visual exam. The duct tape had not been removed from her eyes and mouth. Her hands were still bound behind her. The chain that had been used to tether her to the cement block was still wrapped around her body. Emily left everything in place until she had photographed all sides of Savannah's body.

Flora finally took a look. "Why is her skin so saggy?" she asked.

"It's part of the decomposition process. After a person dies, the body releases methane gas, which causes bloating, especially in the abdomen. That stretches out the skin, and when the gases are all released, the body deflates. That, along with the breakdown of tissue, loosens the skin."

"Kinda like a helium balloon?"

"Exactly. Her skin is saggy because once we got her out of the cool water, which was slowing down the decomposition process, the ambient air temperature began to accelerate it."

Next Flora helped Emily undress Savannah. Emily taught her how to collect, record, and store all the items and clothing found on a victim. She was a quiet assistant, taking it all in. Once the body was undressed, Emily took another round of photographs, employing Flora's help to turn the body and lift the limbs. When that was complete, Emily took out the scales, knives, and saws she would need for the internal examination.

"You ready for this part?" she asked her niece, who had relaxed more into her position of assistant.

"I think so." But Flora's tone was uncertain.

"I'll walk you through the process so there won't be any surprises."

Flora nodded. "Will there be a lot of blood?"

"Some. But not like you see on TV, because the heart is no longer pumping," Emily assured her. "Your job is to be my scribe. I'll tell you what to record, and you write it down. There'll be a lot of technical terms and numbers. So if you have any questions, ask me to clarify."

"Is this how you learned from your dad to become a doctor?"

"It was a good training ground, and it definitely gave me a head start on anatomy. But there's more to it."

Emily moved Flora to the side of the table. "Let's make an exterior examination of the body first. We may get clues about what happened to her even before she's opened up."

Emily glanced over her shoulder at Flora. Her face had blanched.

"You okay?"

Flora nodded.

"You feel sick?"

"No. And I don't smell the decomp anymore."

"Good. You have any questions?"

"She's so young."

"Just a few years older than you." Emily sat in the moment, awaiting her response.

Her father had given her more than anatomy and medicolegal training. He was wise enough to guide her psychologically and emotionally through death investigation. Between the incisions and the dissections of organs, he would marvel over the mystery of humanity. "We are so much more than bone and tissue. We are beings with spirits and souls connected to something much greater than us."

"I was wondering . . ." Flora's voice cracked through Emily's memory. "What is it like to die underwater?"

Emily paused to gather her thoughts. Drowning was one of the worst ways to die.

"There are two ways to drown," she said. "There's a wet drowning, in which a person breathes in water that fills their lungs. And the other is called a dry drowning, where water in the throat causes a laryngospasm. This closes the airway, and the person can't breathe. When the brain can't get the oxygen it needs, it dies."

"Is it painful?" asked Flora in a small voice.

"When you're trying to hold your breath, your lungs start to burn. At some point, a person's involuntary response is to breathe. But obviously the lungs fill with water, not air. As the brain loses oxygen, the body convulses. Mercifully, a person loses consciousness before their brain shuts down and dies."

"A small gift of grace in a horrible situation," Flora observed.

"I like that you see it that way," said Flora. "Drowning is actually a diagnosis that medical examiners make after all other causes of death have been ruled out because it's hard to prove it definitively."

"So do we know she drowned?" asked Flora.

"First I have to do process of elimination."

"What do you mean?"

"Let's think about possible means of dying, starting with unnatural ways. Do we see any gunshot entry or exit points?"

Flora glanced at Savannah and shook her head.

"Any places on her body where she was struck? It's called bludgeoning."

"What would that look like?"

"Broken skin. Contusions. Indentations on the skin or skull. Large welts. Broken bones. Sometimes even protrusions of bone through the skin."

"I didn't see anything like that."

"Me neither." Emily drew Flora to Savannah's upper body. "We will also have to rule out heart attack, drug overdose, and any disease. But I won't be able to do that until we look under the skin and get her blood work back."

"What if she was strangled? What does that look like?" Emily recognized the growing interest in Flora's tone. When she had been learning with her father, Emily was a bubbler of questions. Even if he had been exhausted or overtired, Dad would entertain every last one of them, drilling into her the fine details of a system of organs, or the chemistry of the blood, or the pathology of a disease.

"If she was strangled, you would see evidence of torn or bruised skin around the neck," said Emily. "Do you see any of that?"

Flora looked at the girl's clay-colored skin. "It's hard to tell with the coloring, but I don't see anything."

"Let's feel around the neck." Emily guided Flora's gloved hand over the neck bones, esophagus, and throat. "It takes a solid knowledge of anatomy and good old experience to know what you're feeling for, but you'll have to take my word for it. There's no damage here.

"There's one more thing we can check for," Emily continued. "If she was strangled, the blood vessels in the eyes and throat would hemorrhage. We won't be able to look at the throat until we open it." Emily inched the duct tape off slowly, then pried the lids of Savannah's eyes open. Flora jerked back.

"You okay?"

"It's just weird. Her staring out like that."

Emily understood that it could be disconcerting to look into a dead person's eyes. In the living, eyes reflected the soul of a human being. Once a person died and the soul left, the eyes became just another pair of organs.

"When there are little broken blood vessels in the whites of the eyes, they are called petechial hemorrhages."

"Her eyes look clear to me."

"That's a correct observation." Emily nodded, and Flora jotted it down on her notepad.

"So I'm still not sure how we know if she was drowned," she said.

"We need to look at her lungs. If they're hyperinflated and if the lung tissue is blue tinged on the surface, it's another good indicator of drowning," Emily explained. "But we already have strong physical evidence that Savannah was drowned because of how she was found: in the water, chained to a cement block, her mouth taped shut, hands tied behind her back. All of this points to the cause and manner of her death."

"What's the difference between cause and manner?"

"Cause describes what led to a death. For instance, asphyxiation is a cause of death that happens when airflow is restricted. Then you have the manner, which is the nature of a death. There are just five manners of death we can list on a death certificate: natural, accidental, suicide, homicide, or undetermined."

Emily glanced up at her niece, who was turning green.

"Flora? You feel okay?"

Flora shook her head slightly.

"Let's get some air."

Emily grabbed her niece by the arm and rushed her out of the morgue.

CHAPTER 23

The baby had been with Raven forty-eight hours when the Freeport Police Department called on Sunday in the late afternoon. She listened to the voicemail from a Detective Ishkode Aditson, who wanted to stop by to ask her a few questions about a case he was working on. He'd wondered when would be a good time, asking her to give him a call back, please. She flung her phone onto the sofa as if she were shaking a snake off her arm.

No. This can't be happening.

Raven paced the room, her eyes on the baby sleeping soundly in her blanket cocoon on the floor. Eventually she retrieved her phone from between the couch cushions and called Colton. His voicemail answered. The message she left him was curt. Maxie had told her the news about Savannah. He had lied to her. And although it wasn't the first time, this was grave business he'd roped her into. "Call me. Now!"

Her list of questions was growing. First and foremost, would Colton admit to killing that girl? Second, why had he let the baby live? Was it as simple as wanting to profit from a black-market baby adoption? Next, when was he coming back to get the kid? Did he know there was a detective on her ass? And what did he want her to tell the detective?

Raven rang and rang him, but Colton never answered. Finally she texted him one simple message: *I know what happened to this baby's mother!*

After hours of pacing the apartment and trolling the locals' social media, which was abuzz about the missing girl, she'd discovered the baby's name was Brooklyn.

Late in the afternoon, Colton texted. His instructions were for her to leave and take the baby north: *Don't use 75. Take* two-lane *roads all the way up and cross the Mackinac Bridge to the Chippewa reservation.* They could be under the radar there because Native Americans had their own law and their own police. Colton gave her the name of an old friend, WaliYona, who would house them until Colton could get up there and make other arrangements. As soon as he could, he would meet her there, and they would cross the border and disappear into Canada until they could locate a network to sell the baby.

Raven wasn't sure whether to trust him on this. She made herself a sandwich and picked at it. She downed a shot of bourbon. Then another. Within a few minutes, her nerves were less frayed and her mind a bit clearer. She could call a couple of the girls to pick up shifts for her. She'd tell them she needed to get away for a couple of weeks. At the Slipper, requests like this went unquestioned. Like when she'd disappeared for two weeks after the abortion.

Raven packed her bag and baby Brooklyn and headed out. What choice did she have?

With Colton's plan swimming through her mind, she sat in the driver's side of her Rav4, gazing at the baby asleep on the passenger seat. Raven tucked the blanket around the girl's tiny body.

As she did, Brooklyn's eyes popped open. Her little fists punched at the sky. Raven saw a look of confusion sweep over the infant's face. Brooklyn's thin lips quivered, then released a bloodcurdling wail.

Poor thing. No doubt she was wondering why her mama wasn't here to soothe her.

"Shhh. It's okay. Quiet now." Raven took hold of the girl's fists, folding them into her palms. "We're just going for a ride." It felt weird to have these apparently maternal instincts for a complete stranger. She imagined what it would have been like to have a baby of her own.

Raven rubbed the infant's back, and she stopped crying.

"Are you hungry?" She had no idea how often a baby should eat.

She dug into the diaper bag for a premade bottle of formula. She hoped she had applied the directions properly, since she didn't know exactly how old Brooklyn was or how much the girl weighed. Did she need two scoops or three? Raven had erred on the side of "less is more."

As she brought it to Brooklyn's lips, the baby latched onto the bottle with both hands and started to suck. What if she had given her too little? Brooklyn's eyes went wide as she drank, barely stopping to breathe.

"My goodness, look at you go." She should have put in three scoops.

Raven couldn't take her eyes off the baby.

I did that. I soothed her. I fed her.

Such simple acts of care had opened a well of compassion and confidence in Raven.

What if she drove to Canada instead? She could easily cross the border and pass as the baby's mother. She and Brooklyn could disappear into a new country, and Colton would never find them. She'd take on a new name. Get a job. Start over. Save the girl. But then again . . . . living on the run. All at her own expense and risk. Just the prospect of all that effort sent a wave of exhaustion over Raven.

No way. She had a life here.

Colton was a pathetic excuse for a man, and this innocent child didn't deserve to be trafficked or sold into a life of slavery.

What kind of monster kills the mother of a baby?

And Raven had let him seep into her life again and again! Even after he had persuaded her to kill their baby in the womb. Anger at him reached a boiling point. Her heart thumped at a runner's pace as she felt a panic attack coming on.

Brooklyn whimpered. Raven glanced over as the baby made a complete rollover in the seat. In the next second, she'd be onto the floor. Raven grabbed Brooklyn by the waistband of her pajama pants to tug her away from the edge. The baby rolled back into place and let out a little laugh.

"Was that funny, little girl?"

Raven smiled and tickled Brooklyn's tummy. She giggled again and squirmed in delight.

Raven laughed back. How quickly a bond could be formed between a woman and a helpless creature. It was unexplainable, like her friends who had children were always telling her.

She felt sorry for Brooklyn and ached for her own loss. She would have been a great mother.

For a moment Raven settled into the thought. She liked it. When would she have this chance again? The sand in her biological hourglass was thinning to the last granules. She turned again to the baby. Her flawless skin. Her bright eyes. The way her cheeks puckered when she grinned. Those pudgy little toes.

The wonder of this new life faded into the shaded realization that being in possession of Brooklyn meant Raven was an accomplice to a serious crime. She couldn't keep her here and risk that detective stopping by.

And that bastard Colton didn't care what happened to her. Just like he hadn't cared about their unborn child.

Raven threw the small SUV into drive and pulled out of her parking spot. She'd make her own plans, none of which involved being a criminal or a fugitive.

CHAPTER 24

Flora barely managed to hold down her lunch until Emily got them a few steps out the back door of the hospital. Then she bent over, spewing digested turkey and cheese on wheat onto the parking lot. After the last heave, Emily came up alongside her and rubbed her back.

"It's okay, hon. Happens to the best of us. I've seen men six foot six and two hundred fifty pounds blow chunks all over a crime scene."

"You're making that up," Flora moaned.

"I'm not. Next time you see him, ask Detective Aditson about his first autopsy."

"What if I'm not cut out for this?"

"It gets better. Don't give up yet."

Flora uncrooked herself. Emily walked her away from the mess on the ground.

"Take a few deep breaths."

After she had cleared her lungs, Flora's color returned.

"Feeling better?"

Flora nodded. Emily handed her a clean paper towel she had managed to grab from the dispenser on their way out. "Here. Clean yourself up."

After Flora wiped her face and took a few more deep breaths, she turned to her aunt with a pale face. "Her death seems so awful, so violent."

Emily nodded. She wasn't going to sugarcoat this for a young woman who had just stepped into her first postmortem examination. "It was violent. It was ruthless and evil. And that's why we must be absolutely thorough and search her body for any clues that might help build a homicide case. Everything we find could be a connection point to her killer."

"Whoever did this to her . . . is a horrible person." Flora was full of emotion.

Emily saw it was the right moment to dip into an even tougher conversation.

"Does it scare you that a man can cause such harm to a helpless woman?"

Flora's eyes met Emily's. She responded with a slight nod.

"This is going to sound strange, but good. I'm glad you're scared."

"Why?"

"Because a healthy fear drives us to prepare and protect."

"What do you mean?"

"We don't know all the facts of Savannah Browdey's story yet." Emily sighed. "But if I had to guess, there may have been some point where—had she made a different decision—she might be alive today."

"Are you saying it was her fault she got killed?" Flora sounded indignant.

"Never. I'm saying that as women, we know we are prey, and we should always be trying to lower our predator risk level."

"I never thought of myself as prey before."

"When we let our guard down, our risk level increases. We may not even be aware we're doing it. Especially if it's with people we know or are comfortable with. We need to always be aware of what situations or people might put us at risk of becoming a crime victim."

"How do we know that?" Emily could sense Flora's discomfort.

"Your mom has probably drilled into you not to talk to strangers, right?"

"Stranger danger."

"But most victims of crimes know their assailant. They aren't strangers. Savannah may have known her killer. Or maybe he was a friend of another friend. Maybe she took a ride with him? Maybe he cornered her somehow, got her alone?"

"Okay, this is scary. How am I ever supposed to trust anyone?"

"Going out with a group is a good start. And don't let yourself get separated from your friends."

"But what if I'm not with other people?"

She was asking all the right questions.

"That's next-level personal protection. But I think we've covered enough for one day. Let's revisit this before you go to your first dance."

"I haven't said yes."

"But you already kissed him." Emily grinned at her niece.

"Aunt Em! How did you know?"

"You really have to ask?"

"My mom cannot keep her mouth shut."

"So? How was it?"

Flora shrugged. "All of my friends have gone further."

"Forget your friends. You're on your own timeline. Do what's right for you," Emily assured her. "You know, my first kiss was at fifteen."

"It was?" Flora said.

"Maybe late bloomers run in the family."

"Nick?"

Emily nodded. "What kind of person is Noah?"

"Great eyes. Athletic. Popular."

"Okay. But what kind of person is he when he's with you?"

"Kind. Funny." Flora thought for a moment. "I'm still vetting him."

"And that's why you haven't said yes to the dance yet?"

"That . . . and I'm building up anticipation," Flora said confidently.

Emily laughed. "My sister has taught you well."

CHAPTER 25

Back when Emily was a teenager, she and her father had a tradition of going to the local diner for a burger and fries after working on an investigation. Dad said it gave them a much-needed mental, physical, and emotional buffer between death life and home life. Emily decided she and Flora would reinstate the tradition but with a tweak.

"What are your thoughts on a stop at Brown's?" said Emily, referring to her friend Delia Andrews's bakery in downtown Freeport.

Flora turned to her aunt with a look of relief. "Oddly, a cinnamon roll sounds really good right now."

Emily grinned. "That's my niece."

She pushed the pause button on the postmortem and returned the body to its secure place in the cooler. She locked up the morgue, and from the hospital it was just a short walk into Freeport's downtown district. When they arrived at Brown's Bakery, the locals were taking their late-afternoon coffee breaks. Every time she went there, Emily lamented the fact that she wouldn't see her old friend, a retired FBI agent who'd assisted

Emily with some hairy cases since Emily's return to Freeport. During the last one, Delia had called upon another former FBI agent, Dutch, who'd been living up north on a secure compound. After that case, Delia and Dutch rekindled a romance.

Emily couldn't begrudge her "second mom" the happiness of lost love found. Now Delia was living up north on Dutch's compound, happily and reclusively in love. Emily was thrilled about the love part but missed Delia and wondered how long the fiery, extroverted woman could last sequestered in the northern pines. She'd made a secret bet that in three months the honeymoon would be over, and Delia would resume her station as queen bakery bee and gossip-train conductor. But a half year had passed, and Delia had only made visits every other month to Freeport. She had proved she could run the bakery competently from a distance. Still, Emily and the regulars complained that it wasn't the same without Delia's perky presence.

Flora found them a café table while Emily went to the counter to order cinnamon rolls, a double espresso for herself, and a caramel latte for Flora. She was tapping her credit card on the reader when she heard, "Emily?"

She looked up to see the barista, Sadie, reaching over the counter with her two beverages.

"I haven't seen you in like forever." Sadie had been one of Delia's baristas when Emily first arrived back in Freeport. Back then, she'd been a high school senior, about to head off to Michigan State on scholarship.

"I thought you were off at MSU," said Emily.

"I am. I was. I'm just here for a few days, filling in."

"How are studies going?"

"Great. I'm a senior now. Prelaw."

"Good for you. Got your sights set on any law school in particular?"

"I'm thinking warm winters," Sadie said, grinning. "ASU. UCLA."

"I can't blame you, but that's pretty far away."

"I won't be gone forever. You know what they say: 'You can take the girl out of Michigan, but you can't take Michigan out of the girl.'"

Emily smiled at just how accurately this described her life.

"We're all talking about the BOLO on the baby police are looking for. So scary," said Sadie. "Is that Savannah Browdey's daughter?"

Emily was surprised by the direct ask, since no names had been used in the police alert. "How did you know?"

"I went to school with a girl who was Savannah's cousin—Charlane. Laney, they called her." Sadie lowered her voice. "Are you working on her case, Dr. Hartford?"

Emily nodded. "Did you know Savannah?"

"I met her once or twice at a football game when Freeport was playing Rock River. I know she and Laney were the same age. More like sisters. Savannah came up to Freeport a lot to visit."

"Are you still in touch with Laney?"

"Not for a couple years. She went off to community college. Got her cosmetology license. Moved to Oak Creek for a salon job. But after I heard about Savannah, I reached out."

"What did she say?" Emily prodded.

"She was pretty much in shock. It's so crazy this happened to Savannah, especially after everything else she went through."

Emily leaned in slightly, angling her body to keep others from eavesdropping. "You mean her sexual assault?"

"Yeah, that creepy old guy. He was like forty or something."

Emily kept a straight face. Forty wasn't so old now that she was thirty. But when she'd been Sadie's age, forty was darn near elderly.

"You know, Laney was there that night," Sadie said.

"What night?"

"The night Savannah was killed."

"She was? She tell you that?"

"Yeah. She said she dropped Savannah off at her friend Jonah's house, but she couldn't stay, because she had to get back to some family dinner thing. She told Savannah she could watch Brooklyn overnight."

"She offered to babysit?" Emily said, realizing how differently this all would have turned out if Savannah had just said yes.

"Laney was mad that Savannah was bringing a baby into a drug house."

"A drug house," Emily repeated.

"Everyone knew Jonah dealt." Behind Sadie, a baker slid a tray of fresh cinnamon rolls into the case. "Such a shame. Maybe the baby wouldn't be dead now."

"Hey, we don't know what happened to Brooklyn," Emily said, but Sadie didn't hear her.

"How many did you want?" Sadie asked, slipping on a plastic serving glove.

Emily glanced back to where Flora was now sitting with a bunch of her girlfriends. "I'll have six, please."

"It was good to see you," said Sadie.

"You too. Good luck with your law school applications."

Sadie handed her a small plastic tray with the warm rolls on pieces of parchment paper and forks wrapped up in napkins on the side.

"You know, Sadie, we could use a few more good attorneys here in Freeport."

The young woman smiled at her. "These cinnamon rolls might just be worth moving back for."

Emily wound her way to where Flora had pushed together

two café tables and was now chatting with a circle of girlfriends. Emily plastered a smile on her face to greet them.

"Hi, girls," she said as she placed the tray of rolls in front of them.

They chittered back their greetings. Emily's heart was breaking into pieces as she gazed at these innocent faces. A scene like this might have included Savannah when she was their age, not that long ago. How quickly innocence could be ripped away. Emily's resolve to get justice in Savannah's case grew. She couldn't imagine such a horrific thing happening to her niece.

After their coffee break, Emily drove Flora home and then returned to the morgue to finish Savannah's autopsy and write up her report. It was just after 10:00 p.m. when she sent off a summary of her findings in an email to Aditson. Emily concluded that no injuries to Savannah's body were sustained, other than a few bruises on her arms and legs, probably from being thrown into and overboard the boat. Savannah Browdey's cause of death was asphyxiation. What she and Aditson had suspected all along was correct. She had been drowned.

CHAPTER 26

Ruby must have fallen asleep outside again. She awoke under the pines to a light morning rain misting her bare skin. She unfolded herself and shook out her limbs to pump the blood back into them. She picked her way through the forest back to her farmhouse, thankful for the clear head a good night's rest had brought her.

She'd stopped worrying long ago about why she sometimes found herself sleeping overnight in the forest. She never felt in harm's way.

Her stomach grumbled, hunger driving her back home. When she was still a distance away from the farmhouse, her attention centered on the army of wilted sunflowers covering her property. In that moment, she realized they could satiate her hunger, and she recalled her intention to harvest and store them.

Ruby spent much of that day in her gardens, deadheading the stalks and nibbling on the raw seeds. By late afternoon, her stomach felt less cavernous.

Up near the road that she couldn't see from the house, she heard a car slowing down, and then the crunch of the tires pulling into the drive lifted her spirits. He had come. *Finally!* She abandoned the mountain of sunflower heads in her wheelbarrow and bustled toward the driveway to greet her son. But as the car appeared on the rutted drive, she saw it was bright blue and didn't recognize it.

Ruby went to await the visitor on the front porch. Once the car was parked, a young woman with jet-black hair jumped out, an earnest expression on her face. Ruby recognized this pretty girl. She'd been here before with Ruby's son. A large bag swung by the girl's side, and Ruby hoped there were potato chips in that bag—the wavy kind she'd been craving lately.

The girl smiled as she drew closer to the front porch. "Hi, Ruby. It's so nice to see you again."

This one, Ruby recalled, hadn't put on airs. She was a nice girl, and Ruby smiled back at her.

"Do you remember me?"

A memory was triggered by the gorgeous dark tresses cascading down the girl's shoulders and ending below her waist. Jet black, like a . . . "Raven. You're Raven," said Ruby, pleased to recall the name.

"Yes," Raven said with another smile. "That's right. How are you?"

But Ruby didn't respond, for that was when she noticed the beautiful strawberry-blond baby riding on Raven's hip.

CHAPTER 27

"What if Chauncey handed over Brooklyn to one of his family members? Does he have family around here?" asked Emily as she and Aditson parked his truck near Lake Isabella Monday morning. They both got out and began the short hike to the southern bank, where there were several more cops and a drilling crew complete with divers, who were gearing up to go into the water.

"It's rumored his father left years ago to marry a woman in Indiana. Never been seen since."

"Is his mom alive?"

"I can't find anything to locate Ruby Chauncey. No address, telephone number. She never had a driver's license."

"Maybe she's deceased as well?"

"Or living out of state. Colton Chauncey has four siblings. One is dead. One lives in Iowa. Two live in Michigan: one in Detroit and one on the other side of the mitten, in the thumb," Aditson said, using the colloquial term for the shape of Michigan.

"Maybe Chauncey's hiding out with one of them?"

"My assistant, Skylar, is in the process of tracking them

down." Skylar Jensen was a six-foot-one former college basketball star who'd recently earned her bachelor's degree in criminalistics. After sustaining a sports injury in her last season, she had been forced to hang up her jersey and follow her second passion: criminal investigation. She was currently being trained in digital forensics.

Approaching from a distance, they watched as the drilling crew on the lake plunged a large rock drill into the lake bed. "Looks like you got your funding."

"More like I got lucky."

"How so?"

"The driller's wife is good friends with Savannah's grandparents."

"Small-town connections."

"It's very kind, but I think it's going to be short-lived. We're only going to drill and dig at the two locations where the cadaver dogs indicated."

"Better than nothing," said Emily, hopeful. They moved around the lakeshore toward the small crowd. "I'd like to better understand this sexual assault claim on Chauncey. What happened?"

"Savannah and a friend had been in Freeport County, hanging out with Jonah Hampton at his trailer. They stayed up late playing euchre. Around midnight, Savannah wanted to go home. Her friend was supposed to take her, but he'd been drinking. A lot. Savannah didn't want him to drive. Her statement said she left the friend's house with Colton Chauncey, who offered to drive her home. Instead, he took her to the woods, assaulted her several times, and left her to find her own way home."

Horrific. "What did Savannah do?"

"Walked back to Jonah's house. Which was at least five or six miles."

"And let me guess, he didn't call the police," said Emily, remembering what Lynne Hampton had told her earlier.

"Savannah told Jonah what had happened, but she didn't want him calling the police. Jonah came forward to make a statement to the police only after Savannah had already come forward with hers."

"Jonah doesn't drive, so how'd she get home later?" asked Emily.

"She called her brother, Peyton, to come pick her up. He arrived around five a.m."

"Did she tell him what had happened to her?"

"She did not."

"So when did she report the assault?"

"Not for several weeks."

"Why is that?"

"Fear of Colton Chauncey."

A legitimate concern.

Emily's eyes were drawn to the hydraulic dredging machine floating near the shore. The flat barge platform held a submersible pump with a long tube that was used to suck up debris from the bottom.

"Do you know what convinced Savannah to finally report her assault to the police?" Emily inquired.

"Peyton Browdey, Savannah's older brother. He was taking out the trash and found her crumpled-up dress in the outdoor bin. He thought it was weird because Savannah had just bought that dress. When he took the dress out, a pair of dirty panties dropped out. The dress had blood on it. He went to his sister, and she admitted to him that Chauncey had raped her the night he'd picked her up from Jonah's. Peyton insisted she go to the police, and finally they went together to make a report."

"He brought the dress and underwear?"

"Thank God, yes. They were admitted as evidence and sent to the crime lab, where they were able to get a sperm sample and pubic hairs off Savannah's underwear. The blood was Savannah's. They arrested Chauncey and took a saliva sample from him. It matched the DNA profile from the semen on Savannah's panties."

Emily's heart twisted in knots.

In the lake, the drill operator was moving the drill bit lower and lower into the pond at the speed of refrigerated molasses. Aditson and Emily stopped talking to take it all in. The machine's gears shifted, grinding to a stop.

The production near shore halted.

"We're at sixty feet. It feels like silt all the way down. How far should I keep going?" shouted the dredging operator from the machine's cabin.

"That's not good," Aditson commented. "If they can't find solid ground at the bottom of the pond, then . . ." He stopped.

Emily looked at him. "Then what?"

"Send in the diver now!" the supervisor onshore shouted back.

Nearby, a jockey-size man began squeezing himself into a full black wet suit.

Aditson turned to her and continued his story. "Before giving birth, she stated that she wasn't sure if the baby was Chauncey's or her boyfriend's."

Insult to injury.

"Who's this boyfriend?"

"André Simon. Lives in Rock River south of the city, almost in the next county."

"Did she do a daddy DNA test?"

"Not that we can find." Aditson paused. "But André is African American."

Emily understood what he was implying. Brooklyn was a

light-skinned child whose features favored Colton Chauncey, a white male. Still, Emily had known mixed-race children to look completely different from one or the other of their parents. Only a DNA test would tell them for sure who Brooklyn Browdey's real father was.

"How did Chauncey post bail?" asked Emily.

"It was only set at four thousand dollars. Records show that Raven Kane paid it."

"I'd like to know the story behind that."

"Stopped by Raven Kane's apartment twice. No vehicle. No answer. But I'll keep trying."

"I wonder if Savannah knew she bailed out Chauncey," Emily said rhetorically. "Did he try to get in touch with Savannah after being released?"

"There's no police record of a complaint against him by her."

"And did she ever file for a restraining order?"

"Nope."

Emily groaned. But even if Savannah had, it wouldn't have stopped a cold-blooded criminal bent on revenge or silencing a witness. "Is this as cut and dry as it seems?"

"You couldn't write a more perfect script."

"And still no trace of Chauncey anywhere?"

"Now you see why I'm trying not to panic," said Aditson. "They're finding the silt might be too deep to search. They want to see how far down a diver can go."

The diver attached himself to the scuba equipment, and then the supervisor wrapped a cement block around him, just like the one that had been chained to Savannah's body. He quickly sank into the water. Emily felt herself holding her breath as he disappeared under the murky surface.

After a minute that felt like a half hour, she said to Aditson, "What is he doing down there?"

"They're trying to see how far he'll sink into the silt when weighted."

Savannah's body and the attached block had gotten caught on a log, which had prevented her from sinking into the silt and disappearing forever into the bottom of the pond. What if nothing had caught Brooklyn's body? She might be down there in the silt. How far down could they go in order to search for her?

Suddenly the diver emerged, he and his equipment coated in silt. He was so weighted down in the muck that it took the supervisor and two cops all their strength to pull the man ashore. When he was able to remove his headgear and catch his breath, he told the waiting crowd, "I was down to twenty feet under the silt. And I would have kept sinking, but the scuba gear was getting clogged. I woulda been dead."

"That's terrifying," Emily said under her breath to Aditson.

"Go get cleaned up. I think we're through here," the supervisor said with a nod to Aditson. Aditson nodded back.

"If Brooklyn is under there, no way we'll ever find her, is there?" Emily said solemnly.

"We had to try."

"We don't know for sure that she ever was here," Emily said, attempting to infuse hope into her tone.

"It has been difficult keeping Savannah's family from finding out about this," said Aditson. "We didn't want to upset them at the prospect of little Brooklyn's body possibly being here."

"I won't say a word about this. But speaking of them, I have to meet the Browdeys at the morgue later," Emily said, checking the time. She wasn't looking forward to this meeting. The most heart-wrenching part of her job was explaining someone's cause and manner of death to their loved ones. It was always painful to envision what your beloved had gone through in their last moments of life.

"You've made your ruling?" he asked.

"Drowning. Homicide." She emphasized the last word. "And do you consider Colton Chauncey an active threat?"

"Absolutely," said Aditson. "Police were called fourteen times in the past five years regarding complaints against Chauncey. Many of them not in Freeport County."

"Tell me about that."

"He was renting a room in a house in Rock River with several other tenants. One of the renters complained he went into her room and exposed himself to her. He was also caught in the same house rubbing himself while watching a thirteen-year-old girl. Later, a friend of his reported him for trying to get into bed with the guy's wife and grabbing her breasts."

"This guy is disgusting," Emily said.

"That barely scratches the surface. He was at card games where he pushed a man to the floor and held him by the throat. Another time he was at a friend's house when he grabbed the man's wife by the hair and slammed her head against the wall while punching her face. When their young son tried to intervene, he tossed the kid across the room. He's pulled guns on neighbors, followed women in their cars, and set a neighbor's house on fire while they were sleeping. Fortunately, and for whatever reason, the house didn't catch."

"Is that all?" Emily was being sarcastic.

Aditson went on, "I haven't even started to detail the reports on abuse to people's pets."

"No. I can't go there." Emily held her hand up. "I don't get how there were no arrests for any of these?"

"All of these instances should have been investigated further and resulted in arrests, but no one wanted to press charges."

Fear of retaliation.

Anyone who got in Colton Chauncey's way or even

ticked him off could become the next victim of his barbaric behavior.

It was too late to vent her anger at the judge who'd given his recent case too much leeway. His bail should have been set at seven figures. The justice system had failed Savannah and Brooklyn. But that was about to change: Emily would do everything she could to make sure Chauncey did not get away with so much as a parking ticket.

"Let's go talk to Raven," Emily suggested, hoping that she would give them a clue to finding Brooklyn.

CHAPTER 28

After Colton killed the Rock River woman in the first-floor apartment, he used it as a home base while waiting to question whoever was squatting at Terrell's place. The woman had been easy to get rid of. He'd stuck her body in a laundry sack, and then, under the cover of night, he lugged it down to the river. Crouching on its banks, he retrieved a boulder from the shore and placed it, too, inside the sack. Then, wading into the water, he dragged the sack behind him. The river pulled at him, and he was just on the edge of being unable to resist its coursing flow when he let go of the bag. The mighty current yanked the sack below the water's surface while it took the woman downstream.

Saturday he kept watch on the apartment. He spotted a teenager entering Terrell's place in the late morning. Not even thirty seconds later, the kid burst out of the apartment and went barreling down the staircase and out the front door before Colton could get on his shoes to pursue. He hadn't seen him return. Now it was Monday morning, and he felt he was wasting time here. Raven was on his ass and threatening him. Stupid bitch. Couldn't even take care of a little baby for a couple of days. He was grateful he'd forced the abortion on her last spring. She would have been a terrible, needy mother. He already had one of those. He didn't need another.

Time was running out before some busybody or cop would be knocking at the woman's door, wondering why she hadn't shown up for work or answered their calls. Colton decided to give up waiting for the brat to come back. Before leaving the building, he broke into Terrell's apartment again and tore the place apart, this time not picking up after himself.

Still, no box of valuables. He was going home empty handed, which really pissed him off.

CHAPTER 29

"Raven Kane lives in Unit 207," said Aditson, exiting his vehicle.

"Lights are on. Curtains pulled back. Good sign," said Emily. Raven Kane had a one-bedroom apartment overlooking the back property, which had a small man-made pond with a waterfall feature. Several warped picnic tables were clustered on the waterfall side. And a large weeping willow hung over half the pond. These offered the soulless, square block building the weak facade of being a resort.

Raven answered the door after the third, more serious knock. With porcelain skin and jet-black hair that ended just above her waist, she looked like a character on the cover of a manga that Emily had seen Fiona reading.

Raven's apartment was dusty and cluttered. Every surface was covered with something that needed to be put away. Cleaning products. Work clothes. Magazines. Moldy take-out containers. A gel nail polish kit and an army of polishes. Costume jewelry. Bills, junk mail, and pizza flyers. A bowl of water and another of half-eaten pet food sat just past the kitchen threshold.

Aditson sneezed after thirty seconds. There had to be a cat. Or cats.

"Are you allergic?" Emily said under her breath.

He sneezed his reply.

Raven offered them a love seat in the living room. They had no choice but to sit on the furry couch once she removed a stack of clothing so they had space. "It's the only piece of living room furniture I own." She pulled up a folding chair from the kitchen table and sat across from them.

Emily noticed a baby bottle on the coffee table, and her heart fluttered. Brooklyn could be on the other side of that bedroom door! "You have a baby?" she asked sweetly.

Raven scrunched up her nose. "Oh, that. My sister's kid comes over sometimes. She must have forgotten it."

"Oh, niece or nephew?" asked Emily.

Her nose scrunched up again. "Ah . . . it's . . . a boy."

"What's his name?"

"Um . . . Carter."

What's with the hesitation? Emily and Aditson exchanged a glance.

"I have two nieces," Emily offered.

"I have three," Aditson said, also trying to break the ice. "In the UP."

"Oh. That's nice," Raven said with an uninterested tone.

"Do you like being an aunt?" asked Emily.

"It's okay. I . . . He's a good baby. It's easy. I guess."

"It's more fun when they're older," said Aditson. "You'll see."

Raven pulled a pack of cigarettes from her purse and slid one out. "Yeah. So what can I do for you?"

"We understand you know Colton Chauncey?" said Aditson.

"Yeah. I know a lot of people."

"How much do you know him?"

"He comes into the lounge sometimes."

"Were you with him Saturday night?"

"Look, lemme shortcut this for you," Raven said. "I know what you're after, and I was with Colton the night that girl, Savannah, went missing."

"Why don't you tell us about that night?" Emily coaxed.

"I'd love to." Raven hunted for a lighter on the coffee table and found it under a magazine dated two years ago. She lit the cigarette and took a drag. "Don't I need a lawyer or something?"

Emily smiled to put her at ease. "You're not under arrest or suspicion."

"But Colton is," Raven said.

"Did you know about his rape charges?" Aditson interjected.

"Of course I knew. But he didn't deserve to be in jail."

"Why do you say that?" Emily felt a flash of heat on the back of her neck spread down her spine.

"'Cause that skank seduced him."

"She gave a pretty convincing statement," said Aditson.

"Big shock. The real story is, Colton cheated on me with her and knocked her up. Then she claims it was rape. Real convenient, right?"

"That's what you think happened?" Emily asked.

"Colton was here the night she disappeared. I made dinner. He spent the night."

"What time did he arrive?" asked Emily.

"I dunno. It was dark already."

"What did you do when he got here?"

"Made dinner."

Raven was going to make them tease out every answer, like pulling a long string of taffy.

"What did you make for dinner?" asked Aditson.

Emily turned to him and raised a brow. *How's that important?*

Raven paused. "Chicken legs. On the grill."

"Where's the grill?" Aditson asked.

Raven cleared her throat. "In the closet off the patio."

"Are you sure that Colton didn't leave in the middle of the night and come back?" Aditson asked.

Raven got up and went to the dining room table. She pulled a T-shirt from the laundry basket on the table and began to fold it. "Yes. I am sure."

"Mind if I take a look at that grill?" Aditson asked, rising.

"Whatever."

Aditson rose and opened the sliding door to the postage-stamp-size patio off the living room. He stepped outside to search the storage closet.

"How can you be so sure he didn't leave?" Emily asked Raven.

"Because, yeah, I didn't get much sleep that night. We did it, like, several times." Raven set the folded shirt on top of a stack of magazines and took out a pair of jeans.

Aditson returned, closing the door behind him. "I see you have one of those little egg-shaped ones. I heard those work really good."

"I guess so." She shrugged.

"How long have you been with Colton?" Emily asked.

"Off and on for about eight years."

"Were you off or on when Colton spent the night?"

"We were working it out, I thought."

"Working what out?"

"Colton's older than me, and it was sorta becoming a problem."

"How much older?"

"He's forty-four and I'm twenty-nine."

"Was it a problem for him or you?" Emily continued.

"It was for him. He's jealous. He didn't like me working at the Silver Slipper."

"You get hit on a lot there?" asked Emily.

"It's part of the job. I'm not complaining. It brings in great tips."

Emily could see how Raven might do well at the Slipper. She had an exaggerated hourglass figure that Emily bet had been enhanced by cosmetic surgery.

"How else was his jealousy becoming a problem?" she asked, since rarely did jealous people stop until they got their way.

"The demands. The yelling. I'm getting too old for that crap. I'll be thirty next summer. I want to settle down. Have my own little pack of brats running around."

"Did he ever get physical with you?"

"He could be handsy."

"Did he ever hurt you?"

"Colton can be a real jagoff sometimes. But if he even tried to touch me, he knew what would happen to him."

"What?" Emily asked, curious about what Raven might be planning.

She made the sign of a knife slicing the air. "Off with his dick and balls."

"Are you serious? Really?"

"Believe me: It would be so easy. Get him drunk and passed out. Then, swish."

Emily glanced at Aditson and saw he was trying his best to remain composed as the woman described an imaginary assault.

"Raven, do you know where Colton Chauncey is right now?" Aditson asked her plainly, pinning her with his look.

"Colton is no killer." Raven had reached the bottom of the laundry basket, picking out a handful of thongs and folding them into little triangles.

"That's not what I asked you."

She wouldn't look at them.

"What do you think happened to Savannah's baby?" asked Aditson.

"Well, it's a shame her mom got killed, but she didn't deserve to die too," said Raven, piling folded clothes into the basket.

"You think Brooklyn is dead?" said Aditson, searching Raven's face for a reaction.

"I'm guessing so." Raven didn't glance up.

"Do you know where Colton is?" he asked a second time, still holding his gaze on her.

Raven picked the basket up, pressing it against her torso. She rejoined them in the living room, and standing over them, she announced, "He took off Saturday morning after we had a big screaming fight. That night, he came to the Slipper after my shift to try to apologize. I wasn't having it. He's an ass."

A flicker of movement at the cat's bowl caught Emily's eye. He glanced over at a gray animal with a black mask feeding on the cat food.

Aditson saw it too. "You have a raccoon? As a pet?"

Raven turned to look, then laughed. "Oh, that's Hercules. He's harmless."

"I don't think that's a good idea," said Aditson.

"Don't worry. He doesn't have rabies or anything. He has his vaccines."

"You can do that?" Emily was aghast.

"Yeah, he has his own crate. He's actually pretty cuddly. Loves to be petted."

"Why do you have a raccoon as a pet?" Aditson asked, unable to hold back his disgust.

"Hercules was here when I moved in. Someone had obviously cared for him before I got here."

Aditson gulped and formed his face into an expression that told her that owning a pet raccoon was not okay. Time to leave.

Before they could get off the sofa, Raven got up, opened the bedroom door, and shooed the raccoon in. Emily craned to see inside the room. It was just as unkempt, but there was no baby.

"Thank you for your time," Aditson said. "We can see ourselves out."

After Emily and Aditson got outside, they spent five minutes cleaning raccoon fur off their clothes and gulping fresh air.

"Now I'm gonna have to bring this uniform to the cleaners. Disgusting," groaned Aditson.

"You don't for a second believe she has a nephew, do you?" asked Emily.

"Not a chance. But she doesn't have Brooklyn either. I'll have her followed for a few days. See if she leads us to the infant."

As they were about to get into the patrol car, Emily turned to Aditson with a questioning look. "What was with all that 'what's for dinner' and 'where's the grill' business?"

"It's usually the mundane details that give people away."

"What did that grill give away?"

"Everything. For starters, that grill hadn't been used in a long time."

"How could you tell?"

"The grates were brown and rusty. If they had been grilling chicken legs a few days ago, there would be black char marks on the grates. And debris on the bottom of the grill. There wasn't any."

"So a hundred percent she is lying."

"Chauncey was not here for dinner that night."

"Why cover for him?" There was so much wrong about Raven, even beyond the pet raccoon. "Despite being a little eccentric—"

"That's putting it graciously."

"—she doesn't seem to me like the kind of person who would put a baby's life in danger," mused Emily. "Maybe she thought to take the child to someone safe?"

"Like Brooklyn's father," said Aditson.

"If she knew who that was."

"Or maybe Chauncey convinced her it was him." Aditson's eyes flashed to hers.

Emily made a desperate wish that Brooklyn did not share Chauncey's DNA.

CHAPTER 30

Emily pulled back the white cotton cloth covering Savannah's body, making sure that she didn't expose the surgical cuts she had sewn up postautopsy. She had cleaned Savannah's face and brushed down her hair so that she more closely resembled the pretty young woman in her photographs.

Her father, Ivan, and older brother, Peyton, nodded, and a broken look passed between them as Emily pulled the sheet back over Savannah's head. Ivan shook in silence until tears spilled over his eyelids. Peyton gripped his father, and they held each other.

Emily hastily retrieved a tissue box from the desk in the corner and handed it to them. Then she drifted back to the desk and pretended she was attending to paperwork. After the weeping subsided, she padded over and opened the door of the morgue that led to the hospital hallway.

"It's chilly in here. Shall we step out?"

Ivan clutched the tissue box as father and son headed for the door.

Emily was eager to ask them questions but waited until

after they'd left the large frigid room, shutting the door behind them. Since the morgue was in the basement of the hospital, no other staff or visitors were on the floor. She and the Browdeys could talk here privately.

"I hope you don't mind me asking, but the topic of Brooklyn's father hasn't really come up. Do either of you know who the baby's father is?" she asked.

"No. Not even Savannah was sure," said Ivan.

"She was waiting until after the trial to do the paternity test," Peyton said.

"Did she tell you who she thought it was?" asked Emily.

"Never. Despite our prodding," added Ivan.

Emily let it rest and handed them a copy of Savannah's autopsy report. "This is my official ruling," she said. "Bottom of page two in the notes."

Ivan flipped right to the word *homicide*. "That bastard."

"Not like it's a big surprise." Peyton sighed.

"You mean Colton Chauncey?" Emily wanted to clarify.

"Who else?" Ivan lashed out.

"About Savannah's assault: I'd be interested to hear what happened from your perspective," Emily said, now that the door had been cracked open to discuss Chauncey.

"She was at Jonah's house that night, playing cards with him and some others," offered Peyton. "Colton showed up, and after a while, he offered to take her home."

"How did she get there in the first place?" Emily asked.

"I dropped her off. But I couldn't pick her up later 'cause I had to be at work early the next morning."

"Why do you think she took Colton up on his offer of a ride?"

"First of all, everyone else was too drunk to drive. But mostly, she trusted him because he was a friend of Jonah's."

Emily knew this to be common logic women used to head off with men they barely knew. Predators took advantage of "friendly connections" to isolate their prey.

"Did Savannah have any contact with Colton Chauncey after he got out of jail?" she asked.

"Not that I'm aware. She was really afraid of him," said Peyton. "The last night we saw her alive, she was going out to meet a friend."

"André Simon?" asked Emily.

"No. They'd broken up. She didn't tell us, but I guess it was Jonah."

"Sounds like she and Jonah were close."

"They worked together at Sam's Club for a while. Until his back pain forced him to quit and go on disability," Ivan said. "There were also a few incidents at work due to PTSD from his time in Afghanistan."

"What kind of incidents?" Emily asked.

"Savannah said he had panic attacks," said Peyton.

Emily couldn't help her thoughts springing to Nick and his current condition. She wondered how much emotional trauma was beyond the physical issues.

"Was there ever anything between Savannah and Jonah?" Emily said.

"Nah. She spent a lot of time with him, but they were just friends. She helped him out at home. Cleaning. Doing laundry. Running him to doctor's appointments."

"What happened with Savannah and André?" Emily asked.

"After she got pregnant, things got sketchy between them," said Peyton.

"What did André think about the pregnancy? Was he happy? Angry? Upset?"

"We don't really know him well," explained Ivan with a shrug.

"I only met him a few times," Peyton said. "My sister told me he was pushing for a paternity test."

"Why was Savannah waiting to do a paternity test?" Emily asked.

"It was too much for her to process."

"Once the baby came, André was convinced she looked like Colton Chauncey," Peyton added.

"Do you think that?"

"Hard to say," said Ivan. "Brooklyn looks a lot like Savannah did as a baby. But you know how babies change their looks from week to week. Some days I thought Brooklyn had André's eyes and nose. And then the next day, I'd see only Savannah in that precious face. On the bad days, I'd swear that baby's face was curled up in the same sullen look from Colton's mug shot."

"And you couldn't go by skin color," said Peyton.

"André's a lighter-skinned African American. And we have Italian in our blood. So one afternoon in the sun, and we're the color of rye bread."

"I can see how it would be really frustrating for André not to know," Emily said with an empathetic sigh.

"A few months after Brooklyn was born, he came over to our house, dead set on taking her to get a DNA test. They had a huge fight."

"Was André abusive?"

"Well, there was a lot of nasty talk between them. I wouldn't say he was physically abusive," said Ivan. "But I did have to ask him to leave the house once." He looked to his son, who confirmed the statement with a nod.

"Why did you do that?"

"I didn't like how he was speaking to her," said Ivan.

"How did André react to being asked to leave?"

"He was more hurt than angry," said Peyton.

"He felt rejected," Ivan added.

"What was Savannah's reaction to all this?"

"She said she was grateful to me for getting him off her back. But later I heard her tell him on the phone that he couldn't see her or Brooklyn anymore if he was going to act like that."

"And you believe she held to that?" asked Emily.

Ivan exhaled a frustrated sigh. "As much as any father can believe his strong-willed nineteen-year-old daughter."

Emily glanced at Peyton. She suspected he knew more than he was letting on. She felt a twinge, remembering herself as a teenager. She'd been so strong willed she ran away from home at sixteen to live with Aunt Laura in Chicago, abandoning her father after her mother's death. Emily hadn't come home for ten years.

Peyton hesitated, then said, "They were in touch."

"How often?" asked Emily.

"They would text and call each other all the time. My sister would send André pictures of Brooklyn. I saw them in her text chain one time when she asked me to hand over her phone."

"There's nothing wrong with the kid, mind you," said Ivan. "I just don't think there was a future there. Savannah needed to be paying more attention to that baby of hers. Not going on some emotional roller coaster every other day with a boy who wasn't taking her seriously."

"Do you think there's a chance Brooklyn might be with André or one of his family members?"

Under the circumstances Ivan had described between André and Savannah, it was conceivable André's fury had built up even further. And after Savannah started hanging around Jonah and his druggie crowd, André might have felt compelled to hatch a plan to save his daughter. Maybe he'd even created the front that he didn't care about Brooklyn in order to distract the Browdeys, then swooped in to rescue his baby daughter from her mother's destructive life.

"I don't know. I've been so distracted putting all my focus on counting the days till the trial, when we could put that bastard Colton behind bars and move on with our lives." Ivan emphasized the last few words and clamped his jaw shut as if to stop himself from uttering a rising accusation.

"How did André react to the sexual assault and trial?"

"He was upset," said Peyton. "Also, he didn't understand how Savannah could have put herself in a dangerous situation again."

"Again? What other trouble did Savannah get in because she hung out with Jonah?"

"She was pulled over by the cops once after leaving Jonah's, and she had a stash of heroin in her purse."

"Savannah used drugs?" Emily asked.

"No. She was making a delivery for Jonah," Peyton said. "She did two months in the county inpatient rehab center."

"When was that?" asked Emily, surprised that she hadn't heard about Savannah's criminal record before this.

"She was just about to turn eighteen. Judge went light on her because she was underage," said Ivan. "Could have been much worse."

"Have either of you talked to André since Savannah and Brooklyn went missing?" Emily asked.

Ivan and Peyton shook their heads.

"Has he reached out to contact either of you?"

"Not a peep," said Ivan.

Emily looked to Peyton, who said, "I texted him when she went missing. He never texted back." In a small voice, he added, "I still want to believe Brooklyn is alive."

Emily gave him a small, hopeful smile. "I do too. And we're not giving up."

They walked through the hospital lobby, and then she turned to head back to the morgue and close it down. She was pleased to have the info about André Simon in her back pocket and couldn't wait to tell Aditson. She suspected André had secrets, and they would pry them out of him one by one.

CHAPTER 31

On Tuesday, Emily and Aditson traveled down to Rock River and found André Simon on break from his job at the Pasta Factory, seated at an empty booth in the food court at the Rock River Center shopping mall. He was scrolling on his phone and sipping a sugary sixty-four-ounce beverage. The young man was professional-basketball-player tall and skinny as a fence post.

"André, you mind if we join you?" asked Aditson.

André looked up at them with large brown eyes that held neither fear nor welcome. He pointed an outstretched hand nearly the length of a loaf of bread to the bench across from him.

Emily slid in first. She offered André a smile and introduced herself as the doctor who had taken care of Savannah after she'd been found. After he provided his credentials, Aditson sat next to Emily and tented his hands together on the table, a sign of peace.

"I was wondering when the police would come trackin' me down," André said.

"Really?" asked Aditson. "Why is that?"

"Because Van and I were together. And Brooks—" André stopped with a catch in his throat.

Emily was surprised at the young man's show of emotion and asked, "Did you think Brooklyn was your daughter?"

He shrugged. "Yeah."

"Do you know that Brooklyn is missing?" asked Aditson.

"Yeah, I know," he said evenly, like he was making an effort to hide his emotions.

"Do you know where Brooklyn is?" Emily asked.

"If I did, I wouldn't be sitting here with you."

"I'm not so sure," said Aditson. "Maybe she's staying with one of your relatives." He got right to the point.

"I don't know where that baby is," André said, glancing away. Emily found it curious that he used an impersonal term like *that baby* rather than a more intimate description like *she* or *my daughter*. It could be a sign that he was lying to them.

"How was your relationship with the Browdeys?" asked Aditson.

"Ivan Browdey?" André snickered. "He was high strung. Never liked me. Sure as hell didn't want me to be his daughter's baby daddy."

"Why not?"

"His reasons are his own, man. He's not worth my time."

"What about Peyton?" asked Aditson.

"He's okay. We steer clear. I don't have problems with him."

Emily shared a look with Aditson, and he passed her the baton.

"You call them Van and Brooks?" said Emily, her voice sympathetic.

"Yeah. That's, like, our thing."

"How long were you and . . . Van together?"

"Off and on for a couple years. We started dating in high school."

"How old are you, André?" Emily asked.

"Nineteen. Same as Van."

"So you were dating, let's say, two or three years?" asked Aditson, wanting him to be more precise.

"Like, since senior year. Off and on."

"André, did you love Van?" asked Emily.

He scrunched his shoulders together behind him, stretching out the front of his broad chest. His arms followed, with a wingspan of at least six feet. "I don't know what true love's supposed to be like, but it hurt when I couldn't be with her."

It was as convincing an answer as a nineteen-year-old could give.

"Do you know what happened to her?" Emily asked, not wanting to presume.

"She was killed."

"Savannah was murdered," said Emily. "Did you hear how?"

André shook his head. His arms crossed over his chest again.

"Do you want to know?" she pressed.

"I don't know. Maybe." He paused. "I guess so. I'm curious is all."

Emily waited a moment before delivering the grim facts.

After André knew all the details, he sat motionless, stunned.

Aditson nodded. "Pretty awful, huh?"

The young man nodded again. Emily saw him ball one of those loaf hands into a fist. He encompassed it with his other giant paw. The veins on the outside of his hand bulged over the smooth, luminous skin. His stoic expression, however, never changed.

After a moment, he spoke. "Look, I'm a second year at Rock River Community College. I'm trying to get my degree. First in my family. I don't want no trouble."

"Why would there be trouble?" Emily asked.

"I know the cops always look to the boyfriend. He done it. But I ain't a killer."

"We're not accusing you of anything," said Aditson. "We just wanted to meet you, inform you of Savannah's death, and ask a few questions."

"I don't like a lot of questions," he said. "Feels like a test."

"It's no test. And these are easy ones," Emily said, looking him in the eye to help reassure him.

"Where were you Saturday and Sunday when she was missing?" asked Aditson.

"I worked Saturday night."

"Where?"

"I got two jobs. At night I stock shelves at the Fresh Mart on East Greenway Beltline. You can check my time card—I was working."

"And who was working with you at the time?" Aditson handed him a blank paper and a pen. "Write their names down here."

The pen didn't hesitate in André's hand. He wrote down four names and one nickname. "I don't know this guy's full name," André explained.

"What time did the shift end?" asked Aditson.

"We finished around two a.m."

"What'd you do after that?"

"I stayed for about a half hour, talking to the guys in the parking lot."

Emily glanced at Aditson, who was making a note to check security footage.

"Then what?"

"Got in my car and drove home."

"Write down your address there too."

André's hand flew to jot it down.

"You live alone?" asked Aditson.

"No. With my family. Mom, dad, little sister."

"Were they home that night?"

"Yeah. Think so."

"Did they see you come in?" Aditson asked.

André hesitated, as if he were running that night over in his head.

"Was anyone up?" asked Emily.

"They were sleeping when I got home. Except my mom was in the living room watching TV. She sometimes has trouble sleeping."

"Did she see you come home?" Aditson asked.

"I said, 'Night, Ma.' I don't know if she heard me 'cause she didn't say anything back." André slid the paper to Aditson. "That's all I know. I ain't got nothing to hide."

"And yet you didn't go to the police when you learned Savannah was dead and Brooklyn was missing?" Aditson asked.

"Guess I was in shock."

"This was your longtime girlfriend. You think you are the father of her child. Weren't you concerned enough to come in and ask?"

"I show up and I look guilty."

"So you just go on with your life like nothing had changed?"

"I wasn't sure what to do," André repeated. "My parents told me to let the cops come to me."

"What do you know about the night Savannah went missing?" Aditson asked.

"Nothing. She said she was going out," André said. "I was working. We said we'd touch base that Sunday."

"Did you ever go looking for your daughter?" asked Aditson.

"If I did, that wouldn't be against the law, now, would it?"

André stood up and shoved the paper at Aditson. "But no, I don't need to."

"Why not?" asked Emily.

André turned to face her and for a moment held her gaze. He looked like someone about to reveal a new layer of information. Emily waited for him to speak.

"Van was a protective mom, but she was also making some stupid decisions."

"Like what?" asked Emily.

"Like hanging out with the wrong crowd."

"Who?"

"Drug dealer Jonah Hampton, for one."

"Did you tell Savannah that you didn't like her hanging out with him?"

"All the time."

Emily decided to prod. "How'd that make you feel when she wouldn't listen to you?"

"I warned her she was gonna find herself in trouble. And then she did." It was the first time André's voice rose. "I told her, 'Play stupid games, win stupid prizes.'"

"You mean when she got sent to rehab?" Emily asked.

"That's when I broke up with her the first time."

"So why did she insist on going to Jonah's?" Aditson asked.

"Van liked the guy," André said, shaking his head. "And she liked helping him out. Made her feel good."

Emily and Aditson fell silent for a moment, letting André absorb the gravity of the situation.

"Were you ever worried about Brooklyn's safety?" Emily asked.

"Every second she was with her mother."

"So you didn't trust Savannah?" Aditson added.

"Savannah always wanted to make everyone happy. I told her she needed to look after herself and the baby first. 'Don't worry so much about what other people want or don't want. They don't run you.'"

Emily could feel the energy of his strong emotions.

"She was hanging with junkies," said André. "That ain't no place for a baby."

"André, do you know where Brooklyn is?" Emily asked again softly.

"I swear, I don't."

"You didn't take her?"

"No. Come on."

"Your mom? An auntie?"

"Why would I need to hide my own daughter?"

Emily's ears pricked up. He had used a possessive word to describe Brooklyn. Maybe he was telling the truth. "Like you said, makes you look guilty."

"We understand that you wanted to save your daughter from that kind of environment. That makes sense for a dad," said Aditson.

"Believe me, I was tempted to take her. Many times." André flipped his phone over to check the time. "I've gotta get back to work." André stared at the numbers on his phone screen.

Emily glanced at Aditson, signaling that she was going to pose the next question. "You don't seem overly concerned that your daughter is missing."

"Missing? Nah." André sighed, and a look of distress crossed his face. "I doubt it."

"Where do you think she is?" Aditson questioned.

"He got to Van good this time. And that means he got Brooks too." André looked forlorn. "What I don't understand is why you all aren't out there arresting Chauncey."

Neither Emily nor Aditson responded.

"Yeah. Thought so. You can't find him, can you?" André glanced at his phone again. "He's a ghost. And no, I don't know where he is either. But if I did, I'd probably go kill him myself." He shifted in his seat and glanced over his shoulder to the Pasta Factory. "Are we through here?"

"Go ahead. We're done," said Aditson.

André slid out of the booth and strode toward the restaurant, where he disappeared into the kitchen.

"Interesting," said Aditson. "He seems resigned to the fact that his daughter is dead at the hands of Colton Chauncey."

"Something else happened," said Emily. "Obviously, the kid's deathly afraid of Chauncey, or he would have come to us sooner." She wondered if André fit somewhere on that long list of assaults Chauncey had inflicted upon the world. That could have influenced André's decision to avoid any involvement in Savannah's case.

Fear of retaliation.

"Weird reactions from him," mused Aditson. "But he's clearly bothered, and it's simmering right under the surface."

"He's not going to show it here in public. And especially not in front of us," said Emily.

They sat in silence, observing the jungle of mall rats teeming around the food court.

"We're not going to get any closer to finding Brooklyn by sitting in this booth," Emily finally said. "And there's only one thing left to do before we leave here."

Aditson gave her a questioning look.

"Scoot, scoot," she said, nudging him from the booth.

"What are you doing?" asked Aditson, getting up to follow her.

"I'm not leaving without lasagna." She headed toward the Pasta Factory.

CHAPTER 32

On his way back to Freeport County on Tuesday, Colton stopped at his house. He'd bought the place after returning from an extended trip out West. He wasn't much of a handyman, nor did he have the funds to keep the place up. But so far the government hadn't taken it from him.

Once inside the house, he saw things out of place. The cops had rummaged around, although nothing seemed missing. He gathered fresh clothes, towels, what few paper goods he had, and a few items from the pantry. He stuffed them into a duffel bag pulled from under his bed. He loaded his trunk with three cement blocks, chains, duct tape, a saw, matches, rope, and a large tarp. You never knew.

A call to WaliYona informed him his awaited guests had yet to arrive. So instead of heading up north to meet Raven, Colton drove to her apartment. It was possible she'd decided to wait there for him. More likely, she'd done something to piss him off. Why couldn't she just follow simple directions?

No surprise: Raven was in her apartment. At the door, she was surprised to see him and tried to keep him out. He pushed it open with a single shove.

"I figured you'd be on the rez by now," she said with a wavering voice, retreating a safe distance behind a chair. He rushed around the apartment, looking for the infant.

"Where's the baby?" he asked calmly.

"I know you killed her mother."

"That's irrelevant to this conversation, Raven. Now where is she?"

"Don't worry about it," said Raven. "She'll never be found."

"Where'd you put her?" He grabbed her by the arms, pinning her to the wall.

"Some detective and doctor chick were here asking questions."

"Where's the baby?"

"I couldn't keep her."

"What did you do with our payday?" Colton punctuated each word.

"I had to get rid of her another way." Raven's voice was cold.

"You killed her? You whore!" He slapped her hard across the face, knocking a tooth loose and bloodying her nose. Stubborn tears sprouted from her eyes.

"No, I did not kill her," she hissed through her pain.

"Well, either way, I'm not going to prison 'cause you felt sorry for that little bastard baby." He punched her in the stomach. Raven gave a sharp cry and crumpled to the floor in the fetal position. Colton followed through with a toe kick into her kidneys. Raven yelped.

"You already cost me." Colton's voice went dark as the devil. "Now it's gonna cost you."

Through bloody teeth, Raven spit the words at him: "Your father shoulda killed you when he had the chance."

Her words were like acid to the face. "You'll always be a wretched, dirty whore." His fist came down on the back of her head with such force that he felt her skull break on impact.

CHAPTER 33

Tuesday night, Emily stopped by the hospital after dinner with her family to check on Nick. She planned to stay twenty minutes max to avoid tiring him out, but also that was how long she could maintain surface-level conversation while keeping Nick's agitation at bay.

"How's the case going?" he asked.

"One step forward, three steps back. Chauncey's still on the loose."

"You think he'll kill again?"

"As much as I'd like to say no, there's too much evidence that supports his motive to do otherwise."

"I could find him," Nick boasted. "I got really good at hunting and evasion while trekking around the globe to get back home."

"I'm sure you did." Emily held his gaze, hoping he might share with her a snippet more about his experiences. He didn't elaborate, leaning his head against the thin hospital-issued pillow.

"Feels like a waste being in here." He sighed.

"Early release is not an option. So don't get any ideas."

"You and Aditson have any good leads on Chauncey's whereabouts?" Nick turned to her, and there was no doubt of the skepticism in his face.

"It's all we think about."

"More action, less thinking," he said.

"We know what we're doing, Nick." She wasn't going to let him offend her or insult Aditson's ability to run an investigation.

"I'm just saying, you need more manpower."

"And that should be you, of course?" Emily suppressed her anger.

"I feel fine. Besides, every day I'm in here is twenty-four more hours that creep roams our streets."

"I want you out of here as much as you do," said Emily, "but I'm not going to risk releasing an infectious disease on the people of Freeport." She didn't want to have this argument. "I'm tired. I'm heading home."

"Fine," he said dismissively. "Catch ya tomorrow, Hartford." He gave her a small wave and reached for the remote control without a flicker of tenderness.

Emily paused, about to call him out on the "Hartford" business. As she glanced back at him, he was already clicking through channels on the TV; then the roar of a football crowd came from the speakers. Next time. She sighed and stepped out into the hall.

Visiting hours were over, and a third-shift quiet had settled over the unit. Several nurses collected at the nurses' station, reviewing charts and entering data into a computer. A nurse assistant rolled a dining cart of empty meal trays toward the elevator. The stillness on the floor only accentuated Emily's angry footsteps as they slapped down the empty corridor of the hospital hallway. She clenched her purse to her chest and told herself, *Be the bigger person. He's not well. Try again tomorrow.*

CHAPTER 34

That night Emily slept like the dead. Wednesday morning, she pressed the snooze button three times, resisting the day ahead. Her waking thoughts were memories of a conversation from a few years back during her residency in Chicago. She'd been assisting an older surgeon, and he'd made her aware of a growing trend in medical tourism: Wealthy people from all over the world would travel to China for organ transplants—not because China had a larger database or an overrun on organ donations. According to this doctor, the Chinese government was allowing the harvest of human organs from its prison camps.

After that Emily had seen numerous articles in medical-community newsletters from an organization called DAFOH, Doctors Against Forced Organ Harvesting. She read an article about a renowned transplant surgeon addressing medical students at Harvard University on the atrocities of the Chinese human-organ trade. There had even been accounts of Chinese medical students being trained in organ transplantation here in the States, then returning home to use their expertise.

With these stories building in her brain, she took a seat at her desk and grabbed her laptop, flipping it open and typing in the words *organ harvesting China*. Emily clicked through the links that populated her search engine. She read until her eyes were strained and a dull headache throbbed at the base of her neck. Most of the information came from alternative news sources, personal accounts, and advocate organizations for organ-harvesting research, but a chilling story unfolded.

China's aggressive organ harvesting had become known on the international scene in 2008. Back then, they created a niche market for foreigners who were desperate for organ transplants but were on long waiting lists in their home countries. This quickly became a billion-dollar industry, but one with a very dark side: They were forcibly taking organs from live, healthy prisoners of the state.

Stats from Chinese studies showed a significant rise in liver-transplant volumes that ran parallel to the persecution of a religious group called Falun Gong. The practice of this religion was not permitted by the government, and therefore its members were often imprisoned by the CCP. The articles Emily read asserted that these prisoners were a main source of trafficked organs. The members of Falun Gong practiced peace, discipline in living, meditation, and good health—the latter of which made them prime candidates for organ harvesting. The CCP saw them as a community to be exploited for organ-donation tourism.

Medical communities and governments around the world were alerted about this potential crime against humanity, but these cries fell on deaf ears. Chinese citizens who objected experienced threats and retaliation from the CCP officials. However, some governments elsewhere were beginning to pass legislation to make it illegal for citizens to travel to China for transplants.

The stories shocked Emily. Why wasn't this news in headlines across every media outlet in America?

Emily slapped the top down on her computer and pushed it away. Her body went into a hot flash. Her pulse raced, her stomach clenched, but she felt too weak and depleted to get up.

She was convinced she knew what had happened to Nick. His mission with the FBI had been to infiltrate the CCP and gather information on human rights violations. In light of the evidence inside his body, it seemed likely that his mission had taken a wrong turn, and he had become a victim of the violations he was investigating. Part of his lung had been removed and given to a donor without his consent. What else had Nick endured?

Emily startled at the knock on her bedroom door.

"Hello? Em? It's me." Anna's voice called out from the other side.

"Come in."

The door cracked open. Anna stuck her nose through. "Got a minute?"

"Yeah." Emily patted the empty spot on the bed. Anna plopped down next to her.

"Whatcha doing?"

"Watching videos. Trying to wind down," Emily fibbed.

"How's the case going?"

"We're on a three-person manhunt to find a father, a baby, and a killer."

"What did the boyfriend have to say?" asked Anna. She knew Emily had been in Rock River interviewing André.

"He seems convinced Brooklyn is dead. Says that if Chauncey killed Savannah, then he killed the baby for sure."

"And Nick? Did you see him yesterday?" asked Anna.

At the moment, Emily didn't want to venture into those dangerous waters. Everything she had just read online was still swirling in her head.

Anna recognized her worry. "You know, you can give yourself permission to talk to a professional."

She wanted to let Anna in on everything, but where would she even start? Emily pursed her lips. She wished that verbalizing it would make the pain and suffering disappear like the dissolving thread she used on patient incisions.

"I'm sorting it out," she said.

"I get it. When you're ready, I can be a good listener."

"I know. And thank you." Emily gave Anna an appreciative look even as a ball of despair grew in the pit of her stomach. "I really don't know what's going to happen between Nick and me."

"I want to offer you the hope you're looking for, but we both know that would just be empty words," Anna said.

"What do I do?" Her voice pinched around a ball that had lodged itself in her throat.

"The same thing you did when he was gone. You get up. You do your job. You be there for your friends and family and this community. And they—*we*—will be here for you."

Emily let Anna hug her until the despair no longer suffocated her. She still felt weak and hungry—a reminder to her of how much Nick had endured being imprisoned, abused, and subject to awful crimes.

It was a miracle that he was even alive. And Emily told herself that the fact that this miracle could occur meant that there could be another one.

CHAPTER 35

The first few days in the hospital, Nick had tried to be a good patient. He lay in bed and tried to sleep. But sleep brought torturous nightmares, so he'd stayed awake. He cleared his email inbox, grew bored of YouTube videos, tired of the rants on social media. Constant pharmaceutical commercials that aired every five minutes between segments of TV shows made him want to find a gun to shoot the television with. All this noise and commercial posturing was meaningless in light of what he had overcome.

Silence was better—or so it seemed at first. Until memories started hitting.

Physical pain prodded places not fully healed. He shifted into another mode of distraction: exercise. Nick started performing routines of light calisthenics in his hospital room. To the capacity that his lungs would allow, he did push-ups, sit-ups, planks, and yoga stretches. After that, he paced the room until the staff showed up and forced him back to bed.

As soon as they left, he was up again.

Four days in the place, and he was crawling the walls and

belligerent with staff. Since his health was improving, they left him alone. Blood work this morning had revealed his TB was not contagious, but his lung scans showed small new lesions, and his oxygen levels often dipped into the high eighties, prompting frequent hours on an oxygen tank. He needed regular monitoring, so his doctor was recommending another one to maybe two weeks of hospital stay.

Meanwhile, he had decided against telling Roe about the missing piece of his lung. He had been officially interrogated several times while at the facility in Rock River. His story hadn't changed. He still didn't remember much of his stay in the Chinese facility, which he now assumed was a hospital. In the past few days he hadn't heard a thing from Roe. Did the FBI even need him anymore? Or worse, were they making arrangements for him to sit out the next twenty years behind a desk?

Nick couldn't stew over it in this cement box one second longer. He needed to have something to do with his mind and hands. He needed to be outdoors. Boots on the ground. Moving. Chasing. Hunting. Living. He had been given a second chance at life—more so than ever, he realized, in light of the missing lung. He wasn't going to waste his precious days in a hospital. Especially when Aditson and Emily were doing such a poor job of tracking Colton Chauncey.

All Wednesday morning and afternoon Nick checked his phone, hoping to hear from Emily. But there was only a stupid meme from his mother encouraging him to "hang in there." His thoughts drifted to what Emily might be doing right now. Probably hanging out with Anna and the girls.

He knew he'd driven her away with his caustic attitude. It ate at him like rust on the bottom of a truck door panel. He didn't know why he had no desire to fix the rusty part of him. Rust didn't stop on its own. It continued to feed and grow. The only cure was to excise it completely from the panel and weld on a new piece of metal, making it whole again.

Why *didn't* he want to be whole?

Before the FBI, being a cop in Freeport had provided great satisfaction. When Nick was patrolling or working cases, he was the glue bonding a broken part of the community. He loved being reliably there for people during their times of greatest need. Now here in this room, he was nothing and no one. He was rusting.

It was nearly 9:00 p.m. when Nick pulled up a Google map of Lake Isabella, zooming in and out of the location where Emily had told him Savannah's body had been found. Emily had shared the details of the case with him, for which he was grateful. Truthfully, they had shared little else of importance with each other. He hated living in that empty feeling and pushed his concentration to the map on his phone. He located the area of the fishing shack. If he followed the county property lines, they went directly through the lake's Y shape, splitting the eastern arm from the western one. The western arm was in Freeport County. But when he looked closely at the county map lines, he saw a thin gray line splitting the lake in two. The eastern arm was in the Manistee National Forest, which meant the lake was partially on federal land. Savannah's body had been found on federal property, not county.

Which meant, Nick concluded, this case was the jurisdiction of the federal government, specifically the Federal Bureau of Investigation.

He ripped out his IV and PICC line. He retrieved his street clothes from a cupboard in the bathroom and quickly changed, tossing his hospital gown into the stall shower. He gathered his few personal items on the sink counter and the slew of medications on his bedside tray table. He stuffed them all and his laptop into his backpack.

It almost felt comical. Here he was again on the run—this time in his hometown. Being an expert at moving about in secrecy, he wasn't much worried about his escape plan. The night shift was thinly staffed.

He stood in the threshold of his room to listen. Down the hall he heard the light chatter of nurses fussing over a patient. No one was in the halls. It wasn't even a challenge. Nick spotted the exit sign over the stairwell door and darted for it.

He was out.

CHAPTER 36

Thursday was a half day at the high school for teacher in-service, and Emily offered to pick up Flora so they could spend the afternoon together. She left the Hartford house a few minutes early so she could stop by the police station first to catch up with Aditson on the Chauncey case.

"Any word on the footage from Hank Shepherd's place on Isabella Lake?" she asked, poking her head into his office. Aditson was focused on his computer screen.

"Your timing is impeccable. Come here." He ushered her around to his side of the desk. "Our forensic IT guy said the only recordings the surveillance device picked up were animals crossing the guy's lawn. Several deer. A bear and her two cubs."

"Cute—I think," said Emily. She watched as the cubs trailed the mama bear across Shepherd's patio. Okay, it was darling, if one didn't think about the fact that Shepherd was sleeping not even ten feet away inside a thin-walled cottage. She kept her eyes on the screen, and after a few minutes passed with no movement, a lone fox stepped onto the patio, sniffing around. Then it slinked back out of view.

"And that concludes our animal parade for the evening," said Aditson, shutting the video off.

"The thing is, there's no direct access to the lake from Shepherd's cottage, so I'm not surprised we didn't see any activity that night," Emily said, moving back around to the opposite side of the desk. Aditson rocked his chair back, staring at the ceiling contemplatively, as if the answers they needed might suddenly scroll across it.

"Have you been able to get any more intel on Jonah Hampton?" Emily asked.

"I reached his girlfriend, Erin. Or so-called. She hadn't seen him for a couple weeks. Didn't even know he was dead."

"Yikes. They were on the outs?"

"You could say that. Erin accused Jonah of spending too much time with Savannah. Moved up north to take a job at a resort."

"Ooooh, a jealous one." They could be both unpredictable and vengeful.

"Where is she now?"

"She's Canadian. She moved back to Port Findlay, Ontario."

"Does she know Chauncey?"

"She's been around him a few times when she was at Jonah's. Always had a bad feeling about him."

Emily was suddenly concerned that Erin might be a target as Chauncey fled the country.

"I know what you're thinking, and the RCMP have been notified," Aditson assured her.

"Does Chauncey know where Erin lives?"

"She says not. But she's wary," said Aditson. "She also mentioned that Jonah sometimes went up to her uncle's fishing cabin on Saint Joseph Island."

"Did Chauncey know about this cabin?"

"I'm guessing there's a good possibility he did, because Erin said Jonah talked about it all the time."

"Do you think it's possible Chauncey fled the country with Brooklyn?" said Emily. "Maybe up to Canada?" It wouldn't have been difficult for him to cross the Michigan border and disappear in the huge neighboring country. And if so, Emily felt some relief at the possibility of Brooklyn being alive, and possibly rescued, at the cabin.

"The RCMP is going to send out a BOLO to the Ontario province and do a wellness check at the cabin," said Aditson. "But for now, I'm going to keep looking for Chauncey and Brooklyn closer to home."

"Did you find anything of interest at Chauncey's house?" she asked.

"Nothing we can admit as plausible evidence for Savannah's murder."

"No duct tape? Cement blocks? A boat?"

"A disturbing book."

Emily looked up from the ground, tossing him a look. "It's not against the law to own a book."

"*One Beautiful Victim*. True crime at its creepiest."

"Disgusting. But not enough to implicate Chauncey as Savannah's killer."

"The weird thing about the book is that the assailant never kills his victim. He kidnaps her and keeps her as a slave. It's all about his psychological manipulation of this young girl."

"Maybe that was Chauncey's goal. Maybe he had been trying to manipulate Savannah, even before the sexual assaults," said Emily. "There probably were times when she and Chauncey were both at Jonah's."

"I've learned over the years that with human beings, anything is possible." Aditson shrugged. "But Chauncey doesn't strike me as the type of guy to have the patience or finesse of a master manipulator. He's an impulse criminal. Acts out of raw rage. He does what he needs to do to suit whatever his goal is at that moment."

With that in mind, Emily asked, "What does Colton Chauncey need right now?"

Aditson's response was swift and exacting. "Escape. Protection. Cover. And most of all, money."

CHAPTER 37

Aditson was off chasing down a lead in the eastern part of the state, where someone claimed to have spotted a baby that fit Brooklyn's description. He'd told Emily to take the day off and rest. She saw this as an invitation to do some more detective work with her niece.

After picking up Flora and her friends Bethani and Noah at the high school, Emily drove them back to Serpent's Trail, near the location where Flora had found the severed radial arm bone. After they hiked back to the spot, Emily explained how to do a quadrant search.

"We start by outlining the larger area we plan to search so we can keep track of where we're going and where we've been," she explained to the teens gathered around her. "Then we divide that space into a grid pattern by marking the quadrants with powdered chalk lines."

"Like the kind they use on athletic fields?" asked Noah.

"Exactly. There will be four grids, one for each of us. Each box in the grid will be about twenty-five by twenty-five square feet."

"That seems small," Flora noted.

"They won't once you're in the box. It'll feel like you're searching an entire football field. This is tedious work."

The team helped Emily mark the outer boundaries. Emily had them wait on the trail while she chalked in the grid lines.

"Noah, you take the northwest quadrant. Flora, the northeast. Bethani, you get in the southwest box, and I'll search next to you in the southeast quadrant."

Heads nodded, but their faces expressed confusion.

"It'll make more sense once you get out there. We're all going to start in the southeast corner of our boxes. From there we'll head in a straight line to the top of the box. Turn one step to the right and then travel down to the bottom of the box."

She scanned the three faces to see if they comprehended. Then Emily handed them each several evidence bags and a marker. "These are for collecting anything you find that looks out of place in a forest setting."

"Like another bone?" Noah's tone was shaded with apprehension.

"Yes. Like a bone. But we're most likely to find partial bones or bone fragments. I want to set your expectations low. Flora got lucky. But it's likely that over time, animals or weather elements scattered any remains. Also, we have no idea how old that bone is. Could be the rest of the body was left far from here."

Emily got them all started in their respective quadrants.

"Be careful where you're treading. And if you find something, signal me and I'll come over to help."

The normally chatty teens were silent and focused as they padded across the forest floor, heads bent, eyes laser focused on the ground. Emily finished her quadrant first and went over to her niece to help in her box.

"Not as glamorous as it is on TV, is it?"

Flora frowned.

"It's good for you to have the search experience. And how cool that your friends wanted to help," Emily said. "I think Noah's trying to impress you."

"Shh!" Flora shot back.

"Have you given him an answer yet?"

"Not yet."

"Playing hard to get, huh?" Emily grinned.

"He's cute, isn't he?"

"He's a doll. What's holding you back?"

Flora shrugged.

"Take your time. And no pressure if you're not into it."

Flora smiled. "No, you're right. I'm playing hard to get."

Emily laughed. "Listen, I wanted you to know that I reached out to my friend Samantha Eckhardt at the university, and she says we can pop down anytime and she'll take a look at the bone."

"We?"

"Absolutely. I want to introduce you to the staff there, and we can see how they do things."

Flora's face lit up. "So cool."

"But I don't want you missing classes."

"We could go Friday. It's another teacher in-service day. No afternoon classes."

"I'll pick you up at noon. Pack a bag, and we'll make it an overnight trip. I'll show you around the campus. Sushi for dinner?"

Flora was beaming at the opportunity. "Love it."

Being a mom didn't seem so hard after all. At least not with a kid like Flora. Emily saw a lot of herself in the young teen. Fourteen going on twenty-four. She couldn't wait to introduce her to the kind of life she might aspire to in the quickly approaching future.

"Mrs. Hartford?" Noah's strained voice called out.

Emily looked up. "It's just Dr. Hartford. No ring on this finger," she teased. "What's up?"

She and Flora were already crossing their quadrant to get to his box. Noah was bent over something in the middle of his space.

"I think I found something," he said, glancing up at them as they approached. "But I don't want to touch it."

"Just leave it. Let me see what you got there," said Emily.

By now, Bethani had left her box and joined them.

Emily knelt down to see what Noah was looking at. The object appeared to be made of wood, but most of it was buried in the ground. She gently dug around the surface to loosen the packed soil. Soon more of the object was in view.

"It looks like a stick that someone whittled," said Bethani.

"More like a wooden handle," Noah said.

Emily carefully jostled the end of it, dislodging it from the earth. When it emerged, she brushed off the dirt. It looked as if something had been broken off the top. The body was smooth and well worn. When Emily gripped it, it fit nicely into her palm.

"What is that?" Flora said, taking a photograph of it with her phone.

"I think it's a handle from a tool," said Emily.

"What kind of tool?" asked Bethani.

"Maybe a hammer?" said Flora.

"The handle's too thick to be a hammer," said Noah.

"I think it looks more like the base of a hatchet or an axe," Emily proposed.

"What's it doing out here?" Bethani said.

"Did you know that this area was covered in virgin white pines that grew over two hundred feet tall?" asked Emily. "It was reforested by lumber barons over a century and a half ago."

"You think some lumberjack lost his axe?" asked Flora.

"Happens all the time," Bethani told them. "My dad's a carpenter, and it seems like he's buying a new hammer every other week."

"It's probably nothing of interest. But let's collect it properly so you can see how it's done," suggested Emily.

She wasn't about to share her honed instinct that this was probably not a lumberman's misplaced axe. It seemed more likely, given that the bone had been found in the same area, that the tool had been used as a weapon, then hidden.

CHAPTER 38

Nick stood on the north banks of Lake Isabella, looking across the water. After a good night's sleep in his own bed, he'd risen late Thursday afternoon. A quick shower and bite to eat, and he was out the door to Lake Isabella. He had wanted to survey the area methodically and slowly; thus, he'd chosen to hike to the fishing shack from the two-track road that led from the main highway. Even this moderate distance of three miles had caused his compromised lungs to grow tight with pain. He paused to catch his breath and allow his heart rate to come down. Nick gazed over the property. If what Emily had told him about the location was correct, the body had been found on federal forest land, not Freeport County property.

If Savannah Browdey's murder had occurred on federal land, it was rightfully a federal case. Nick saw this as the perfect opportunity. His return to active duty would be predicated on his seeing a therapist, but he figured he could show up and bullshit his way through a few sessions if it meant taking on this case. Nick was dizzy with the anticipation of getting back into the field. His mind buzzed with plans to track the suspect. He knew the Colton Chaunceys of the world well. Means always justified their ends.

Nick had begun formulating his argument to his boss when the churr of a small saw starting up penetrated his eardrums, sending a prickle from cervical to lumbar vertebrae. His gaze circled the woods, searching for the source. But he couldn't spot a single person.

The churring took a deeper tone as it droned on. Nick felt it grating up and down. Curious about its source, he began to run the circumference of the lake toward the sound, which seemed to originate from the east side of the Y branch. His feet plodded through the soft, sandy bank, his steps interspersed with the intermittent revving of the machine. Before long, Nick's lungs were taxed, and he became lightheaded. But he refused to slow down.

The lack of oxygen put him in a brain fog. The scene before him distorted and blurred, and he weakened and dropped to his knees as images warped time and space.

Nick was dragging himself through the camp-like setup of a war hospital. He was visiting a place he'd been before. The dingy room was familiar. He knew these cement walls, cement floors. The backdrop to it all was the whirring and churring of machines. Thick gray curtains blocked light from rectangular windows located just below the ceiling. The room was stuffy, humid. A lack of airflow wrenched his lungs. Nick's thin cotton robe was drenched in sweat. He slogged ahead, planting each footstep into what seemed like wet cement, down the center of the room, past rows of bodies on cots, all covered by white sheets.

The room had no end, but Nick persisted, his shoes coated with wet cement. He was being dragged by two men dressed in military uniforms through the door to a surgical area. Each held him on either side as he trudged farther, his legs growing weak. He struggled for each sip of air.

The revving notched up as he moved across the massive room. Heart monitors beeping. Bone saw whirring. The low chatter of Chinese. The clatter of surgical instruments. With every step, it extended beyond his reach until he couldn't see the end of it. He couldn't see faces. Above it all, the distressed sobs were taking over every thought in his mind.

A figure dressed in a medical uniform came into view. *Hurry. Hurry. Hurry,* they chanted in soft whispers.

Nick circled them, but they paid him no attention. *What are you doing?* he screamed, but no sound came out. *Stop. Stop it!*

The fever dream was broken by a deafening *ca-caw.*

Nick froze. Less than eight feet above his head, a flock of black birds jutted straight up from the surface of the lake and soared across the water. Nick was caught in the thrust of their takeoff. Arching his neck, he watched them until they disappeared over the tree line. Then he stumbled back from the bank, gasping for breath. He wasn't going to make it.

He fumbled for his phone and tapped on Emily's number. The signal was weak and refused to connect. Nick shook his phone as if to harness the radio wave. It was futile, of course. He glanced from the screen and looked up into the sky, struggling for the shallowest of breaths. He grabbed at air as his vision blacked out. With a thud, Nick collapsed, his body sinking face-first into the damp, mucky shore.

CHAPTER 39

Ruby never let Strawberry out of her sight. When meandering around the house or the yard, she wore her in a sling made of a bedsheet torn in half. She told the baby happy and sad stories of all those who'd lived and died there. She showed her the sunflower fields and the stock of seeds in the cellar for next spring.

And yet, every night in the old house, Ruby heard in her dreams the haunted cries of her lost babies. No sooner would she drift off to sleep than those babies released their wails, so near it felt like they were hiding in the walls of her farmhouse. In Ruby's dreams she trolled the house, trying to find them in her bedroom, and even the bedrooms that she'd locked up years ago after the kids had left. She went down into the cellar and peered under every bushel basket, bucket, and tool her husband had left. They weren't behind or in the furnace either.

But when Ruby awoke, she felt joy, for there was precious Strawberry, a real, alive, breathing baby for her to care for. This sweet baby giggled and reached out her chubby arms for Ruby, and the old woman's heart melted.

Unfortunately, there was the problem of food. The fridge

and pantry needed a restock. When the baby had been dropped off by that girl, there'd been no potato chips in the bag—in fact, there'd been no food except for half a can of powdered milk formula that she'd mixed with tap water and fed to Strawberry. But now the powder was down to its last few scoops.

Ruby thinned out the baby formula, even as she knew it wasn't enough to satisfy a baby's belly. She rocked little Strawberry and sang to her.

Those blue eyes close tight.
Bright angels are near.
So sleep without fear.

Strawberry wiggled her body and cooed, encouraging Ruby to sing some more.

She plotted their survival. She'd been here before and had scavenged from the woods. She needed the comfort of her land.

Late-season berries might still be on the bushes. And wild apple trees could be found in the back of their fifty-acre pasture. Ruby could make juice from them for baby Strawberry. And Ruby could eat the pulp. It would be pleasant out there tonight, especially during this warm spell setting in. Her outdoor thermometer told her it was near sixty degrees.

At nightfall, dressed in her thinning flannel nightgown, matted chenille robe, and slippers with holes in the bottoms, she set out from the house. Cradling Strawberry, whom she swaddled in a tattered crocheted blanket, Ruby moved through her long-dead sunflower gardens and across the expanse of the field toward the wooded area at its far end. Entering the woods at the mouth of the worn path, Ruby followed a snaking dirt trail to a back corner of her property, which butted up to a hiking trailhead maintained by the state forestry department. She made her way to a pine tree cluster and ducked underneath bowed branches that formed a pine tent.

This was a lovely spot. She'd collect apples later, for sweet Strawberry had fallen asleep in her arms and Ruby didn't want to jostle or wake her. Her arthritic bones knelt on the soft-needled ground. She lay down happily, never letting go of the beautiful child curled warmly and safely into her chest.

And finally came a deep and restful sleep.

CHAPTER 40

Twenty minutes after he passed out, Nick regained consciousness and found himself gasping for air. Even in this groggy state, he managed to turn his face to the sky, sucking in large gulps of oxygen. He pinched his nose to force out muck clogging his nasal passages and sat up. He had been on the ground long enough to garner itchy patches of red welts around his ankles and forearms, where the flesh had been exposed to insects. Nick got to his feet and stumbled his way back to the trail as the blood flowed back into his legs. Once the tingling went away, he tried to pick up his pace, but it taxed his lungs until it felt like a hundred knife points were pricking them. What had he been doing on the ground, nearly drowning at the lake's edge?

He checked the time. Then he recalled the whitewashed memory of the past that had meshed with the whirs of machines. His ears pricked, trying to hear it again, but captured no more sounds. Walking the wooded trail from Lake Isabella to the roadside parking lot was more miserable than going the other way had been. The entire trek back to his truck, he listened, wondering if he'd really heard any of it at all.

Nick was relieved when thirty minutes later he turned into the driveway of his lakeside home. Once inside, he set down his things and went to the kitchen for a glass of water and a bag of microwave popcorn. He laid it on the microwave turntable and started the two-minute cooking cycle. He hadn't taken any of his meds. He knew he should. Feeling lightheaded, he sat down on the barstool at the kitchen island and placed his head into his hands. He gulped down the glass of water and felt better. It was nothing. He was probably just a little dehydrated.

He checked his phone. Emily had texted. *How are you doing today?*

He pinged her back. *Tired. Bored.*

Three dots pulsed.

Want a visitor?

Not today. Call you tomorrow Hartford.

Emily sent back the thumbs-up emoji along with a heart kissy face.

Nick texted Roe next. *Time to talk?*

By the time he was shaking out the popped corn into a large bowl, the link to a secure video-call link was posted to his FBI email inbox.

Nick clicked on it and waited for Agent Roe to connect on the other end. Nick looked at himself on the screen. Flecks of grass and mud splotches clung to his cheek where he had face-planted onto the ground. He wiped them off. His forehead sported several red bugbites. How was he going to explain those?

The screen split into gallery view as Agent Roe joined the call.

"Larsen, looks like you've been playing rugby," his supervisor joked.

Nick grinned. "Was outside doing some light yard work," he lied.

"You're home?"

"Early release for good behavior."

"Thought you were still quarantined?"

"I'm no longer contagious."

"Haven't seen a medical sign-off."

"It's coming."

"It better be. And how are you feeling?"

"Doing much better, sir." As they spoke, Nick saw Roe studying him. Watching Nick's reactions, his facial tics, his eye tracking. It was classic behavioral observation. Any involuntary movement might give away something about Nick's current state of being.

"What's the cause of this urgent call?" asked Roe.

"I want to go back to work."

"You do?"

"And I found my in."

"Isn't that my job?"

Nick grinned. "I know, but I discovered something close to home that needs FBI attention."

The supervisor leaned slightly toward the screen, and Nick knew he'd gotten his boss's attention.

"There was a recent homicide here in Freeport County. A local police detective has been working the case, but he shouldn't be."

"I don't understand."

"The murder victim was found on federal land." Nick pulled up the relevant images from his app and the map link.

His supervisor scanned the images, seeing the same thing Nick did. "And they didn't bother to call this in to the feds?" asked Roe.

"To be fair, I don't think they know."

"And this is in your hometown?"

"Smack dab in the middle."

"You'll need to pass psych first."

"I'm working on it. I've picked a therapist in Rock River."

"I can't let you out there yet."

"I'm going crazy—or should I rephrase that?"

"Putting you back to work before you're ready is a risk. For all of us."

"I've been cooped up in that hospital room, and now you want me to stay home and just sit around?"

"Didn't you used to like hunting and fishing?"

"That's not the point. I get to being alone, and then . . . it all comes back."

"All the more reason for therapy."

"I'm doing just fine."

"And what about when you encounter intensely stressful situations? How do I know you can navigate and execute according to orders?"

Nick rocked back on his chair, exhaling his frustration. "I can do whatever the job requires."

On-screen, his supervisor didn't break his gaze.

Nick could tell he was thinking it over. That was a good sign.

"I will see if we can make this a probationary case," said Roe.

"What does that mean?"

"You need to wade before you can swim."

Nick wasn't stupid. "Sounds like there are strings attached."

"We partner you with another field agent who will be evaluating your progress."

"I don't need a babysitter."

"You're right. You need a partner."

Nick's jaw locked, and his words seethed out. "Look what that got me in China."

"We didn't know he would—"

"Don't start." Nick pointed a finger at him on the screen. "I don't want to hear it."

His supervisor backed off but kept his eyes locked on Nick's.

"I don't want any help," said Nick. "I need to work this alone. Get back on my feet."

"Nonnegotiable."

A tightness constricted his throat. Nick's face reddened as he fumbled for words.

"Nick—you okay?"

He held up a finger to the screen. *Give me a sec.*

"Are you at home?"

He gave a shallow nod.

"I can call 911."

He wagged his head. He stepped away from the computer screen, drawing in long inhales.

"Nick? Larsen?" his supervisor's voice called out through the laptop speakers.

He breathed through it until his nerves relaxed.

"I'm calling for help."

Nick slid back in front of the screen. "No, no, I'm totally fine." He gave his supervisor a thumbs-up. "All good."

"Didn't look like it."

"I'm rapidly improving."

"That looked to me like a panic attack."

"It wasn't."

"If you say so." Roe clicked his tongue. "I need that sign-off and proof of therapy appointment. Before I even ask."

Nick struggled to keep his voice steady. "I am always going to have trust issues."

"Understandable."

"But do you really?" Nick asked. "I was betrayed, then left for dead."

"We got the guy, Larsen. It's over."

"Fine. But I want . . . I *need* my life back. And I don't have time to play silly trust games with a new guy while working a highly sensitive murder case."

For a moment, neither spoke. His supervisor tented his hands in front of his mouth and took several breaths. In a slow descent, his hands moved under his chin.

"There are only two options here, Agent Larsen. You accept a partner. Or you walk away and we reassign the case."

"This is my hometown. My people."

"So you'll accept a partner?"

Nick chose his next question carefully. "Does this partner have to be agency?"

"What do you think?"

"You bring a stranger . . . a federal agent, no less . . . into this community, and people will clam up. And that will make my job difficult because it may stall or tank the investigation."

"You're telling me people in Freeport won't cooperate with an investigation to help one of their own?" Roe crossed his arms and stared at Nick from behind the screen. "Given your circumstances, what about the local detective?"

"Aditson?" asked Nick. "He'll be in my way."

"Is this the trust thing again?"

"I barely know him."

"He's already working the investigation. It's an easy way into the case."

"I could do this job single-handedly. And I have."

"Stop wasting my time, Nick. There are rules. Are you in or out?"

"I have someone else in mind."

"Who?"

"An old friend."

"Which means you trust this person?"

"With my life."

Agent Roe nodded, considering. "Okay, put him in touch with me. And then we'll see."

Nick nodded. Fair enough. They ended their call, and he stood to fill up his water glass. Lightheadedness swept over him. He shuffled toward the living room, the sofa calling him. Just a quick nap.

Then he'd get Emily to agree.

CHAPTER 41

He didn't usually visit Ruby in the middle of the night, and he hoped she'd be fast asleep. As he pulled into the long drive with his headlights off, he noticed the work she'd done cutting off the sunflower heads. Kooky old woman and her flower fetish. He imagined the thousands of seeds she had harvested and was drying and storing in the cellar. How was it possible that this creaky woman had enough energy to get all those seeds into the ground each spring? It was something of a miracle, or maybe just the workings of a lunatic. Either way, he was grateful for the coverage they'd provided for various graves he'd dug on the property in the past.

Colton decided to bury Raven toward the back of the property, where there was little chance of her body being discovered. The land abutted a national forest that was rarely, if ever, explored, even by rangers. His truck bobbed and rocked through the unpaved field. He stopped at its far end, which bled into a thick forest. He would dig the grave just inside the family's property line.

He glanced over the field to a grove of pine trees clustered together. He and his brothers and sisters had used the space underneath as their private fort. In summertime it was cool under the pines, and they'd have picnics and play board games. In the winter, the branches sheltered them from the snow. The pine needles that fell to the floor formed a bed so soft he often wished he could make a mattress of them. And . . . *What the hell?*

His mother was lying under the pines with the baby spooned up against her belly, both sound asleep. This had been Raven's brilliant maneuver? Leaving a baby with a batty old woman? And what in holy's name was Ruby doing out here in the woods?

The two of them didn't stir as Colton watched them sleep. He had never seen his ma look so peaceful. Maybe it was the night shadows on her face, but he thought he saw the corners of her lips curled up in a content smile. This vision drained any temptation he had to wake them.

The baby seemed all right. He'd take her later. Now he had business to finish.

Colton slowly backed away toward the car and drove to the other side of the property. The manual labor was backbreaking and took several hours. Just after 4:00 a.m., the last mound of soil was set in place and patted down.

Colton drove to the house, where he went upstairs and slept in his old room. After his ma got back, he'd reclaim the baby. But he expected it was going to be a struggle to tear her away from the tough old bird.

CHAPTER 42

"He just up and left in the middle of the night?" said Emily, who had popped up to Nick's room to check on him and bring a treat from Brown's Bakery.

The second-shift nurse handed her Nick's chart. "Poof! Gone."

"What time was this discovered?"

"When the night nurse went in around three thirty in the morning, the room was empty."

Emily scanned the chart. The last entry had been made at 8:06 p.m. Just after seven, the attending doctor had ordered Nick to stay another seven days, pending retests. Nick's chart eased her concerns that his TB might still be contagious. But why flee under the cover of darkness?

She rummaged through the drawers under the countertop. None of Nick's things were there.

"And no one saw or heard him leave?" asked Emily.

"It's not a prison. And he was cleared."

Emily stuck her head into the en suite bath. Empty. "Anyone check the security cameras?"

"Why? Is he wanted for a crime?" The nurse side-eyed Emily with the little dig.

"No. But he's sure acting sketchy, skulking out of here in the middle of the night." Emily sighed and plopped down on the edge of the hospital bed.

"He wasn't exactly a model patient," said the nurse. "I'm just happy he didn't bleed all over the floor when he ripped out his IV. I hate cleaning up that mess."

"What about his meds?"

"They weren't here. I'm guessing he took them." The nurse nodded toward the door. "I've gotta disinfect this room for the next intake. Do you mind?"

Emily went out and planted herself in the hallway.

First she tried calling Nick, but before the first ring, it went to voicemail.

She phoned his mother next.

No, Bernadette hadn't heard from him since yesterday morning.

Yes, she'd give him a call and check his house.

And yes, like Emily, she was worried.

Earlier in the day Emily had gotten a text from Aditson saying the potential sighting of baby Brooklyn in eastern Michigan had been a false lead. Someone had spotted a scruffy older man with a blond, blue-eyed baby in his shopping cart at the Safeway grocery store and called it in. It was confirmed by the infant's mother that the man, who was babysitting for the day, was the grandfather. Now it was Emily's turn to share bad news, and she called Aditson.

"Nick fled the hospital, and now he's not answering my calls and texts," she told him. "Can we send out a search party?" She was only half kidding.

"He's not missing."

"How do you know?"

"Because he left my office five minutes ago."

A long pause followed. Emily fidgeted.

"Don't keep me in suspense," she said.

"Larsen's taken over the Browdey case."

"On what grounds?"

"Funny you should choose that word."

"What word? What are you talking about?"

"Apparently, Savannah Browdey was murdered on federal land."

Emily hung up and texted Bernadette. *Meet me at Nick's.*

This would require a tag team.

CHAPTER 43

What was Nick trying to prove, stealing this case from under Aditson's nose? Emily blazed a hot trail to his house right after texting Bernadette. She lived close by, and when Emily arrived, she was already in Nick's kitchen, pulling out ingredients to make spaghetti and meatballs.

"What are you doing?"

"Making lunch."

"Where is Nick?"

"Said he had an errand to run."

Emily knew better but kept that to herself. "He should be in the hospital."

"Maybe I should see if he wants to recover back at my place so I can take care of him," his mom suggested. "Or I could move in here."

Emily thought both were horrible ideas. And now she was worried about what he was doing out on the field at the moment.

"I'm sure he would be bored stiff anywhere we try to confine him. Could never keep that kid still," said Bernadette.

"Maybe so, but *that kid* really shouldn't be out and about doing anything but recovering."

"I say we make him a nice meal. The way to a man's heart and head is through a pot of pasta." Bernadette took a block of Parmesan from the crisper drawer. "Does Nick have a cheese grater?"

Yeah, let's reward Nick's bad behavior with Mom's home-cooked spaghetti. Emily was about to go full snark on Bernadette. Instead, she regained her composure and pulled the grater from the drawer. She was about to hand it over when Bernadette put the block of cheese in front of Emily.

"Will you grate me about a cup of that, hon?"

Emily bit her lip. Bernadette poured a box of noodles into a pot of boiling water.

"Has Nick talked to you about what happened to him over there?" Emily fished for information.

"Of course not." Bernadette's hands went to her hips. "You?"

"Not a peep." Emily wasn't going to give her anything to chew on.

"He will when he's ready, I'm sure," said Bernadette. "You can hardly blame him for wanting to get out of that hospital room."

Yes, Emily could. Right now Bernadette's precious son was his own worst enemy.

Emily tucked both lips in and felt Bernadette's stare on her.

"Em? What do you know?"

But she couldn't let those worms crawl out the can. "Nothing," said Emily. "He's told me next to nothing."

"Next to nothing is something. What is it? Something terrible?"

"I can't tell you anything about his health. It's against HIPAA."

"I'm not asking about his health. What happened to him over there?"

"That's for Nick to say." Emily noticed a Ziploc baggie of medications on the kitchen counter. At least Nick had had the presence of mind to bring his drugs. But from the look of the sealed foil pill packages, she didn't think he had taken any.

"For Pete's sake, you were almost my daughter-in-law."

Were?

The implication of a missed opportunity singed Emily.

"I'm not going to pass along speculations as fact," she said.

"I forgot how stubborn you can be." Bernadette stirred the noodles, splashing hot water onto the gas burner with a sizzle. "I am making my son a hot meal. It's the least I can do."

"When is he supposed to be home?"

"He didn't say. You can stick around and eat with us or not. Your choice."

Nick got his toughness from his mother, no doubt about it.

"I've got to get to work." Emily grabbed her purse and keys. She felt an urgency to find Nick. If he wasn't taking his antibiotics, he might be getting sick, and he wouldn't feel it until his whole body went septic.

"You sure you don't want to stay?" asked Bernadette.

"Have to finish some paperwork," Emily lied.

Emily wove all through downtown Freeport, looking for Nick's truck. She called him fifteen times and sent eleven text messages. No response. After an hour of driving aimlessly, exasperated and getting hangry, Emily pulled in front of Brown's Bakery.

She trudged in, eyeing the bakery case of goodies. No trouble was so large that a gooey carb-and-caffeine extravaganza couldn't take the edge off. She only wished Delia were here.

"What can I get for you, Dr. Emily?" Emily glanced up to see Sadie the barista behind the case, smiling at her like it was Christmas every day. Cranky Emily found herself judging this pretty book by its cover, the innocent expression and cherry-sweet smile indicative of Sadie's youth. How nice to be so untouched by life's deep cuts.

"Cinnamon roll. And a cappuccino, triple shot of espresso," Emily said in a deadened voice.

"That is the order of a woman in need," said Sadie. "I'm adding extra frosting on the side."

"Thank you." Emily placated the girl with a tightly drawn smile. She slid a ten over the counter and told her to keep the change. Which amounted to about seventy-eight cents. She was about to leave the counter but guiltily drew back, pulled another dollar from her purse, and stuffed it in the tip jar.

Emily took her treats and found a small café table in the corner where she could tuck herself away unnoticed. The warm roll melted in her mouth and was down the hatch in several large bites. She took her time with the cappuccino, savoring it with little sips and licking the residual foam around the rim of the mug.

She checked her emails. A message from Samantha Eckhardt at the forensic anthropology department confirmed their meeting tomorrow. She wrote that she was looking forward to reconnecting and meeting Flora, the budding forensic scientist. Emily scrolled to the signature line. Samantha Eckhardt was no longer "Research Assistant." Instead, the letters *PhD* sat behind her name, along with the title of *Head of Genetic Genealogy*. Good for her!

Emily confirmed that they would arrive by late morning.

Her phone buzzed. An incoming text from Nick.

Can we talk?

CHAPTER 44

Ruby entered the kitchen with the baby on her hip, and her heart skipped a beat at the sight of a brown paper grocery sack on the kitchen counter. Her son had been here! He hadn't forgotten his ma. She shifted the baby onto her left hip, and with her other hand she riffled through the bag to see what he'd brought. Dry beans. A block of cheese. Noodles. Three cans of tuna. Enough food for a month. Maybe more.

"Hi, Ma."

She startled at the voice. And when she looked up, she barely recognized the disheveled man standing in her kitchen. Colton had grown a beard to his chest, and his long peppered hair was mangy. His clothes hung on him, and he smelled of body odor and dirt. He gave her a stern look as he stepped toward her. "I need that baby."

"She's beautiful, isn't she?" Ruby said with a grin. "Has your nose. Your cheeks. A perfect little Strawberry—that's what I call her."

"You named her?"

"After her beautiful hair and the fuchsia sunflower that blooms in June."

"I need to take her." He hovered over her.

Ruby stepped back, hugging the infant to her chest. "No, Strawberry was given to me to care for. She'll make up for the others . . . This is her home."

"She can't stay." His voice was calm and gentle as he reached for her. "Ma, she don't belong to you."

Ruby clutched the baby harder, who whimpered. "I wouldn't let Thomas take you away, boy, and I ain't letting you take this one neither."

"Give me the baby, Ma."

"It's another chance for me."

"Ma, she's not yours," said her son.

"She was given to me."

"It was by mistake that Raven brought her here," growled Colton.

"Babies are never a mistake," Ruby cooed into Brooklyn's ear. "I loved being a mother, and now . . . I can save this baby."

"I have two bags of potato chips." He held up the bags, and Ruby's hand instinctively rose to grab them. "Give me the baby, and they're yours."

"No. She'll die for sure if I let her out of my arms."

"She's not gonna die."

"But so many did," Ruby insisted. "Six before you. And then two after."

"This baby's going to be just fine, Ma."

"I protected you. And I'm protecting this one."

Ruby wasn't sure if he knew about his lost siblings. Thomas had abused all thirteen of Ruby's babies. Only five of them had survived past infancy.

"You're not taking this one, Thomas."

"I'm not Thomas." His voice was gravelly. "That was my

daddy, and you know he's dead. Now give me that kid. She's not yours, Ma."

Ruby scooted out of his grasp and balanced herself against the kitchen counter for support.

"You are not taking this baby, Thomas."

"Mama, it's me. Your son." He moved slowly toward her, scanning the kitchen. When his gaze landed on a spool of twine resting on the kitchen table, she knew he would use it to restrain her.

Ruby turned slightly toward the kitchen counter, where she'd been deseeding sunflowers with the tip of her butcher knife. It was buried under a thin stack of old newspapers.

She hadn't been able to stand up to protect the others, but she'd save this wee one. She gathered all the strength and motivation left in her wizened soul. With the reflexes of a much younger woman, Ruby felt for the worn wooden handle of the knife. Her bony fingers wrapped around it.

"Gimme that kid!" Colton shook Ruby good, and her arms went to jelly. The baby slipped down her hip. He scooped up Strawberry, then dashed out of the kitchen.

Ruby stumbled across the front porch after him. Too feeble to stop him by physical force, she looked down and saw that she was still holding the butcher knife. She raised it over her head and launched it like a javelin. The tip met its target, but lack of force caused it to bounce off and fall to the ground.

Colton spun to look back, and little Strawberry slipped from his grasp, tumbling over the porch railing.

Maternal instinct in overdrive, Ruby dove over the porch rail after Strawberry, her body tearing through the bushes planted along the front of the porch. As she landed on her back, she felt a bone snap in her hip. Above her, Colton towered with a twisted look she had seen a thousand times. Never mind him. Little Strawberry was safely in her arms.

CHAPTER 45

Emily agreed to meet Nick at the Freeport Memorial Park.

He was forty minutes late. Her three texts to him went unanswered. Emily planted herself against her Yukon and checked the time. She'd wait five more minutes. And then she was done.

Three minutes and seventeen seconds later, Nick pulled up in his truck.

When he exited the vehicle, Emily was surprised at how good he looked. His color was back. Despite the lackluster hospital food, Emily thought that he'd gained a few pounds. Being in his street clothes and not in a hospital gown hooked up to an IV helped too. He almost looked like the Nick who'd left two years back.

"Sorry I'm late, Emily," he said, looking truly penitent.

"I was less than two minutes from leaving."

"I could explain, but—"

"Don't waste your breath. You haven't the lung capacity."

"I've missed your sense of humor," he said.

"Don't placate me."

"Sorry about disappearing, but I was going nuts in that

place." He tried to meet her eyes, but Emily looked away, determined to remain immune to his charms.

The case against him was significant. "You went against doctors' orders," she started, "then you bounced from the hospital, then plotted how you could insert yourself back into the workforce at the FBI by stealing other people's cases?"

"That's a pretty good guess, though it wasn't exactly in that order," he said playfully. "But facts are facts, Em, and Savannah Browdey was murdered on federal land. It was only a matter of time till Aditson had to hand over the case."

"She was *found* on federal land. We have no idea where she was murdered."

"That's stretching it, Em. You're the ME, and you ruled her death a drowning."

"She could have drowned somewhere else."

"Occam's razor. When you have two competing theories, the simpler is preferred."

"Are you purposefully trying to make me mad?"

"Absolutely not," he said with a half laugh. "But please stop being obstinate. Especially about casework."

He had her. She was too good to bend her professional integrity.

"Nick, you and Aditson could be working together on this," she told him. "He's a talented investigator."

"Well, yes, his investigation brought information I can springboard from," said Nick. "But he's not up to the task of tracking this guy."

"Oh? And you are?"

"You and I both know that I can find Colton Chauncey. If nothing else, I know these woods as well as anyone."

"But what if he's not hiding in those woods?" she asked. "Anyway, I'm not questioning your investigative skills. I'm worried your body won't cooperate with your brain's plans to catch a serial murderer."

"I survived worse than what I'm dealing with right now," said Nick. "Look at me. I'm up for the challenge." He raised his arm and flexed a muscle.

Emily smiled, and she had to admit that he didn't look half bad. Or at least he had improved quite a bit. In truth, she wanted to believe he was getting better. And she also knew her line of reasoning was not convincing him.

"Think about it this way," he said. "Me taking the case frees Aditson up for his other local law enforcement duties."

"How benevolent of you," said Emily. "Is that how you sold it to your boss?" She crossed her arms over her chest, protecting herself. "So what did you want to talk with me about?"

"I thought you should hear it from me—not Aditson."

"Too late."

"I need the Browdey and Hampton autopsy reports."

He was within his rights to request this public record. Still, she said, "Ask politely."

"Please?"

"I can email all of it within the hour." She shifted her stance but kept her physical distance. She sensed another ask in the works. "Is there anything else?" she said, averting her eyes from his face—his handsome face.

"I've only been allowed on the Savannah Browdey case on probationary status," he said.

"Probationary—that's good. At least Roe might still have some sense."

"But I need a medical sign-off note. And I was hoping that . . ."

"You've got to be kidding."

"I feel good, Doc, and I'm taking my meds."

"And your activity level should be moderate," she said, every bit the doctor. "Can you promise me that? I doubt it. And if I remember correctly, you also need to pass a mental health exam."

"That's all arranged." Nick held up his phone to show her his appointment calendar. "Next week, Tuesday. Ten a.m. Rock River. Dr. Patricia Haines, psychiatrist. She's supposed to be very good."

"I'll believe it when it happens." Emily glanced away. "Have you considered the fact that if I sign off on you, I'll have to disclose to Roe what was found on your lung x-ray?"

"I was hoping you might finesse that, make it more general. Fit to return to work, that kind of thing." He sighed, and their eyes met. Nick's expression and voice conveyed sincerity. "I'm not a cog in some confounded mission. This is . . ." He pointed to his chest, and his voice dipped to a near whisper. "This is hard to take."

Witnessing Nick's vulnerability, Emily also recognized her own rigidity. Coming to terms with the fact that part of his body had been stolen from him had to be surreal. Anyone would need time to sit with that. And all things considered, he was doing pretty well.

If it had been her, she would have expected Nick's support. Where was hers for him?

"I guess missing body parts is not something most people deal with every day." She gave him a soft smile.

"I haven't been able to find the DSM listing on organ heists."

They smiled, and then Emily broke the gaze.

"Let me think more about how I can phrase the release," she said. "But think long and hard about how and when you'll tell Roe about what happened to you."

"I will. I am." Nick sighed with relief. "Thank you, Em. I really need this."

She could think of a hundred other things he really needed.

"There's something else I need to ask," he said. "As I mentioned, I can only go back to work if I have a partner."

Someone to pick him up off the floor when he's gone into a PTSD puddle. She sighed. "I hope it goes well. There's a lot at stake."

"I was allowed to choose you."

"Allowed?"

"Normally, I'd have to choose a bureau agent."

"Please tell me you are kidding. Choose me? Like I'm a truffle in a chocolate-store window?"

"You're even better than chocolate," he said, "and the only one I want on the case."

"Why?"

"You know Freeport and have a good rapport with people."

"So does Aditson."

"But I want you. I'm comfortable with you. And right now . . . that's what I need."

"And if I don't want to be your 'partner'?"

"An agent from the Detroit office will be assigned. Someone who doesn't know this place or its people like we do."

Emily didn't love the thought of a stranger snooping into the community. The layers were only beginning to unfold; Savannah's case was going to need a tough hand but a tender touch. And it needed someone whose focus was on finding Brooklyn.

"Did you know the Browdey family?" Emily asked. Both her family and Nick's had deep roots in this community.

"I don't remember any of them," said Nick. "You?"

"Never heard of them. Or the Chaunceys. But this is our hometown, and you know how quickly a reputation can get dragged through the pigpen by outsiders."

"I do. And in case you've forgotten, I was loyal to this town long before you returned."

"It's not a pissing match," she bit back.

"I'm not trying to start things between us—" Nick sighed. "I want you with me, Em."

On this case or in your heart? Emily held it back, searching the face of a guy she once thought she knew so well.

"When would I start?" she asked.

"Right now. I have a lead. That's why I was late getting here."

"So you're here to pick me up?"

"As I remember it, you never could walk away from a good case."

"I hate that you know me so well."

Nick gave Emily a look that melted her a little. "Everything's under my jurisdiction now. Aditson gave me the case information, including a rundown of Savannah's case and Chauncey's assault reports. Just waiting on those autopsy reports."

"C'mon, Nick, are you sure you're up for this?" she asked. "The guy's extremely dangerous."

"I know exactly how to deal with this savage," he said, and she almost believed him. "So what do you say, partner? It'll be like old times." He was putting on the charm with the accent of a salty noir detective. The thing was, in those black-and-white movies they'd watched together in high school, the female lead rebuffed the detective until the last scene. And for good reason. She had her own path to follow.

"The old times?" she asked. "As I recall, there were only two cases of those so-called old times. And both were highly problematic."

"But in the end, it was bliss." Nick gave her a broad, sexy smile, one of his best tricks for getting her to say yes. "And we caught the bad guys. We can do it again. This is big, Em."

Emily unfolded her arms and dug for the truck keys in her

jeans pocket. "I can't be your partner," she said. She held up her index finger. "Your *only* partner, that is."

"What do you mean?"

"Aditson. We do this as a team, or I'm not on board."

Nick was cornered.

"Do I hear a yes?" she asked.

"Fine."

She saw a flash of familiar rebellion behind his eyes that told her Nick was going to play by his rules no matter what he agreed to. But at the moment, Emily would take what she could get.

"One thing," she said. "You'll have to get started with Aditson first without me. I have an appointment to keep."

CHAPTER 46

Hank Shepherd was building a small screened-in patio on the front of his lake house with the goal of being able to sit outdoors without getting eaten up by mosquitoes. He'd thought by late fall the bugs wouldn't be a problem, but they were; if not mosquitoes, there were flies or gnats. He was also sick of the little crawling creatures—probably mice by the size and shape of the droppings—that were always making a toilet of his patio furniture. And he might feel a bit safer watching nature from an enclosure, not fully exposed, especially after that bear-and-cubs sighting.

It was getting dark this late Friday afternoon when he nailed the last piece of the framework in place and stopped to take a drink break. It was cold and gray with a slight breeze. Not freezing temps yet but hovering somewhere near forty degrees. Hot green tea from his Yeti thermos warmed him from throat to chest to belly. He emptied half the thermos while contemplating his wooded lot. Not a day had gone by that he'd regretted coming up here.

He was screwing the lid of the thermos back on when a

crying sound echoed through the woods, coming soft and distant off the lake. Shepherd thought he was just hearing things, but when his dog, Milton, perked his ears and lifted his head at the sound, he knew he had not imagined it. He froze in place and strained to listen.

Ever since that girl's body had been found, something heavy and clandestine separated the two halves of Lake Isabella's Y, like a veil. And he had no desire to cross it.

He had not seen a human soul or heard a human sound from the other side of Lake Isabella. Neither had he been keen on trucking down there to check things out.

At Brown's Bakery in Freeport, which he frequented once a week to stock up on bread, he'd received a BOLO on his phone about a baby missing. Based on the timing, he guessed it was the daughter of the murdered girl. So tragic. And so unsettling to live so close to where the dark deed had taken place.

The small cry sounded across the lake again. He was glad to note that it wasn't a cry of distress, more one of discomfort. And he was sure this time that it was human. But a baby? Out here? He hadn't heard any vehicles in the area. It didn't make sense. He must have heard wrong.

But Milton's head was cocked toward the lake, and he was standing at full attention.

Shepherd's humanitarian side trounced his stay-out-of-it side. He put down his thermos, grabbed Milton's leash, and attached his leather collar. Shepherd was about to start for the lake when he thought he'd better grab his pistol. If he was going to cross the veil of darkness, he'd better have a means of defense.

CHAPTER 47

On the way to Ann Arbor Friday morning, Emily stopped at the Browdey home in Rock River to return Savannah's personal items. Flora was sound asleep in the passenger seat as Emily pulled into the driveway of a modest Cape Cod, probably built right after World War II, judging by the look and feel of the cookie-cutter homes lining this well-established neighborhood on the southwest side of Rock River. Parked in the driveway was a 2008 Honda Civic with rusted wheel wells and a sun-damaged paint job on the hood.

Emily supposed it was Peyton's car. And she was right. He answered the door.

"Dr. Emily Hartford," she reintroduced herself.

"Yeah, I remember."

"Is your dad here?"

"At work. Do you need him? 'Cause I can call him. Or give you the address to his job."

"No. It's okay. I was in the area, and I thought I'd save you all the trip up to Freeport to get your sister's things." Emily held out a paper bag.

"Oh." Peyton scrunched up his face and didn't reach for it. "Are you here to tell us you're releasing her body?"

"Not yet, I'm afraid." Emily searched his face. "How are you and your dad doing?"

"All right, I guess."

"It takes time," Emily said in an effort to comfort him.

"There's something . . . Do you have a minute?"

Emily glanced back at the front seat of the Yukon, where Flora was still sleeping. "Yeah, I have a minute."

Peyton held the door for her, then led her to the small family room.

"Make yourself at home. I gotta get something from my room." He disappeared through a door leading upstairs.

Emily took a couple of steps into the family room and scanned the tidy area. It was clean but dated looking, furnished with a brown sofa circa 1990 and two pleather recliner chairs. A baby's car seat was stashed on the side of the sofa. On a glass-top coffee table were magazines, a TV remote, a baby bottle half filled with juice, and a teething toy. Near the doorway to the kitchen was a playpen with toys and a blanket lying inside.

She heard Peyton's footsteps coming downstairs. When he appeared, she asked him, "Having a hard time removing her things, I see?"

"I know it's weird."

"It's actually not as weird as you might think."

"This is how it looked the last time Savannah left with her."

Emily searched Peyton's face, twisted in grief. "And you have to see this every day?"

He nodded. "When I tried to put the car seat in the basement, Dad came home and went crazy on me."

"Wow. That's a lot, isn't it?"

He didn't answer, instead saying, "Have you found Colton?"

"Not yet." Emily glanced up at him with a confident look. "We will."

"I didn't want to mention this in front of Dad, but about a month after Brooklyn was born, he came here hunting down Savannah."

Emily nodded. "What did Savannah do when Colton showed up?"

"We both freaked out. I told her to get up to her room and hide there with Brooklyn. Then I ran around the house, making sure every door and window was locked."

"What was Colton doing this whole time?"

"Banging on the front door. Shouting at us."

"You could hear him through the door?"

"Oh yeah."

"What was he saying?"

"He wanted to know if he was Brooklyn's dad. He thought that'd guarantee a guilty verdict at his rape trial."

"Did he have a gun?"

"We couldn't tell. Who knows what he had in his truck?"

"Did you call the police?"

"I did. But Chauncey disappeared before they got here."

"Did you make a report?"

"Yeah. But what could they do? He was gone. There was no proof he'd been there. It was our word against his."

"Were you . . . Are you . . . afraid of Chauncey?"

"I'm always watching my back." Peyton's voice trembled. "Especially now."

"You did the right thing. And don't be afraid to do it again." Emily nodded in empathy. "What was it you wanted to show me?"

Ivan held out two opened white envelopes. "These letters came a few days after Savannah didn't come back home. Whoever wrote them was pretending to be Savannah."

"Why do you say that?"

"Read them."

He handed them to her, and she slid a letter from one. Emily read a few lines to herself.

Dear Daddy,

I met a guy named Rodney that I never told you about and we're headed for Florida. He wanted to take me and Brooklyn on a vacation to Disney World. I knew you'd be mad and wouldn't want me to go. That's why I didn't tell you. Please don't be mad. He's a good guy. Brooklyn's doing great.

"These letters are a joke. There is no Rodney," Peyton said. "Savannah didn't write these. She doesn't talk like this. She never called our dad 'Daddy.' And she wouldn't just take off for Florida without preparing for it. She only had enough of Brooklyn's clothes and diapers in her bag for one night."

Emily searched his expression. "Why did you want to show these to me?"

"I just wonder, if Brooklyn is still alive, maybe Colton's got her in Florida. Like the letter says."

Emily scanned the postage stamps. One had been stamped from the Rock River post office on the Monday after Savannah was killed, the other on the Wednesday after. *Whoever sent these didn't think her body would turn up.*

"When did you get the second letter?" she asked.

"Thursday. Then on Friday, her body was discovered, and with all that going on, Dad and I kinda forgot about the l etters."

"So you never contacted Detective Aditson to report these?" Emily tried to keep the tone of her voice from blame, but she would never understand why people held anything that could assist an investigation back from the police.

"No. We weren't sure if it was just some cruel prankster. I think Dad would have burned them if I hadn't taken them and hidden them in my room."

Emily didn't want to touch them and contaminate them with her fingerprints. "Peyton, I want you to seal those for me. Do you have food storage bags in the house?"

"Why?"

"We need to preserve these in the event we can pull some DNA or prints off them. In the meantime, I'll alert Aditson. My guess is that he'll let law enforcement in Florida know."

Emily followed Peyton into the kitchen, where he pulled a clear gallon storage bag from a drawer and slid the stack of envelopes inside.

"Do you have anything else written in Savannah's handwriting? A sticky note, some old school paper, a list?"

"I think there's a couple old school notebooks in her bedroom."

"Can you check? We can use them for a handwriting comparison."

Peyton scurried back upstairs. Emily gave the room a second scan, her eye catching a framed photograph on the shelf of a corner bookcase. It was the classic shot of a mother meeting her baby for the first time in the hospital. Savannah looked very young, dressed in the hospital gown, with no makeup and loose hair. She was ruddy faced and beaming at this new creature, so swaddled that the only visible part of Brooklyn was a perfect, tiny hand reaching out to her mommy's face. A tidal wave of maternal emotions overtook Emily so strongly that she jumped when Peyton said, "Here you go."

He stood behind her, holding out one of Savannah's composition notebooks.

"Plastic bag?" Emily said, refocusing.

"Right."

"Thanks for sharing these, Peyton. You just never know how something like this could be helpful in an investigation." She made her way to the front door to wait for him. She glanced out the window and saw Flora waking up with a confused look.

Emily opened the front door, waved at Flora, and called, "I'll be right out."

Flora fluttered a wave back to acknowledge.

"Your daughter?"

Emily turned to see Peyton looking over her shoulder.

"My niece. But I love her like a daughter."

"I was a good uncle." He said it as if he needed to convince someone.

Hopefully you still will be, Emily wanted to assure him. But his chilling account of Chauncey terrorizing them churned her unsettled fears.

"You take care and be safe, Peyton," she warned him. "Lock doors and windows at all times."

CHAPTER 48

When they were back on the highway heading to Ann Arbor, fresh coffees in hand, Emily told her niece, "You know, there was a time I toyed around with the idea of a career in forensic anthropology."

"Why didn't you pursue it?" asked Flora, sipping on her caramel-mocha, extra-shot latte.

"I realized I liked dealing with fresh bodies more than dry old bones." That was only part of the truth. The other part was that Emily had a run-in with the head of the department, who'd only wanted to use her and her skills for his own professional gain. The same old academic crap. After he'd tried to steal her research, she no longer trusted him.

Speaking of men and trust, it was time to have that talk with Flora.

"I wanna have an aunt-to-niece chat," Emily said with a glance to her niece in the passenger seat, who was giving her a wary look. "Have you given Noah your answer yet about the dance?"

"He called last night. I told him yes."

"Congrats on your first date acceptance."

"It's not a date. We're hanging with a group of us."

"I like that," said Emily. "There can be a lot to deal with in girl world. And it can come at you pretty fast."

Flora's face twisted. "Just spit it out, Aunt Em . . . Date rape."

"Yes. I'm just saying, it often happens with someone you already know and trust. How much has your mother talked to you about personal self-defense?"

"I mean, like, I have pepper spray."

"That's a good start. Let's talk about a few steps before you'd ever have to use that."

"You mean, like, use a buddy system. No means no. Pick a line you won't cross before you get into it with a guy."

"Yes. To all those things." Emily was grateful Flora was open to the discussion and already had so many good plans in mind. "And always be aware of your surroundings. No walking in public with your nose glued to your phone. Seek to lower your risk level."

"Got it."

"Has your mom talked to you about what to do if you find yourself in a really scary situation?"

"She's told me to trust my intuition and get out of there."

"Also great advice." *Bravo, sis.*

"Mom sends me stuff all the time," said Flora.

"Like what stuff?"

"Articles and videos and stuff."

"About what exactly?" Emily wanted to make sure this convo didn't go too far off the rails.

"Like how to get out of zip ties and duct tape if someone kidnaps you. And how to escape a sinking car in a lake."

Oh boy. Being a YouTube voyeur was one thing. Being in the situation and keeping a level head was a whole different ball of wax.

"I'm sure those are very informative. And let's hope you never need to use that information."

"I know to never get into a car alone with a guy. Never walk alone at night. That kind of thing."

"All good. But even if we do those things and are super careful, sometimes things happen. I'm not trying to scare you, but do you understand what I'm saying?"

Flora shook her head.

"You know Savannah Browdey, the case that—"

"Of course," Flora said solemnly. "From the morgue. I will never forget her."

"Savannah was the victim of another crime even before she was murdered."

"I heard she was raped by that old guy," said Flora.

"Yes. But how . . . where did you hear that?"

"Her cousin Laney's little sister, Celia, is a senior at Freeport. It's all over school."

Of course it is. Freeport.

"Savannah waited to tell the police," said Emily. "I understand why it was hard for her. It's horrible what she went through. The thing is, it's not unusual for women who were assaulted to *not* go to the police. Unfortunately, that's when important evidence can get lost. And then—"

"The guy gets away with it," said Flora.

"Exactly." Emily nodded. "If anything like this ever happens to you, even with a young guy, even with a guy you know and like, but he just took it too far, even after you said no, please, Flora, come to me or your mom. Promise me?"

"I promise."

"And most importantly, remember it's not ever, ever your fault."

"I got it."

"And we're with you, every step of the way. Always."

"Good talk, Auntie."

Emily grinned at her niece. The loss of innocence tugged at her heart. It was a hard thing for women to come to terms with the idea that they were prey and that sometimes they had to fight back. Emily wanted Flora to know that she had an army behind her in case she ever needed to go into battle.

They arrived at the University of Michigan just after 11:00 a.m. Emily took Flora on a brief tour, zigzagging the U of M's main campus, stopping briefly at a coffee stand to grab two more cups of caffeine. Flora's was diluted with pumps of caramel syrup and steamed milk, while Emily took a double shot of espresso.

Just before noon, Emily was knocking on Professor Eckhardt's door.

The woman recognized Emily right away and ushered them inside.

"This is my niece Flora, and she recently made a discovery," Emily told Dr. Samantha Eckhardt.

"Nice to meet you," said Flora. Instead of holding out her hand, she nervously extended the bone in the bag.

Dr. Eckhardt laughed. "Too bad that guy doesn't have a hand attached."

"Sorry."

"Don't be. I like your sense of humor."

"I wasn't trying to be funny."

"You should be. Gallows humor is always welcome around here."

Emily smiled at her niece to ease her nerves.

"Tell me what you have here," asked Dr. Eckhardt.

"Aunt Emily thinks it's a radius bone," said Flora, her voice gaining in confidence. "I found it in the woods when I was hiking with friends. I think it looks like a human arm bone."

Dr. Eckhardt took the bone from the bag and turned it over. "I think you're right. It's definitely human. But what's this smooth edge?"

"We don't think it's a natural break," said Flora.

"Troubling," said Dr. Eckhardt. "But my job isn't to figure out what caused that. I'm just here to confirm it's of human origin."

"We're working on it." Flora beamed. "We searched the area where I found it, and we found an old wooden handle."

"I'm going to have a tool specialist analyze it," Emily explained.

"That's interesting," said Dr. Eckhardt. "And we'll get a lot of information from this little guy too."

"Really?" asked Flora.

"First, we'll run a DNA test on it so we have our original source. But of course, we'll need something to compare it to in order to make a match. We will have to use our genetic mapping system to try and find out who it belongs to."

"Sounds so easy," said Emily.

"In theory, it is. But we never know if a match will show up."

"Do you use places like 23andMe?" asked Emily.

"Exactly. Along with AncestryDNA, MyHeritage, GEDmatch, FamilyTreeDNA, and DNA Painter."

"That's intense," said Emily.

"We turn over every rock we can. Of course, not everyone in the world is in a DNA database."

"How do you find the right match?" asked Flora.

"We extract the DNA, then perform genome sequencing and bioinformatics."

"What's that?"

"It's something you'll learn more about if you join us next week."

"For what?"

"I'd like to make you an offer, Flora," said Dr. Eckhardt. "I'm hosting a two-day forensic camp for high schoolers who want to explore forensic investigation. We'll be working closely with local law enforcement agencies on some of their oldest cold cases to try to find DNA matches through genetic genealogy. Would you be interested in participating?"

"I'd love that!" Flora burst out.

"After she asks her mother, of course," Emily added.

"Right. Yeah, I have to see." Flora grinned. "But I'm sure she'll say yes. Right, Aunt Em?"

"Can't speak for my sister, but I'd say the odds are in your favor."

"I'll hold a spot for you," said Dr. Eckhardt. "Just get back to me in the next couple of days, okay?"

"I will. Thank you." Flora rushed at Dr. Eckhardt and embraced her.

"Oh! My." She nearly knocked the wind out of the woman.

"Flora, relax. She needs to breathe." Emily tapped her on the arm. "We're a family of huggers."

"I like it." Dr. Eckhardt embraced her back. "Not much hugging goes on in the forensics department."

Flora unwrapped herself. "Sorry, I'm just really excited."

Emily turned to Dr. Eckhardt. "She wasn't even this excited when I took her to the morgue."

"And I haven't even told you the best part," Dr. Eckhardt said to Flora. "Each student gets assigned a case study to work on."

"That's cool."

"Not as cool as when the case has already chosen you." Dr. Eckhardt held up the bone.

"You want me to work on that?"

"You found it. Let it come full circle. Wouldn't that be amazing if you could find out who this bone belongs to?"

"It would," said Flora, turning to her aunt. "My very first case! At age fourteen."

"It's unheard of, isn't it, Dr. Hartford?" said Dr. Eckhardt.

Emily smiled. *Sure.* Someday she'd tell Flora about her first case at age eight. The airplane crash she'd worked on with her dad. As they'd collected various body parts scattered across the airfield, her dad explained how the body systems worked together. "Every single human being is a miraculous thing. Fearfully and wonderfully made," he'd told Emily. "There are no mistakes when it comes to human life." Yet Emily mused now, as she had then: *Why do people treat each other so badly if we are all miracles?*

CHAPTER 49

Twenty-three-year-old Georgia slammed on her brakes and screamed as a giant dog bounded across the road in front of her car.

Her best friend, Freeda, sitting in the passenger seat, swore in a high-pitched voice. "What was that?"

"A small horse." Georgia was teasing, but the animal was huge.

"Poor guy. It looks like he's lost," said Freeda, turning back to look at the large dog prancing down the embankment on the other side of the road.

"Poor guy? I'm shaking!" Georgia extended her hand for her friend to see.

"Stop the car," said Freeda.

Georgia pulled her car onto the shoulder of the two-lane county highway. Middle-of-the-afternoon traffic was light. They both got a better look at the unfazed dog, who was now trotting down the ditch.

"He's clearly well taken care of, and he's got a collar." Freeda was a volunteer at the Freeport animal rescue.

"Is that . . . Is he dragging a leash?"

"Let's see if we can get him in the car," said Freeda, giving Georgia no choice in the matter.

"I just vacuumed, and he's ginormous."

"This guy needs us," Freeda said, jumping out.

Georgia got out to help her friend.

"Hey, buddy," Freeda called in a friendly voice as she slowly made her way toward the large canine. "I'm not gonna hurt you. I just wanna talk."

The dog stopped and looked at the girl.

She kept approaching while talking sweetly to him. Eventually he trotted toward her. She held out her hand for him to sniff. He gave it a lick, giving Freeda permission to pet him. Freeda rubbed the back of his ears, making her way to his neck so she could read the tag on his collar.

"His name's Milton," she told Georgia, who had stayed back by her vehicle.

"Is there a phone number on it?"

"Yeah, dial this number."

Freeda called out the digits, and Georgia punched them into her cell phone.

The line rang a few times, then went to voicemail.

"Should I leave a message?" she asked Freeda.

"No. Let's get him out of here." She was now holding Milton by the leash as she stroked his back. Milton was loving it. "We can try the owner again once we get him to the rescue."

CHAPTER 50

"So . . . how was your trip to meet Dr. Eckhardt?" Anna asked Emily when she returned to the Hartford home late that afternoon. Flora joined them in the living room. Anna was dressed in comfy clothes and tucked under a blanket with her iPad. Emily took a glance at the screen and saw it was displaying a design catalog.

"Working on a new project?" Emily asked, kicking her shoes off and sinking into the sofa.

"Window-shopping for a new client." Anna had worked as an interior designer since her college days. First for high-end furniture stores, then with an interior design firm; after the divorce, she'd branched out on her own, taking on clients as they fit into her parenting schedule.

"I love U of M, Mom," said Flora, squeezing in between them. "And I've been invited to a camp!" she exclaimed.

"You hate camp. Two days into summer camp, and they called me to take you back home."

"It's not that kind of camp."

Emily chimed in, "It's a two-day mini forensic-investigation workshop for high schoolers sponsored by U of M. Each student gets to work on a project using genetic genealogy techniques to try and solve it."

"Can I go, Mom? Please?"

Anna turned to Emily for sisterly guidance. "I thought you were just going there to get a bone checked out."

"We did. It's human, and now I'm going to find out who it belongs to," Flora blurted out.

"How, exactly?"

"At the camp. It's going to be my project."

"When is this camp?"

That was the kicker. "It's next Tuesday and Wednesday," Emily said.

"You have school," said Anna.

"Please, Mom. It's a great opportunity."

"Dr. Eckhardt invited her personally," Emily looked to Anna to reassure her.

"I'll get all my assignments from my teachers so I don't miss anything."

"I know you've got your hands full with Fiona and now this new client," said Emily. "I can take her down."

"Can you afford to take off work?"

"I consider it an extension of my job," said Emily. "I'd like to learn more about genetic genealogy. It's fast becoming an emerging practice in the field of forensics now that we can tap into public DNA databases."

"I can't argue with you two." Anna sighed.

"Thanks, Mom." Flora gave Anna a quick hug.

"Go unpack, then check your emails. I saw a bunch of them come in from your teachers."

"Homework on the weekend?" Flora groaned.

She was on her way out of the room when her mother told her, "Hey, a boy called for you."

Flora darted back in. "Noah?"

"Yes. He asked when you'd be home," Anna told her.

"What did you tell him?"

"To call back tonight. But not after ten."

"I'm a little confused," Emily interrupted. "I thought it was all texting these days. Since when do kids call each other?"

"When their parents make them." Anna grinned. "I've already talked to Noah's mom at school."

"You did?" Flora said with horror.

"Remember what I said about an army?" Emily said to her with a wink.

"What's that?" Anna challenged.

"Nothing," said Flora. "It's between me and Aunt Em." She took off for her room.

Anna groaned. "I thought thirteen was a challenge. Now I have to worry about young men prowling around."

"It could be so much worse," said Emily. "Flora could be hiding it from you."

"I did that with my first boyfriend, Cody," said Anna. "We managed to keep our secret for a whole three months."

Emily grinned. "How did your mom find out?"

"Caught us at the movie theater."

"What'd she do?"

"Nothing right then, thank goodness. But when I got home, I was grounded for a month. Then she insisted that she meet Cody's parents. He didn't want any part of it and broke up with me two days later."

"What a jerk."

"He was," said Anna. "I'm not sure I picked them much better after that."

"Don't be so hard on yourself."

"Look at my track record." Anna and her ex-husband, Kyle,

had divorced after she refused to put up with his affairs. She and the girls had jumped at the chance for a fresh start when Emily suggested they move to Freeport.

"Now you have me to vet your men," said Emily. "We'll find you a good one."

"I'm pretty comfortable where I'm at in the moment." Anna smiled as she curled the blanket up to her chin. "The only thing that would be better is a pint of mint-chip ice cream."

Emily rose to head to the kitchen. "I'll get two spoons."

As she opened the silverware drawer and took out the spoons, Emily's phone rang: Aditson. She tapped accept and greeted him.

Aditson's strained voice struck a chord of concern. "How soon can you get to Lake Isabella?"

"Again?"

"Bring your kit and a bag."

"Water or land death?"

"Chauncey's fishing shack."

"It's not—"

"It's not Brooklyn."

"I'm on my way," said Emily as she set one spoon back into the drawer. At least Anna could enjoy the ice cream.

CHAPTER 51

"Are we sure this shack is on federal land?" Emily asked Aditson and Nick. As she approached them outside Emmett Johnson's old fishing shack, she noticed that both men's heads were buried in their phones, and they were not talking to one another. Aditson looked up first.

"Double-checked the property lines with the county clerk's office," he said. "The shack is on federal land. But the dirt road to get to it is county property."

Nick tucked his phone in his pocket, barely glancing her way. "We should get going before we lose daylight hours."

The trio went into action, each taking a piece of the investigation.

"Have you identified the body?" Emily asked.

"It's Hank Shepherd," said Aditson.

Emily was grieved at the news; then her gut twisted. His dog. "Where's Milton? Is he in there too?"

"No. He's safe and healthy at the animal rescue. But he's the reason we found Hank."

"How's that?"

"A couple of young ladies almost hit him on the highway. They brought the dog to the rescue, and when they couldn't reach Hank, a couple of the other volunteers looked up his address and decided to deliver Milton home. They got worried because when they arrived at Hank's cottage, it was wide open, his car was there, but he was nowhere around. They were trying to decide if they should call the police when Milton started acting funny. He led them to the shack."

"Unbelievable. What a good dog," said Emily, wondering what might become of the pet now that he'd lost his owner.

"We're gonna lose the light soon, folks," Nick said.

They began their investigation with the exterior of the dilapidated building and a set of tire tracks that led up to it. Aditson offered to collect a mold of the tracks while Nick photographed them. Emily watched Nick, thinking he looked pale.

"How was lunch with your mom the other day?" she asked.

"Cold. She left before I got home."

"She didn't seem too worried about you leaving the hospital."

"She knows I can take care of myself."

"How are you feeling?"

"Fine."

"You taking your meds?"

"You're worse than my mom."

"Maybe because I'm more worried than she is," Emily said.

"You shouldn't be."

"Okay. These are done. Just need to wait about thirty minutes for them to set," said Aditson.

He stood to admire his work, and a light breeze fluttered a nearby cluster of leaves. They blew over the freshly poured plaster.

"Oh crap." He dove to retrieve them. Emily pitched in.

"What's this?" Nick was pinching a piece of paper off the ground from where the blown leaves had been.

Emily looked over his shoulder to see a pay stub from a Social Security check. She could make out a name and address on the weatherworn sheet: Terrell Nalene of Rock River.

"Wonder what that's doing up here?" said Emily.

Nick slid it into a clear plastic evidence bag. "Maybe this guy comes here to fish. It is public property. I'll look into it. Maybe he was up here and noticed something."

Emily went inside the shack first, as medical examiner and the only professional in this situation who was legally permitted to examine Shepherd's body. The two men stayed back while watching her every move to make sure she didn't disturb anything they thought was part of the crime investigation. Which, it turned out, was almost everything. And almost impossible not to tamper with, given the space limitations and the fact that whatever had gone down here before Shepherd's murder was nothing short of a fight for his life.

The rickety shack had been torn apart, with items scattered every which way.

"I see at least two gunshot wounds to the chest. Small caliber. But he must have fought hard before he was shot," said Emily.

"Against whom? And why?" said Nick.

"There's a gun on your right, three o'clock," said Aditson. "I can see the tip of the barrel sticking out from under that old tackle box."

"Noted," said Emily. "Can I take a look?"

"Go for it," said Aditson. "Just don't get your prints on it."

Emily lifted the box so they could see the small pistol.

"I wonder if Shepherd was shot with his own gun." Aditson leaned into the shack to get a better look.

"Is that a twenty-two?" asked Emily. She would need to look for bullet casings inside the body when doing the postmortem.

"Yes," confirmed Aditson and Nick at the same time.

"Not a powerful bullet," commented Nick, "but, at close range, effective when it hits vital targets."

"Like the heart and lungs." Emily sighed. She had gotten the feeling when they'd met Shepherd that he was a decent man simply wanting to live out his golden years in peace.

When Emily was done registering livor and algor temp, she stepped out of the matchbox-size cabin. "There's not much more I can do with him until I get him on the table. Your turn, guys."

Both men stepped up at the same time, blocking each other in the doorway.

"Do I need to flip a coin?" Emily teased.

"Federal first." Aditson graciously deferred to Nick, who Emily noticed already had his boot across the threshold.

She stepped back to give them both breathing room. They needed it. But she stayed close enough to observe. Aditson held his ground at the doorway. Nick took two careful steps inside the ten-by-ten-foot box. He scanned the premises, his mind working like a tracking device. He snapped photographs of the room to document how the crime scene looked as they found it.

"We can get through this faster if we divide and conquer," Emily offered.

"What do you have in mind?" Aditson asked.

"Nick, you search and photograph. Aditson, you collect. I'll record."

"I'm good with that. Nick?" Aditson asked.

"Fine." He didn't even look back.

In small, calculated movements, the team began collecting, removing, and documenting items of interest. They moved left to right across the room. When they reached a flimsy twin-size cot that had been overturned, they made a discovery that chilled them.

Nick had flipped the cot on its right side and found a baby's diaper bag underneath.

"It has to be Brooklyn's," Emily announced, feeling both excitement and dread.

"I suspect Shepherd wouldn't have ventured down here unless he suspected a baby was on the premises," posited Aditson.

"And possibly in trouble," added Emily. "I wonder why he didn't call the police, knowing what he knew about the crime here." She didn't mean to heap blame on the deceased man. She was just frustrated. One call might have given them a triple win. Shepherd would be alive, Brooklyn saved, and Colton Chauncey arrested.

She glanced at the baby bag and pink onesie they'd placed in a clear plastic evidence bag. Aditson put a gentle hand on her shoulder. Emily nodded, thankful for his reassuring touch at this moment.

"I know you're reeling. Try not to go there."

"Em, the more time goes on, the less hope there is for her survival," Nick said.

But she refused to give up on Brooklyn. "We still need to try."

Nick sighed, his glance grazing the baby bag. "None of the others made it."

Emily stopped what she was doing. "None of whom made what?"

Nick's gaze bounced up and locked on his phone screen.

"Nick?" she said louder. "What do you mean, none of the others made it?"

"Huh? I don't know."

"You just said none of the others made it. Who are the others?"

A confused look flashed over Nick. "I said that?"

"You did. I heard it. Aditson heard it."

"Brain drift, I guess." Nick looked at Emily.

"You feeling okay?"

"I'm fine. And I wish you'd stop asking."

"Okay. Then let's remove the body," she said, changing the subject—for now. "I'd like to get started on Shepherd's postmortem."

"I'm good in here," said Nick. "Aditson?"

"Let's wrap it up."

"Will either of you be joining me?" Emily asked, readying to leave.

One man looked to the other. Neither was going to be the one left behind.

CHAPTER 52

That jackhole, nosy neighbor had come over and cocked everything up. All Colton had wanted to do was leave the sleeping baby in the shack for a few hours while he went to Rock River to get Terrell's Social Security check. From there, the plan was simple. Easy. Come back, retrieve the baby, then drive up four hours to WaliYona's in the UP. Once on the rez, he could lie low for a few days, maybe a week, in case he was being hunted by the cops. After he felt it was safe, he could take a couple of hours' drive over the border to the remote Saint Joseph Island. He'd be home free to find a buyer for the baby, and then he could do as he pleased. With all that money, maybe he'd roll up the Saint Lawrence Seaway to the Atlantic and catch a ship down to the Caribbean. The fishing was good down there, he'd heard.

His head and arm throbbed. He had a goose egg on his temple, and he was pretty sure his wrist was fractured from wrestling the gun from that wiry city dweller with the Great Dane. He had fought hard. Harder than Colton had thought the retiree was capable of. Colton had not been prepared to take such a beating. Then he found out the guy's gun hadn't even been loaded. Not a single bullet in the chamber. And now this idiot was the reason his ribs were so sore he couldn't take a full breath.

Never mind the pain. He had to come up with his next steps. It was evident in light of what had just happened that he couldn't take the chance of anyone else finding her. Nor could he risk the baby getting hurt or maimed. A healthy baby fetched a better price. He would need to stash the kid with someone reliable but pliable. Maybe even expendable.

Think. Think. Think. Think. Think.

Eventually, someone came to mind. He'd let the dust settle and stalk her for a few days. But he didn't think she'd cause too much trouble. Not once she saw the infant.

CHAPTER 53

Aditson was at Emily's side, gowned and holding a clipboard to take handwritten notes for her, a job he had performed many times when they'd worked cases together. Nick was across the room, searching the drawers for a gown and goggles. During the years Nick had been a local sheriff, he, too, had filled this assistant role, but beside Emily's father, Dr. Robert Hartford, the practicing medical examiner. Dr. Hartford taught Nick many things that had made him a better detective.

Now, on such a fraught and sensitive case, Emily was grateful that all hands were on deck. This meetup in the morgue was also an opportunity for the three of them to regroup and plot next steps.

Emily broke the ice. "Aditson, how was the follow-up with André's family?"

"Oh my goodness. I must have talked to forty-five relatives: parents, aunts, uncles, and lots of cousins. All said they didn't know where Brooklyn was. His alibi held up. I even had Rock River send a patrol to follow André for forty-eight hours.

Home. Work. School. Home. Rinse and repeat. The guy was never alone."

"Probably too scared to be," said Emily.

Nick pointed to a cooler with a lock on it. "Is Savannah still in there?"

"Of course," said Emily. "I'm waiting for your approval to release her body to the family."

"Let's hold on to her for a bit," Nick said.

"Reason being?" she asked.

"Three bodies and possibly a dead infant in less than a week. Tell me it hasn't slipped your attention that we have a serial killer in our midst."

"The autopsy report and death certificate are filed. There's no more evidence I could take from her body. Meanwhile, her family's in limbo, suffering."

"We should push the pause button in case there's something else we overlooked."

Emily took offense. "Are you saying I didn't do my job well enough?"

"No. I just don't see the harm in waiting."

She shrugged. "Your call. But if the Browdeys ask, I'm sending them to you."

Nick cast a glance at Aditson. "Do you have any qualms if I send the evidence we collected from the shack to the FBI lab?"

"Be my guest," said Aditson. "Saves on the county budget."

Nick stepped up, gowned and gloved, and Emily gave him a handheld recorder. She had learned to use this backup note-taking system, especially when dealing with cases that were sensitive, violent, or likely to end up in court. "Point this at me, please." She began dictating. "Two gunshot wounds to the chest, one at the heart, one near the lungs. Strangulation marks on the neck. Slight bruising by the hyoid bone." She palpated the area with her index finger. "I can feel it's been broken."

"So Chauncey tried to strangle this guy first?" Nick asked.

"The bruising would indicate that. But I'd like to take a close look at the lung tissue before I make that ruling." Emily took her time, noting the condition of Hank Shepherd's extremities. Arms. Legs. She glanced over to where Nick had sat on a stool near the countertop, looking ashen. When Emily made the first incision of her autopsy, Nick rose from the stool and began pacing, recorder in hand. She noticed beads of sweat on his temples. He had been a witness to hundreds of autopsies with her dad. This shouldn't be affecting him.

"You feeling warm?" she asked.

"A little." He let the recorder drop to his side.

"Nick, can you please point that recorder toward my mouth?"

He picked it up and came closer, extending his arm toward her but keeping his face turned away from the dead body.

"There are hairline fractures on several ribs," she said, "which would indicate that Mr. Shepherd was also struck in the chest."

"Brutal," Aditson said under his breath, shaking his head.

Emily announced her next step: "I'm now going to cut through the rib cage to expose the lungs." She engaged the electric bone saw. The soft, whirring sound of the motor echoed through the sterile, sealed room. From the corner of her eye, she saw Nick panting, thwacking the side of his hand against his thigh.

"You okay?" Her voice rose over the sound of the saw.

"I'm good. All good." But he didn't look good. The color had drained from his already gaunt face, and his breathing had picked up. Sweat ran down his forehead.

"Give the recorder to Aditson and step outside. Get some fresh air," Emily coaxed as she worked her way around the murdered man's lungs, detaching the tissue and gingerly placing the organ on a scale mounted to a metal tray with wheels. She'd want to make a slide of the tissue and take a look under a microscope.

Nick froze in place, his focus trained on the organ she was weighing. The voice recorder went skidding across the floor as he dropped and gripped the sides of his torso.

Emily recognized the signs. He was about to vomit.

"Detective?" she asked. "Can you—?"

Aditson flung the clipboard onto the countertop and rushed Nick out of the morgue.

CHAPTER 54

Nick lost the contents of his stomach on the hospital hallway floor. It was mostly stomach fluid.

"When did you last eat?" asked Aditson.

Nick dry heaved two more times, then stepped away from his puke puddle.

"That was embarrassing," said Nick as Aditson handed him a wad of paper towels he had retrieved from a nearby bathroom. "It's probably just the antibiotics upsetting my stomach."

"Did you take them with food?"

Nick didn't answer.

"I should get back in there, give Emily a hand. Take your time out here. I'll call housekeeping to clean this up."

Nick rested his back against the wall. "I think I'll sit this one out."

Aditson had his hand on the morgue door when he turned back to Nick.

"From the first moment you got back to Freeport, I've seen that demon circling you," said Aditson. "How long are you going to ignore it?"

"There's no demon. I just need a little food. Like you said." Nick focused on the tension curling around his muscles.

"None of this is going away until you're willing to accept that what happened to you was not your fault."

"You don't know that."

"Why are you shouldering burdens that aren't yours?"

"This is none of your business. And I don't appreciate Emily talking to you about me."

"Emily has told me nothing. I can see it for myself."

"Can't you see how pointless and irresponsible it is for us to be sitting around here when a serial killer is at large?" asked Nick, almost shouting.

"Let's talk about our next move then."

"I've got my next move. And I don't want you or her getting in my way. Got it?"

"We're supposed to be a team."

"How many more people have to die before we stop this animal?" Nick angled toward the exit sign that led to the hospital's parking lot. "This part of the hunt I do on my own."

"What's your plan, Nick?" Aditson asked sternly, blocking his path to the door. "I have your back on this."

Nick scowled at Aditson. He couldn't trust him. He couldn't trust anyone anymore. His partner had abandoned him the morning he had been kidnapped. The FBI had given up on him. How did he know that Aditson wasn't just looking for an opportunity to report him to Roe? Even Emily wanted him back at home, quarantined and resting.

Nick was on his own. And he would be better than fine. He would come out on top when he found and captured Colton.

"Excuse me," said Nick, sidestepping Aditson. He marched toward the exit, ignoring Aditson's calls to come back.

CHAPTER 55

Aditson was quiet when he returned to the morgue, and Emily decided not to ask him anything right away. He went to the work counter and began removing Brooklyn's items from the baby bag: diapers, baby bottles, a package of wipes, three pacifier rings, and an extra set of clothing. He laid them out and began to photograph, collect, and record each thing.

"Well?" Emily said, unable to keep quiet any longer. "How's Nick?"

"He took off. It seems he doesn't think we're determined enough about finding Chauncey."

"He has hero syndrome."

"He's worried about the body count."

"So am I."

"He's off to hunt Chauncey on his own."

"What? Where?"

"Wish I knew."

"Why didn't you go with him?" she asked.

"That wasn't going to happen," Aditson said. "Technically,

this investigation is out of my jurisdiction. Second, he's out of my sphere of control."

Emily sat with it, dictating the last of her notes on the post-mortem. She then draped Hank Shepherd's body with a thick white sheet and rolled his gurney into one of three refrigerated drawers. Aditson was documenting the last of Shepherd's belongings. When he finished, he handed Emily the clipboard.

"Skylar's going to find and notify Hank's next of kin," Aditson told her. Emily thought again about Milton.

"What about the dog? Who's he going to end up with?"

Aditson shrugged. "He's at the dog rescue last I knew."

"Skylar should let his next of kin know about Milton."

Aditson was checking his phone and didn't hear her.

"What do you think we should do about Nick?" she said. "Should I call Agent Roe?"

"Tattle on him? What good's that gonna do any of us? Or this case?"

"I want you to be honest with me. Do you think he's stable enough to be back on the job?"

Aditson glanced away. Emily had her answer.

"Doc, I think we need to finish up here," he said. "Then you and I can regroup and figure out next steps."

Emily didn't like his answer, but she had to accept it. For now. She dug through the baby bag's compartments. She thought Aditson had emptied it thoroughly until she slipped her hand into the outside pocket and discovered that the plastic-coated lining had peeled away from the exterior shell of the bag, exposing filler inside. She felt something stiff and crinkly.

"What's this?"

Aditson looked over as she reached in and pulled out a mailed envelope. It was addressed to Savannah Browdey from a company called BetGen in Lansing, Michigan.

"Do you know what BetGen is?" Emily asked, taking out the single-sheet letter inside.

"Haven't got a clue."

"It's addressed to Savannah at her house in Rock River." Emily's heart raced as she scanned the page. "I think we just hit the jackpot." She looked up and saw Aditson was staring at her, awaiting her next words. "It's a paternity test. Postmarked five weeks ago."

"What does it say?"

Emily scanned the letter. "Dear Ms. Browdey. Enclosed please find the log-in and passcode to your results." She pulled out her phone and did a search for the company. "BetGen stands for Better Genetics. It's a genetic-testing company." She glanced up from her phone. Savannah had gotten a paternity test after all. Did she share the results? Had she told Chauncey?

"Let's see who the father is," said Aditson.

Emily scanned the QR code printed on the lower third of the paper. The company website popped up. "Read me the passcode."

Aditson read the convoluted string of numbers and letters. Emily typed them in carefully.

An "invalid passcode" message came up on-screen. "Try it again."

She retyped. Another "invalid" message popped up.

"What am I doing wrong?" Emily said, frustrated.

"Could be the code expired."

"Is that a one or a lowercase *l*?" She pointed to the character in question.

Aditson squinted. "It looked like a one to me."

"Okay, I'm going to type in an *l* and see if that works."

Aditson looked over her shoulder, double-checking. This version of the passcode was accepted, but a secondary authentication code was sent to Savannah's phone, which they hadn't been able to locate.

Emily sighed and set the paper on the bench to photograph it. She flipped it over to record the back side and saw a name scribbled in the bottom left corner.

"Aditson. Look. Who's that?" she said as Aditson leaned over to read the name.

Bradley Leland.

"Her dad and brother never mentioned anyone by that name," Emily said. "Could this Bradley guy be the father? Why else would she have written down his full name?"

"No idea, but Bradley Leland was subpoenaed by the defense to appear at the trial," Aditson said.

"Maybe they intended to use Bradley's paternity to support Chauncey's exoneration from Savannah's rape."

"Let's find Leland." Aditson grabbed his phone. "I'll get Skylar on it." He called his assistant.

Emily took a deep breath, trying to shuck off the despondent fog that had settled over her. Something didn't feel right. Something beyond the Chauncey case. It had to do with Nick's panic attack and sudden departure. She felt wrong *not* calling Agent Roe. Nick was putting himself at risk.

She felt a sudden urgency. "Certainly Chauncey knew Bradley Leland was on the witness list, and likely he wanted him out of the picture. He might still act on that. Chauncey's rape trial isn't going to be thrown out just because Savannah is dead," she said. "We should notify Nick."

"I say we move forward and first try to locate this guy. We'll reach out to Nick after we have something useful."

He had a point. Nick had ditched them, not the other way around. He certainly wasn't keeping them informed on his case developments.

Aditson's phone rang, and he took a quick call, then said, "Skylar found Bradley Leland. He and Savannah went to high school together."

"That was fast."

"Gen Z. Gotta love 'em. Skylar downloaded Savannah's socials days ago. Bradley Leland popped up in several of her posts."

"That generation may never value their privacy, which sure comes in handy during times like these," Emily said. "If they were high school friends, he must be living in Rock River."

"Actually, north. Traverse City."

"Really? Why there, I wonder. It's off the beaten path."

"Skylar said he's hiding out," said Aditson. "Disguised as a raccoon character named Oliver."

CHAPTER 56

Saturday morning, Nick drove to Rock River. The Social Security number belonging to Terrell Nalene listed his address in a dodgy area near the Rock River, the city's namesake because it snaked through downtown. His neighborhood was rife with the homeless, drug addicted, and indigent.

The elevator to his apartment building was broken, so Nick climbed the interior set of cement steps that spiraled up to the fifth floor, apartment 504B.

When he reached the top, he was gasping for breath and paused outside 504B. He checked his phone and saw a text from Roe.

Status report.

With shaky hands, Nick texted back.

Recon on person: Terrell Nalene.

Report requested.

That would get Roe off his back for a few days.

Once he got his breathing regulated, Nick gave several knocks on Terrell's door. No one answered, but it drew out a man from the apartment across the hall.

"He's not in," the man barked.

Nick spun to face him. His wrinkle-free face made it hard to tell how old he was, but rough, cracked hands told the story of decades of hard work.

"Do you know Terrell Nalene?" Nick asked him.

"Who's asking?"

"I'm Nick Larsen. Know where I can find him?"

"Nick Larsen? Who *are* you?"

"Someone who thinks Mr. Nalene's been the target of Social Security fraud."

"You a fed then?"

"I want to see he gets his money."

"He's not here."

"Know where I can find him?"

"Haven't seen Terrell in over a year." The man shut the door, and Nick heard the lock latch.

He knocked on the man's door. There was stirring inside, and then the volume of the television went up. It was futile. Nick looked down the hall. Maybe another resident on this floor could give him a morsel. He began knocking on doors and was partway down the hallway when he heard Terrell Nalene's apartment door open.

Nick spun around to see a teenage kid slinking his way out.

"Hey."

The kid sprinted for the fire escape.

"Wait!"

Nick ran after him, catching him by the tail of his coat on the first landing.

The kid wriggled to get free. "Get off me!"

"You're not in trouble," Nick assured him. "And I'm not going to hurt you."

"What do you want?"

"What's your name?"

"Jasper616."

"That's a funny name. What were you doing in that apartment?"

"I live there."

"Then why were you running from me?"

"I'm gonna be late for school."

Nick laughed. It was nearly noon. "That ship has sailed, buddy."

"You gonna hit me?"

"Why would I do that?"

"You're a cop, aren't you?"

Nick shook his head and let go of the kid's coat. "Most cops aren't like that."

"Whatever." The kid stared him down.

"I'm looking for Terrell Nalene."

"I don't know him."

"But you just came out of his apartment."

"I said I don't know him."

"I don't believe you."

"I'm not doing anything wrong."

"Aren't you?" Nick stepped back to show the kid he wasn't a threat.

"I pay the rent."

"How old are you?"

"Eighteen."

"Try again." Nick flashed his FBI badge.

"Sixteen."

"I wouldn't say a day older than fourteen."

Jasper616 glanced down the hall, his foot tapping against the baseboard.

"How do you pay the rent?" asked Nick.

The kid shrugged. "It's not illegal."

"Great. Then you can tell me, and nothing will happen to you."

Jasper616 paused, searching Nick. "I'm a gamer."

"As in video games?"

"Yeah. They pay me to play."

"Who?"

"Advertisers."

Between the calluses he noticed on Jasper616's fingers and the truth behind those young eyes, Nick was willing to give him the benefit of the doubt.

"Are we done?" asked the kid. "I'm gonna be late for algebra."

"Very funny. Where do you play?"

"The Silver Key. It's a game shop downtown."

Nick tapped it into his phone and confirmed. This kid clearly had more problems in life than could be addressed in their short conversation.

"Give me your phone," Nick said.

"What? No." The kid backed away.

"I want to give you my contact info."

"Why would I need that?"

"I can only guess. But you may want it someday."

"Whatever."

"If you come across Terrell Nalene or anyone who knows where he is, will you contact me?"

"Why should I?"

"'Cause I think someone did him wrong."

"Everyone gets screwed at some point."

"Maybe. But you can do your part to stop that. And I never forget a favor."

The kid held out his phone, and Nick entered his name and number. In the "company" line, he typed *One of the Good Guys*.

Jasper616 slid his phone into his backpack and started down the stairs. Halfway down the next flight, he stopped and looked up at Nick, who hadn't budged.

"Terrell took me in when my mom . . . died."

"I'm sorry to hear that. What happened?"

"She got a bad pill."

"Fentanyl?"

The kid shrugged, lowering his guard a smidge. "I guess."

"Where's your dad?"

"I stopped asking that after my fifth birthday."

"Sounds like Terrell was kind to you. What happened to him?"

The kid shrugged again. "He disappeared one day."

"What's your best guess?"

"The river."

"Suicide?"

"Nah. Not Terrell."

"Why do you say that?"

"He was always a happy guy. Lotta friends. Coming and going. Day and night."

"Does Terrell sell drugs?"

The kid laughed. "Of course you would think that."

"Enlighten me."

"He was a jazz musician—I mean, like, back in the day or whatever. But he didn't play gigs anymore."

"So why all the people coming and going from his apartment?"

"They came to play with him or to just hang out and smoke weed."

Happy guy.

"Why do you think he's in the river?"

"It's a metaphor, man. Terrell's dead."

"You sure?"

"Isn't that your job, Good Guy?"

Nick grinned. *Touché.*

"You're not gonna bust me, are you?"

"For what?"

"Squatting."

"You said you paid rent."

"I do."

"Then you're not squatting," said Nick. "But I'd really like to take a look around the apartment."

"I told you, I'm late."

"Just give me ten minutes."

"I don't play, they don't pay."

"Do it for Terrell," said Nick, showing the kid a fifty-dollar bill.

The kid paused and snatched the money from Nick's hand. "Whatever. Just don't touch my stuff." He walked back up the stairwell, went to the apartment door and unlocked it, then let Nick inside.

CHAPTER 57

Strawberry was gone.

This was Ruby's first thought when she regained consciousness. How long she'd been lying behind the front bushes of the house, she had no idea, but now it was dark, and the pain in her hip was agony. A broken hip was death to the old and frail. She was willing to accept her fate. She had even been prepared. This was a long time coming.

And she could die knowing she had saved Strawberry's life.

Ruby managed to crawl to the back of the house, where she'd dug one final grave: her own. She had wanted to be buried alongside the shallow graves of all the little ones Thomas had killed. Three feet wide by three feet deep. But Ruby's empty plot was twice that size, as she'd been digging for a few seasons now.

She dragged her spindly, veiny legs over the edge of the open hole, then rolled herself into it. Every inch she dropped brought excruciating pain until her body settled on the floor of the pit. She lay on her back, staring up at a cloudy Michigan sky that reflected in her own gray eyes.

Behind those eyes, Ruby saw the memories of a lifetime. When she was a girl living with her mother and father and three sisters in the fishing shack on that little lake far, far in the woods.

They were bathing and swimming in that lake, the four girls, Ruby and her best friends.

They were roasting chicken over an open firepit in the yard.

They were playing in the woods during a rainstorm.

They were planting seeds in the south patch of earth near the fishing shack, one seed for each little thumb-pressed hole.

Ruby inhaled the scent of wet dirt and felt a tug on her heart, like someone squeezing a tennis ball. It didn't hurt, but she found it hard to take the next breath. Her heart squeezed again, and she found she was in her summer garden with dinner-plate-size sunflowers. Rows and rows of sunflowers bowed to greet her, then became the faces of all the babies she'd loved. Ruby drifted past each one of them.

When she came to the end of the last row, she rose up from the earth, breaking through the ethereal veil between worlds. She chuckled at the vision of herself down below, planted in the earth like a sunflower seed. And then Ruby saw the whole magnificent field, as the Creator did, looking down from heaven. She hoped someday Strawberry might come back here and plant sunflowers where she lay.

CHAPTER 58

Jasper616 showed Nick a coat closet where he'd boxed up Terrell's things. Several saxophone cases. A box of Terrell's clothes. Two coats were pushed to the far right of the coat bar. Shoeboxes overflowed with Polaroids. Nick flipped through them: Terrell playing his sax in clubs, Terrell and friends.

"You know any of these people?" Nick asked Jasper616.

"Nah. Before my time."

Another bin near the bottom was filled with old *Time* magazines. A plastic file folder wedged in the back of the closet had what Nick was looking for: receipt tabs from Terrell's Social Security checks.

He thumbed through the orderly stash. The check dates stopped December of the previous year.

"When did you last see Terrell?"

"About a year ago. It was right before Christmas because I got him a new set of reeds for his sax as a present. But he never got them. He never came back."

"Did he say if he was going somewhere?"

"Terrell never went anywhere except long walks along the

river. And to church. Went to Mass every day. Used to burn smelly incense crap in here too."

"You think there's any chance he's still alive? Maybe went to live with a relative somewhere?"

"He didn't have any family that I know of," said Jasper.

"Do you think he's dead?"

Jasper shrugged. "The guy was solid. Too nice for his own good. Probably got caught at the wrong place, wrong time."

"Too nice for his own good," mused Nick.

"Too trusting. Too giving. People took advantage."

Nick let the idea sink in as he pulled up a picture of Colton Chauncey on his phone. He held it out to Jasper616. "You recognize this guy?"

Jasper616 studied the image and shook his head.

"Never saw him around the building?"

"I don't know him."

"Didn't ask if you knew him. Have you ever seen him here?"

"No. Never saw that guy in my life," Jasper616 clarified.

Nick slid his phone back into his pocket. "What did you do with the reeds?"

"I still got them. Wrapped in a box with a green bow." Jasper616 wiped the melancholy from his face before Nick could comment. "I really gotta go, dude. They're texting me to know where I'm at."

"Yeah. I'm good here. Do you mind if I take Terrell's Social Security folder?"

"I guess not. Whatever helps."

"Do you happen to know where Terrell picked up his Social Security checks?"

"Yeah. He went to the post office down on Sycamore."

"And after he . . . didn't come back, did anyone come around asking for him? Checking in on him?"

Jasper616 shook his head. "Guess they knew the music had died."

Interesting turn of phrase.

"I can see you miss him."

The boy shrugged. "What good does that do?"

Nick followed Jasper out of Terrell Nalene's apartment building, which was set along the river that ran through the middle of the city. He texted an inquiry to Roe, then wound down the sidewalk from the apartment to the river walk, strolling north, away from the city. Nick walked the banks for fifteen minutes while waiting for Roe to get back to him. Terrell sounded like the sort of person who could have been easily conned by a criminal like Chauncey. It would have been convenient and quite simple to get rid of him. Terrell's unreported death meant the Social Security checks would keep coming. And Chauncey would be right there to collect them. It was a cruelly clever scam.

Nick's phone pinged. Roe had the info he needed: The Social Security office reported that Terrell's next check would arrive at the Sycamore post office tomorrow afternoon around three.

It wasn't worth the trip back and forth to Freeport. He'd wait to see if Chauncey showed up to pick up the check tomorrow. Looked like Nick would be spending the night in his truck.

CHAPTER 59

Sunday morning, Skylar texted Aditson and Emily her notes on Bradley Leland. She had worked all day Saturday to track and research him. He was twenty years old, had no criminal record, and was taking courses at a community college. His last known address was in an apartment in Rock River near the college. A call to his mom revealed he was working at the Great Wolf Lodge, a wildlife-themed resort and indoor water park in Traverse City, where he shared an apartment with several other wildlife-character actors.

After an hour-and-a-half drive north, Emily entered the lobby of the Great Wolf Lodge and found Oliver the Raccoon greeting guests in the lobby.

"Bradley Leland?" Emily asked the furry costumed figure.

"Who's Bradley? I'm Oliver the Raccoon!" said a cheery male voice from behind the headpiece of a raccoon costume.

"Bradley Leland, I'm Dr. Emily Hartford, and I need to talk to you about a friend of yours, Savannah Browdey."

"What about her?" Bradley stammered, and Emily knew for sure she was speaking to the right raccoon.

"How did you know Savannah Browdey?"

The figure went still, and the raccoon costume sagged in folds around his wiry five-ten frame. He could easily put on twenty pounds without anyone noticing.

"How did you find me?" The voice was sullen. Emily couldn't get a good look at the man behind the headpiece's mesh breathing panel.

Did this young man really not know how easy it was to find someone in the digital world? "Several recently posted pictures of you were geotagged to Traverse City. Then we confirmed your employment with Great Wolf paycheck stubs, bank statements, and verbal confirmation from your boss. Lastly, your mom told us where you are."

The raccoon head turned from side to side as Bradley glanced toward the dining hall, just past the lobby. It was filling with families for lunch. Several children were already pointing to him in the dopey costume and tugging on their parents' arms to go meet him.

"Is there somewhere else we can talk?" she asked.

"Outside."

"Lead the way."

Bradley's raccoon face glanced furtively across the room to a middle-aged man in khakis and a light-blue polo shirt, who was eyeing their interaction with curiosity. "I need to let my manager know."

"I already did," she reassured him and gave the man a little wave. He nodded back. This investigative incident would give him days of gossip currency with the staff.

Bradley led her out of the dining room, through the kitchen, and out the back of the building. "That's our break area there." He pointed to a grassy patch with a picnic table.

"As long as we don't get interrupted."

"Am I in trouble?" said Bradley, sitting opposite Emily.

"This will go a lot better if you take the headpiece off."

Bradley slipped the raccoon's head off. He had a pale, pockmarked face, gray eyes, and light-brown hair. A thin nose and thin lips gave him a meek, unattractive look.

Emily's tone eased up. "Were you and Savannah Browdey friends after high school?"

"Now and then. Why?"

"Have you spoken to her lately?"

"No. Not in like a month."

"Are you aware that Savannah is deceased?"

"What?" Bradley's already bleached-out face went even paler. "What happened?"

"Savannah was murdered."

"That's why you're here? To tell me?"

"It's a little more than that." Emily showed him the letter from BetGen and his handwritten name on the back. "Let's fast-forward this conversation."

Bradley glanced down. "What's this?" He read the letter inside. "Why is my name on this?" He looked up at Emily, genuinely surprised.

"That's what I was hoping you could tell me. It was in Savannah's diaper bag." She leaned in closer. "Want to tell me more about your relationship with her?"

"We were friends," Bradley said with a monotone voice.

"She submitted a DNA test to either learn or prove Brooklyn's paternity. I'm wondering why she'd write your name on this letter. Are you the father of her baby?"

"What? No. Oh no. I can tell you for certain it's not me."

"You sure about that?"

"Savannah and I never had sex. I'm not . . . I don't like girls. I mean, I like girls, but I—"

"I understand. And that's fine." Emily nodded and put him to the test. "But it doesn't exclude you. If you know what I mean?"

"No, ma'am. We weren't like that. And I have no idea who Brooklyn's father is."

The BetGen results had been subpoenaed and were being sent to Aditson. Emily would soon be able to confirm if Bradley was telling the truth, but for now she was hoping he'd just come clean if he had something to offer.

"Are we going to have a problem with that answer when I get my hands on the results?"

"There's no problem." He was growing cagey.

"Then why'd you move up north?" she asked.

"More jobs up here." He pursed his lips. Emily knew there was more to it.

"But you had a good job in Rock River. Your family. College. Come on. What's going on?"

"Needed a change of scenery."

Emily searched the young man's squirrelly expression. "Your name's not in the police report. But you were called into court as a witness. Why?"

Bradley squirmed as she said nothing and stared at him for over three minutes.

It never took too long.

"I was with Savannah the night she was raped," said Bradley, his voice trembling at the confession. "I was at Jonah's trailer playing cards that night. Later, when Savannah wanted to leave, I asked for a ride too. Well, 'asked' is putting it loosely."

"What do you mean?"

"I jumped in the car with Savannah and Colton. I didn't think Savannah would be safe with him. About ten minutes into the drive, he pulled off onto the shoulder and demanded that I get out of the car."

"What did Savannah do?"

"I told her to get out with me, but he threw his arm across her chest to block her in."

"Was there force involved?" Emily asked.

"Yeah. He pulled a knife."

"What did you do?" Emily was aghast at his story.

"I tried to talk him down, but then Colton turned the knife on Savannah."

"You were in the back seat?"

"Yeah. I told Colton I knew what he was up to. He said he'd kill me if I ever said anything."

"What did you do next?"

"I froze. I didn't want to leave her. But she looked back at me and told me to go. She said she wanted to be alone with Colton."

"You didn't believe that, did you?"

"Course not." Bradley shook his head. "She was trying to protect herself. And me."

"She sounds brave."

"She is . . . was." Bradley's eyes glazed over at the frightful memory.

"What did you do after you got out of Colton's car?"

Bradley's eyes shifted to Emily's. "I stood there and watched them disappear into the woods on this dirt two-track. I thought about running after them. I knew the road led down to the river, only about a half mile away. I figured that's where he was headed."

"Why didn't you go after them?"

"'Cause it would only make things worse. We'd both end up dead."

"So you left her there. With friends like you, who needs enemies?" Emily glared at him. "You didn't think to call the cops?"

"I left my phone in the back seat of Colton's car."

"What did you do then?"

"I hoofed it back to the highway and managed to hitchhike a ride to Rock River."

"So you let Savannah be subject to Colton's violence."

"It was a zero-sum game." Bradley clasped his hands and cracked every knuckle.

"That was a hard decision. You ever regret it?"

Bradley gave a small nod. "But Colton knows that I know he raped Savannah."

"And that's why you left Rock River?"

Another nod.

"Did Colton Chauncey ever threaten you?"

"He came to my apartment after Savannah went to the cops about the rape, pounding on my door. I didn't open it, of course. Eventually, he left, then camped out in my parking lot, pacing and waiting for me."

"Did you call the police?"

"A neighbor did. The cops came. Talked to him. And then he left." Bradley rocked the raccoon headpiece in his lap.

"Are you afraid Chauncey will try to find you here?"

"It's not over. It'll never be over till he's behind bars."

Emily toyed with the idea of telling him Jonah Hampton was dead but decided against it. She didn't know if he could bear too much more suffering at the moment.

"Do you think Colton Chauncey is Brooklyn's father?"

"No. Savannah was pregnant before Colton did . . . the . . . thing."

"How can you be so sure?"

"Several nights before Colton got to Savannah, we were all playing euchre, and Jonah offered her a beer. She refused, which wasn't like Savannah. Jonah ribbed her a little. Then she told us she was pregnant. But she wouldn't say who the daddy was."

"If she knew it wasn't Colton's baby, why keep it a secret?"

"I don't know. I always thought it was because she was trying to protect the real father."

"Did Colton Chauncey show up at all that night?"

"No."

Emily kept her eyes on the young man, trying to find a thread of compassion for him. He'd done nothing while his friend was being assaulted. "Why is your name on that piece of paper?"

He met her stare. "Before the trial, things were getting bad for Savannah. She kept 'running into Colton,'" he said, using air quotes.

"Chauncey was stalking her?"

"She'd see him at the gas station. Or the grocery store. Even trolling past her house. Savannah called me and said she needed a place to stay. Somewhere safe. I told her to come up here and hide out. We had worked out a plan."

"Her and Brooklyn?" Emily asked.

"No, just her. She was going to have her cousin take care of the baby. She said she'd leave my name in the baby's bag in case her cousin needed to find her."

"When did this conversation between you two occur?"

"Like, the Friday before the trial was supposed to start."

"Why didn't she come up?"

"Her car broke down that afternoon. Then the next day she had her cousin take her to Jonah's. I had to work up here that night and the next morning, but I said I'd come down Sunday afternoon and pick her up and bring her here."

"You lied to me. You knew she was dead," Emily said softly.

Bradley nodded.

A girl's voice called from the back door. "Brad, the kids are mobbing me for the raccoon!"

He looked up and waved at a girl dressed as a squirrel. "Are we finished?" he asked Emily.

"Is your plan to hide in that suit forever?" she asked.

"I just want it to all go away," Bradley whispered. Emily noticed his hands clasped together to stop them from shaking.

"Scurry up, raccoon!" squirrel girl bellowed from inside the building.

"This is far from over for you," Emily told him.

"I'll do whatever I can, but not until Colton is behind bars." He was clearly terrified of Chauncey finding him.

"I hope for that too," Emily empathized. "But if you hear of anything, don't hide behind that suit. Got me?"

He nodded.

"And be vigilant."

"You don't know where he is, do you?" Bradley whispered.

"We're getting close," she fibbed.

Bradley slid his raccoon headpiece on and scrambled away from the table, scampering through the restaurant's back door. Emily worked her way around the building to the front of the resort and back to the main parking lot, mulling over their conversation.

Not once had Bradley asked about Brooklyn. If she was okay or alive. Wouldn't he at least care enough about Savannah to ask about her child?

The base of her skull throbbed with anxiety. She tried calling Aditson, but cell service wasn't strong enough in this thickly wooded area. This agitated her even more. She'd have to drive out to the highway and travel south until she reached better cell service.

Her whirling thoughts were taking everything out on Nick. He hadn't checked in with her or Aditson since he went rogue from the morgue. She toyed with the thought of contacting Roe.

Emily inhaled a long, deep breath and held it for five seconds. She would not let Nick's behavior get the best of her. Nor would she feed her uneasiness about where Chauncey might be prowling and who might be in his path. But if she didn't hear from Nick in the next twenty-four hours, Roe was getting a call.

Emily pulled out of the parking lot and pressed the gas pedal. The Yukon's engine roared as she accelerated ten miles an hour over the speed limit. She cranked the radio to club music and let the pounding beat drive into her. Anything to bolster her spirits and keep her hopes fixed on finding Brooklyn. Alive.

CHAPTER 60

After the fishing-shack incident, Colton fled back to his house with the baby. The police had already been there, and he was riding on the assumption they wouldn't return. What choice did he have?

He squeezed a dropper of liquid Benadryl into the infant's bottle.

Sunday, he lay low, keeping the child sedated and asleep. He, too, slept most of the day.

Early Monday morning, after feeding her another bottle, Colton felt assured no one was coming to the house. He placed the sleeping infant on a blanket on the floor and headed to Rock River.

CHAPTER 61

The rest of Sunday, Emily stayed home, feeling helpless. Aditson was in the office, following up on more potential sightings of Brooklyn across the state and in Chicago. The tip line had been flooded with them, but the leads were going nowhere. Nick wasn't responding to Emily's texts and calls. She was stuck in a black void while Chauncey and Brooklyn were still missing. She tried to distract herself with a long run. She helped her nieces with their homework. And then they cooked and ate an early dinner together. By evening, Emily was so wound up and jittery that Anna decided to give her some time alone, and she took her daughters to see a movie.

Emily cracked open a bottle of red, put on a mindless TV show, and finally crashed on the couch after a single glass of wine. She stirred awake Monday morning to the aroma of coffee brewing. Emily heard Anna and the girls in the kitchen making breakfast. She unfurled herself from the couch and went to join them.

Anna poured her a cup of coffee. "You slept well. Didn't even flinch when we got home."

"I think I wore myself out," Emily said, taking that delicious first sip.

"Eggs? Toast?"

"Please. And thank you," Emily said, then turned to Flora. "You'll be ready to head out after school today?" They were heading to Ann Arbor and Dr. Eckhardt's forensic workshop.

"Yeah, I'm all packed."

"Make sure you get the assignments from your teachers," Anna said. "I don't know why they have to do this during the middle of the week. Don't they know high schoolers go to school?"

"It's fine, Mom. I'm not missing that much."

"And she'll be gaining so much," Emily reminded her sister. The timing wasn't ideal, but she knew how much Flora was looking forward to it. Every time she heard her on her phone, she was bragging about it to a different friend.

Emily was seeing the bottom of her mug when her phone rang from the sofa. She dove out of the kitchen to answer it.

Aditson had sent a video link.

Footage taken earlier that morning at a Walmart entrance.

Every muscle in Emily's body tensed up as she watched a grainy but distinctly identifiable Colton Chauncey entering a store wearing a hoodie and jeans.

She immediately called Aditson. "Is this in Freeport?"

"No. It's the Walmart in Oak Creek," Aditson told her. Oak Creek was a midsize town halfway between Freeport and Rock River. "A store manager spotted him buying beer at seven in the morning and thought it was a little odd. He kept an eye on him and then realized from the BOLOs it was Chauncey. He followed Chauncey through to see what else the guy was picking up. Water, potato chips, and three bottles of Benadryl."

"A killer with an allergy problem?" mused Emily. She sighed. "Have you reached out to Nick?"

"I've left countless messages. No response."

"Me too. I've been trying since Saturday night."

"I'll try him again as soon as I hang up," said Aditson. "I take it you found Oliver the Raccoon?"

"Live, and in the fur."

Aditson chuckled. "How did he take the news about Savannah?"

"He already knew about her death. And he told me that he was with Savannah the night she was raped. He bailed on her after Chauncey threatened him at knifepoint. Later they had plans to hide out from Chauncey together up north. Now he's riddled with guilt."

"Tough call. Some would have stayed and fought. He and Savannah may have been able to overpower Chauncey."

"I don't know if he'll ever recover from it," Emily said.

"Once we catch Chauncey, the state's prosecutor will no doubt also press those rape charges, and Leland will be called to the witness stand."

"I get why the kid wants to steer clear of Freeport County right now."

"And is he Brooklyn's father?"

"Says he's not, and I believe him. He also says he doesn't know who is."

"We'll know soon enough," said Aditson. "BetGen should be emailing me the results today."

"I'll get dressed and come over. I'm driving myself mad being at home."

In the meantime, she was also going to blow up Nick's phone.

CHAPTER 62

Less than an hour later, Emily stood impatiently over Aditson's shoulder as Aditson opened the BetGen email. He followed the link BetGen had sent, then entered a passcode before a PDF of the results appeared. Another click and they were in.

"Scroll down past the STR graphs," Emily instructed.

"Hold your horses." Aditson read a paragraph of text at the top of the page. "Says here Savannah Browdey provided a known sample from a donor and a sample from Brooklyn. The test conclusively matched both samples provided."

"Does it give the donor's name?"

"It does."

Emily read it with Aditson: Gage Chauncey.

"I can't believe it," said Aditson, shaking his head. "If memory serves, that's Colton's younger brother by twelve years."

"Let me see," said Emily. Looking closer, she studied two graphs that represented the samples. Both had the same twenty-one loci required for a definitive match. It was irrefutable.

"Do you know where Gage Chauncey lives?" asked Emily.

Aditson was looking at his notes. "His last known address is in Detroit."

Emily gave a small smile. "Do you think it's possible Colton brought baby Brooklyn to her father?"

"I'm betting Colton doesn't know Gage is the daddy," Aditson said. "I doubt Gage Chauncey even knows."

"We should try to get this info to Nick." Emily grimaced. "Except that he's ignoring me too."

"We can't wait for Nick to come around to us. We need to handle this." Aditson wore an uneasy expression. "Also I'm curious to find out if Gage Chauncey knows he's a daddy."

"If he doesn't, that's definitely the kind of news best told face-to-face," said Emily. "I'd like to be the one who does it."

"Fine by me," said Aditson. "When?"

"I'm taking Flora to Ann Arbor." Detroit was only a forty-minute drive from there. "Why don't I try to arrange a meetup when we're there?"

"I'll have Skylar get his info and set it up. He's more likely to show up if it's coming from us."

"Late afternoon would be best."

"You sure you want to do this by yourself?"

"He's not a suspect, and he has no criminal background."

"You'll call me as soon as the meeting is over."

"Of course. But I hate leaving Nick out of this. Not just because of jurisdiction issues. I—I'm worried about him being out there alone. What do you think he's doing?"

Aditson folded his hands in front of him as a calm came over him. "Nick underwent a great trauma while he was in Asia. You don't have to tell me what it was, but am I right?"

"Yes. It's true."

"That experience caused a separation in his body, mind, and spirit."

"Speak English."

"It's my way of saying he's unbalanced."

"What does this have to do with him not returning calls and running off on his own?"

Aditson remained still and serious as he said, "Balance can only be achieved when mind, body, and spirit reunite. He has to anchor all three parts of himself. But he won't sit still long enough to allow it to happen."

"And how exactly do I get him to sit still?"

"You can't. And that's not your job. But no healing will be accomplished until he stops and addresses this disjointedness."

"Is there anything I can do?" Emily was wrecked inside.

"Only Nick can choose to tie them together."

"How long till he recognizes this?"

Aditson gave her a sad smile. "You should not be tied to him until he does."

Emily gave a slight nod.

"Do you understand what I am saying, Doc?"

She did. "But what if he . . . never repairs himself?"

"You will be holding on to nothing but shreds. And eventually they'll slip between your fingers."

CHAPTER 63

Nick overslept. It was nearly ten when he woke up to muted gray light that made the Monday morning feel more banal than usual. He had been parked overnight in a parking lot outside Terrell Nalene's apartment building, seeded with the hope that Chauncey would turn up. Now he worried that he might have missed the man.

Unlocking his phone, he saw he had fifty-seven missed calls. He hadn't intended to respond to Emily's or Aditson's calls but thought better of it after realizing one of them might report him to Roe if he didn't give proof of life.

"Hey there," he said to Emily, adding a lift to his tone.

"Hey." He sensed relief in her voice.

"What's up?" he asked.

"I've been trying to reach you for days."

"Yeah, I see that. Sorry."

"Where are you?"

"South." He didn't want to reveal much more right now.

"Rock River?"

He didn't answer.

"What are you doing down there? Do you have a lead on Chauncey?"

It took a second for him to find an answer. Whatever he told her would surely get back to Aditson. "I'm working on something."

More silence.

"Okay. Can you elaborate?"

"No."

"Do you need . . . backup?"

"I'm good."

Emily cleared her throat and spoke stiffly. "We are supposed to be a team."

"I've got this," he said, feeling jumpy all of a sudden.

"Does Roe know what you're doing?" Nick thought she sounded judgy.

"I'm good, Em."

"Does Roe know you went rogue?"

His voice rose: "Is that what you and Aditson think?" Then he went quiet.

Nick heard a long, frustrated sigh on the other end of the call, drawing out the conversation's awkwardness. He wanted to make a fast exit, but that would only make her more irritated with him. Would she tell Aditson to alert the Rock River police to find him?

"Are you even curious about what's going on up here in Freeport?" she finally said in an accusatory tone. "Would you like an update?"

"Yeah. Of course," Nick said, his eyes scanning the neighborhood for any activity.

Emily told him about Bradley Leland, the BetGen results, and her upcoming meeting with Gage Chauncey in Detroit.

Nick listened attentively. He didn't like that she was meeting with Gage alone, but he kept his mouth shut about it, knowing any objection from him would rile her up. "I'm sorry I went radio silent. It's just . . . I've been on my own for the last year plus and . . . always watching my back. Reentry has been a bit tougher than I expected."

Emily's voice was softer, more forgiving, when—after a brief silence—she responded: "I wish there was something I could do to make it better. For you. For us."

"Me too."

"We could try. If we spent more time together—that is, outside of working a serial-murder case."

Nick chuckled. "How about we do dinner together after you get back?"

"Will you be back in Freeport?"

"I hope to be."

"I wish you'd tell me what's going on," Emily said.

"Start thinking about what you want for dinner."

"I miss your grilling."

"I'll pick up a couple of steaks while I'm down here."

"That sounds perfect. I can make a salad."

Nick grinned. They both knew darn well that cooking was not Emily's forte. But she could manage putting together some lettuce leaves and veggies.

The moment hung there, neither wanting to be the one to end the conversation. And yet there was nothing more either could say.

Nick broke first. "See you soon."

"I hope so. Be careful. I love you." Emily rushed the words and hung up.

Nick set the phone down with an overwhelming, ravenous hunger. For once, he felt like eating.

CHAPTER 64

Emily and Flora arrived Monday evening at the University of Michigan campus and checked into the dorm where they'd be sharing a room for the night. Then Emily walked Flora to the medical-research building so she'd know where to go in the morning.

They spotted Dr. Eckhardt and her teaching assistant in the lab, setting up for the next day's camp. Emily recognized the testing materials laid on the counter. Test tubes. Latex gloves. Plastic vials to hold saliva. Pipettes. Centrifuge machines. Thermocyclers used to break down and open the cells so DNA strands could be replicated. And of course, the DNA STR—short tandem repeat—machines, which used electrophoresis to test for repeating sequences, which showed if there were common loci between a known and unknown sample. Twenty-one or more shared loci was considered a match.

"Hey, you two, welcome," Dr. Eckhardt called out, scurrying across the room to greet them.

"We didn't mean to interrupt. I have to be in Detroit tomorrow for a meeting, so I wanted to make sure Flora knew how to get here."

"Of course. Hi, Flora, this is where you'll spend all day tomorrow. You'll be assigned a lab partner from another high school."

"Do you still have the bone?" Flora asked. "How are we going to analyze the DNA?"

"Yes, and you'll be fully immersed in the process tomorrow. You're the only one who's going to be doing bone DNA. Congrats on that."

Flora grinned.

"Sounds exciting," said Emily. "Will there be any lecture time?"

"We start off with a general lecture on DNA history, structure, and testing methods. We do our lab portion, then break for lunch. After lunch we'll do another lecture on GEDmatch Pro, which is the database we use mostly. After that, the students can learn how to conduct an IGG search."

"What's that?" Flora asked.

"Investigative genetic genealogy."

"Will we get to test any DNA?" Emily asked.

"Absolutely. We'll conclude the day with another lab where students take an unknown DNA sample and match it against the database. Every team gets a chance to explain their results and how they got there during the Wednesday-morning workshop."

Emily was impressed. "How does that sound to you, Flora?"

"I'm excited," said Flora. "Do you know what's for dinner?"

"Love your priorities." Dr. Eckhardt grinned. "You're a girl after my own heart. You'll be dining at the campus cafeteria, where there's a wide variety of choices."

"Are there any plans for the kids tomorrow evening?" Emily asked.

"We'll walk them downtown to a local pizza fave. Then back to campus to the auditorium for a concert featuring the U of M brass quintet."

"Sounds fun," said Emily.

"Will you be back from Detroit by dinnertime?" Flora asked her.

"Wouldn't miss it."

"Any other questions for me?" Dr. Eckhardt said.

Flora shook her head. "I'm really excited."

"And we're pleased to have you here."

"There's nothing we need to be around for tonight, right?" asked Emily.

"Nope," said Dr. Eckhardt. "Flora, I'll see you tomorrow morning at eight with that bone."

"She'll be here. Thanks, Sam." They left the lab, and Emily led Flora across campus. "Let's head to the cafeteria and grab a bite."

"I'm really beginning to like this campus," said Flora.

"I'm not surprised. It's in your DNA. Your grandfather—my dad—went to medical school here."

"Really?"

"Yup. He and my mom were just married, and they lived in a little apartment on the top floor of an old house pretty close to here."

"Cool. Did you go to school here too? Is that how you know Samantha?"

"No. I did all my college and med school in Chicago."

"How'd you end up there?"

Emily sighed. It was time to tell her the full story. "I was about your age. Just fifteen when my mom was killed in a car accident."

"What happened?"

"The short version is that my mom was struggling with depression, and she thought my dad was having an affair. One morning when she thought he was going to meet his girlfriend, she flew out of the house to follow him in her car. She was really upset—which caused her to take a curve too fast."

"She crashed?"

"Her car went off a steep embankment," Emily said soberly. "I didn't know all this until much later. Dad refused to investigate the accident. He told me a lie about how she died, and later that made me hate him."

"How'd you know he was lying?"

"Because I went to the scene of her accident, and there were tire tracks on the pavement from braking."

"I can't imagine losing my mom." Flora was rapt in the story. "What did you do?"

"I grew up too fast. I ran away to Chicago to live with my aunt Laura on the South Side—or rather live *at* her condo. Aunt Laura was almost never home—she traveled overseas for work all the time. But the worst part was that Dad and me—mostly me—stopped talking. For almost ten years."

"I get being mad at your dad."

Emily empathized with her niece. Flora and Fiona would be working through their own daddy issues for the next decade or two, since their traveling dad had abandoned them in exchange for a woman at every port he visited for work.

"It wasn't my best moment," said Emily. "I was angry and grieving. But what I didn't realize, or have the maturity to understand, was that Dad was grieving too."

"Why do men have to be such scum?" Flora groaned.

"First, not all of them are. Also, it turns out Dad was not having an affair."

"He wasn't?"

"No. He had been communicating with your mom. Anna reached out to him to let him know she was his daughter. Until then, he didn't even know of her existence. But my mom thought she was a secret girlfriend that Dad was on his way to meet. That's why she chased him."

"Why didn't he tell Grandma about my mom?"

"He didn't really know her yet. He wanted to make sure your mom was really who she said she was before pulling his wife and daughter into the mix."

"It's all so sad."

"All over a misunderstanding," Emily agreed.

"After you left home, did he ever try to call you? See you?"

"He did. A lot for the first couple years. But I never responded. After a while, he just gave me space and kept hoping I'd return."

"Obviously, you did."

"Yeah. I came home when Dad had a heart attack. He died not long after."

"And that's when you met my mom."

"Yup, Dad's lawyer told me. That's how I found out."

"Wild story, Aunt Em."

"I wish it weren't. I regret those years because I'll never get him back." Emily looked deep into her niece's clear, beautiful eyes. "I know you're mad at your dad. But even if he has demons to deal with, he loves you, and someday you might want to have a relationship with him."

Flora shrugged. "Whatever."

Only time was going to heal that festering infection. But it was good for Flora to know it need not be permanent. Still, better to let it air out for now.

"I think it's cool you picked up the baton at the ME's office," said Flora with a reassuring smile. "I think he'd like that."

"I do too." Emily met her smile. "And I also know he'd be really proud of his granddaughter."

CHAPTER 65

The lone hiker was on day thirteen of his monthlong trek of the Iron Belle Trail, which traversed Michigan from Ironwood in the Upper Peninsula to Belle Isle down in Detroit. He was winding through forested land, skirting up a small hill that leveled out on a stretch of land bordering private property. His map told him he was in the heart of Freeport County. He had been up since 6:00 a.m. and had at least another eleven miles to go before he'd reach the state campground for the night. The day was unseasonably warm for early November. He guessed high forties or low fifties. Wispy white clouds were painted over a cerulean-blue autumn sky. He stepped out from under the cover of the trees to bathe himself in the light of the filtered sun, then took a swig of his coconut water and enjoyed the view of rolling grasslands as far as his eye could see. This was the perfect day. Breathtaking.

A slight breeze picked up, tumbling the dry leaves across the forest floor and bringing with it a wretched stench that gagged the man. He covered his mouth with his hand and looked around for the rotting carcass. Maybe a deer. The odor was so strong.

Scanning his surroundings, he spotted a mound of fresh dirt, as if an animal had been digging a hole. This was private property, and he knew he shouldn't be trespassing, but no one was around, and curiosity got the better of him.

The closer he got, the worse it smelled. He pulled his neck bandanna over his nose and mouth. When he was just feet away, he saw animal tracks all around the makeshift grave. They'd been digging. Hundreds of flies buzzed around the site. Something moving caught his eye. Getting closer, he realized the moving ground he saw was actually thousands of maggots carpeting a human leg.

CHAPTER 66

Monday, 12:30 p.m. Nick parked his truck down the street in view of the Sycamore Street post office's front door. Folks came and went, and then the stream slowed down to a trickle, typical of a postlunch lull. An hour later, he was still ravenous with hunger. His last meal had been six hours ago. His blood sugar was dropping, and the lack of a good night's sleep was catching up to him. He clenched his muscles from toes to shoulders, limb by limb. He blasted the AC in his face. Despite his best efforts, Nick found himself fighting drooping eyelids.

He slapped his cheeks and blasted the radio.

Forty-five minutes later, a USPS delivery truck pulled in, and a man entered the building with several trays of the afternoon mail. He emerged minutes later and left. The parking lot was quiet again for thirty minutes. It was twenty after three when a homeless man came dragging his way down the sidewalk, pushing a rusty, overloaded shopping cart. A mangy dog sat in the child seat atop a pile of ratty blankets. Nick watched the man turn the cart into the post office parking lot and head toward the front door. He pulled his cart off to the side and entered the building, carrying nothing with him. The dog obediently stayed in his seat.

Nick found this curious. He didn't think it was plausible that a guy who kept all his worldly belongings in a cart would be spending anywhere from five to twenty dollars a month on postbox fees. He jumped from his car and strode across the street and through the parking lot. Just as he was about to pull open the door, it swung open and the homeless man exited, head bent to the ground.

"Excuse me," Nick said.

The man didn't look up as he shuffled past Nick.

"Excuse me, sir?" Nick let the door close. "Do you have a second?"

The man tottered to his cart. Nick needed to know if this was Terrell Nalene, or if he had that check.

"Sir? I'm speaking to you."

He continued ignoring Nick.

Nick raised his voice, trailing him to his cart. "Can you hear me, sir? I'd like to speak with you."

The man picked up his pace, rolling his cart out of the parking lot.

"Sir, I need to speak with you."

"It's a conversation down on Fascination Street," the man muttered under his breath.

"Yes, that's right. I'd like to have a conversation."

The man did not stop, rattling the cart over uneven blocks of cement, then down the slope of a driveway toward the street.

Nick saw the corner of a white envelope sticking out of the pocket of the man's oversize trench coat. "Did you just pick up a letter?" Nick had no intention of using force on the man, but the guy could clearly hear him and was choosing to ignore him.

"Sir, I know you can hear me."

The man looked over his shoulder with a snarl.

"I'd just like to ask you a question."

"You have no right," the man said, quickening his step.

"What did you do in there just now?" Nick asked, hoping to draw him into an answer.

"I can't talk," the guy snapped. "*It's opening time down on Fascination Street.*"

He gave every indication he wasn't playing with a full deck, but "Fascination Street" sounded familiar. Wasn't that from an old Cure song? Emily had introduced him to the band back when they were teenagers.

"Sir, I'm asking you as a law enforcement agent, please stop and talk to me."

The man stroked the top of his dog's head and leaned in to say his next words, which Nick recognized as lyrics from the Cure's song. "Let's move to the beat . . ."

"Sir, please stop walking and turn around," he said.

When the man didn't listen, Nick, in a split-second decision, reached into his coat pocket and snagged the letter.

The man yelped and yanked on the cart to stop it from rolling down the sidewalk's decline. "Hey! You can't do that. Give that back!"

Nick saw that the envelope was addressed to Terrell Nalene.

"Are you Terrell Nalene?" he asked the man.

The man's eyes dodged Nick's. "I picked it up for a friend."

"Do you know Terrell Nalene?"

"Who's that?"

"Don't play dumb. The man whose check you're picking up. Have you ever met him?"

"He's not a good man."

"Who's not good?" The more the homeless man talked,

the more Nick realized how difficult it might be to get a clean answer from him. "Where is this not-good man?"

"Down on Fascination Street."

Nick recognized the lyric. "Are you a fan of the Cure?"

The man laughed.

"What are you doing with Mr. Terrell Nalene's Social Security check?"

"Give it back." He jutted his crusty palm at Nick.

"Who is paying you to pick up Terrell's check?"

"Gimme that. I have a dog to feed."

"I see that. But I can't give this back to you," said Nick, flashing the man his FBI credentials. "This is Social Security fraud. You're participating in criminal activity."

"You need to compensate me. You can't just take that check."

When he saw that Nick wasn't going to give him money, the man turned back to pushing his cart down the sidewalk.

Nick trailed him. "Where are you supposed to meet him?"

"You got money?" The man stroked his dog's head and kept his gaze from Nick.

"What's your dog's name?" asked Nick.

"Bob."

"Hi, Bob." Nick offered a smiley greeting but didn't touch the probably flea-infested canine.

"He's clean," said the man, reading Nick's thoughts. "See. He's got a flea collar."

Against his better judgment, Nick reached over and scratched the dog behind the ears. "Hey, buddy."

This seemed to please the man, who held on to the handlebar of the cart.

"What's your name?" Nick asked.

"Giggs."

"Nice to meet you, Giggs. I'm Nick."

"What do you really want?"

"I know Terrell's roommate, Jasper," Nick revealed. "He's worried about him."

"Why should I believe you?"

Nick dug into his wallet and handed him a couple of twenties. "Do you know where Terrell is?" he asked again, lowering his voice.

The man took the money and shoved it into his pants pocket. "He's down on Fascination Street."

"You said that." Nick buzzed with frustration until he reminded himself that people living in alternate realities played by a different set of rules. He had to go with it. "Can you take me there, Giggs?"

Giggs didn't answer. Instead, he drove the cart forward and let Nick flank him.

CHAPTER 67

The address they'd found for Gage Chauncey had proved erroneous—but Skylar had been able to identify a workplace and his office phone number. He worked in marketing for the Ford Motor Company in Dearborn, but after Emily phoned him, Gage arranged to meet her in the lounge of a five-star hotel in downtown Detroit late Tuesday afternoon. She found him in the lobby, and he led her to a dark corner booth. Once they were seated, she got right to the point, handing Gage the results from BetGen and awaiting his reaction.

Gage Chauncey didn't react. If his unempathetic response was an act, he could have won an Oscar. He calmly shifted one leg over the other, maintaining a professional demeanor that matched his appearance. Slim black jeans and a tailored jacket. Well groomed, fit, and handsome. He strongly resembled a younger, more professional version of his brother Colton. His eyes displayed none of the evil that his older brother's held, at least in the photographs she'd seen.

"Do you know where Brooklyn is?" Emily asked, going on the offensive. "Is she with you?" She searched his face for any clue that might confirm Brooklyn was still alive and being taken care of.

But Gage stared at the paper from BetGen with a blank look that continued to give none of his emotions away.

"Savannah never told you about the baby?" Emily asked.

"I heard from a friend that she'd had a kid. I sent her a text to congratulate her but never heard back. Maybe it crossed my mind that it was possible the baby might be mine. But I also knew Savannah had a boyfriend."

"So you were with her at some point?"

"A one-night hookup." He shrugged.

"Have you ever met Brooklyn?" Emily asked.

"I saw pictures on socials after she was born."

"She has your nose and eyes," Emily couldn't help but add.

Gage glanced up uncomfortably, trying to get the attention of a server across the room.

"Do you know what happened to Savannah?" she asked.

"I know she was murdered."

"And did you also know that your brother is a key suspect?"

"It doesn't take a rocket scientist to figure that out." Gage's eyes traveled back to Emily's, and he asked flatly, "Is the baby dead?"

"I came here hoping to find that she was with you."

Gage shook his head. His posture softened, and he leaned forward slightly, possibly a sign of compassion for the daughter he'd never met.

"We don't know where Brooklyn is," said Emily. "An active search for her is in progress."

"Have you checked the fishing shack?" asked Gage.

"We have. And Lake Isabella."

"And the cottage at the top of the lake?" Gage asked.

"We spoke to Hank Shepherd, who owns it," Emily told him.

"Someone else is living there now?" asked Gage. "That used to be my grandfather Emmett's house."

"I see." Emily wasn't going to tell him about Shepherd's murder. She wanted to be careful with how much information she dished out. Family members often knew more than they let on.

"I guess Colton sold it off," said Gage. "Loser probably needs the money."

Emily noted the way his jaw muscles clenched when he said it. "You seem upset. Did the cottage mean something special to you?"

"No. Yes. At one time, it did."

"Did you spend a lot of time there?"

"When I was a kid, we used to go there in the summer. Swim. Fish. In the winters, we played hide-and-seek in the house."

"Really? It's so small. It must have been a challenge to find good hiding spots," Emily commented.

"You wouldn't believe the nooks and crannies we discovered." Gage paused, smiling to himself.

"Sounds like good times."

"They were practically the only ones that were good."

Emily changed tactics. "Were you close with Colton?"

"Not really. He's twelve years older than me. He was out of the house by the time I was six. I have only a few memories of him."

"And your mother? Is she still living?"

"I have no idea. I graduated high school early and left home at sixteen."

"You don't know where your mother is?" Emily tried again.

"I just said I didn't. Look, my ma was a troubled, sick person. And so is Colton. You should be trying to find him, not interrogating me."

"This isn't an interrogation. And I'm not a cop. I'm a doctor, and I'm also someone who cares about arresting the person who murdered your daughter's mother. I also desperately want to find your daughter. Alive. Therefore, it seems reasonable to me that you'd do everything in your power to help me."

A female server padded up with two water glasses. "Can I get you two anything?"

Gage glanced up at her and said curtly, "We're good here."

"I'll have a soda water with lime," Emily told her. Odd that Gage should assume what she did or didn't want.

The waitress slipped away. Emily waited until she was out of earshot before asking, "How well did you know Savannah?"

"Well enough to get her pregnant," Gage said with a touch of sarcasm.

"Tell me more about that hookup."

"I was in town for a weekend for a friend's wedding, and Savannah was there. It was a big barn-type reception on a farm. Savannah and I ended up taking a walk in the field together when the dancing started. Neither of us are big dancers."

"Were you drinking?"

"We had both had a lot. It was a wedding."

"Friends of the bride or groom?" Emily asked.

"I was friends with the groom's sister. She was a guest of the bride."

"Did you know Savannah before the wedding?"

"Not really. I mean, she's quite a bit younger than me. But you know, everyone's sort of connected in Freeport."

"Did this one-nighter occur at the wedding venue?"

"Yeah. In the barn. After our walk."

"And what happened afterward?"

"I took her home just before dawn. It was Sunday, and after a few hours of sleep, I drove back to Detroit."

"Did you reach out to Savannah after that weekend?"

"I didn't have her number. I figured if she wanted to keep in touch, she would have given me a way to."

"And she never tried to contact you?"

"Never. I only heard about her again when I heard about Colton assaulting her."

"I'm assuming you didn't check in with him over the weekend of the wedding?" Emily asked.

"No, but . . . he showed up at the reception."

"He did? Was he invited?"

"No. It was late and almost everyone had left. Savannah and I were sitting outside the barn talking."

"What was he doing there?"

"Someone had tipped him off that I was home. Typical Colton, he wanted to get some money out of me."

"Has he asked you for money before?"

"Many times. Before I cut him off. Changed my number. Moved and left no forwarding address."

"What did you do?"

"I told him no."

"How'd he take that?"

"Not well. We ended up getting in a fight. He punched me. I punched back. Soon we were on the ground. He's always been stronger than me. I knew better than to pick a fight."

"Sounds like he's the one who picked it. You had every right to say no," Emily encouraged. "What did Savannah do during all this?"

"I think she was shocked to find out we were brothers. She knew Colton from hanging out at Jonah Hampton's. She ran to get some help."

"How did it end?"

"Some of the other guests pulled him off me and dragged

him to his truck. And made sure he left."

"Did anyone call the police?"

"I didn't let them. Doesn't do any good. He gets away with everything."

"I'm sorry that happened. And Savannah? How was she after all this?"

Gage's eyes filled with tears. "Helping me . . . It cost her . . . everything."

"What do you mean?" Emily was relieved to see he wasn't the ice block he feigned to be.

"As my brother was being dragged out, he looked right at me and then her and said, 'You'll pay for this.'" Gage wiped his eyes dry with the back of his hand and straightened his jacket. He glanced around to see if anyone was looking at him.

"And you think his later assault of Savannah was payback?" asked Emily.

"It's his way of dominating. He wanted me to see that he could take anything he wanted from me."

The more she learned about Colton's twisted logic and motivations, the more she realized how uncontrollable he had become.

"Had you known your brother to sexually assault women before?"

"Plenty of times. He couldn't keep his dick to himself."

"Was he always so violent?"

"Since I was a kid, I saw him getting into fights, turning on people. He's the main reason I left Freeport."

"Did it ever occur to you to help Savannah out once she was facing the prospect of a trial against him?" Emily controlled her tone to suppress any judgment.

Gage's face went hard. "Testify against my brother? No, thank you."

"But if you felt responsible for Savannah?"

Gage looked back up at Emily. "Colton has a near-genius IQ. He was a star high school football player. Once upon a time, he had the world at his fingertips. About to get a full scholarship to Michigan State. But after all my father's beatings, several motorcycle accidents, and his time getting tossed around on the football field, his multiple untreated concussions started to affect him. He changed, going from a kind and generous kid to being angry, belligerent, and vindictive."

Emily was aware of the devastating effects of multiple concussions. It could cause atrophy in brain matter—apoptosis, or cell death. And inflammation could lead to neurotoxicity. The results could be depression, cognitive-performance declines, and personality changes. Colton Chauncey seemed like a classic case of cumulative brain damage.

"And you are saying all of this contributed to his violence and crime?" she asked.

"Yes. Combine that with how he started to develop extreme ideas about politics, sex, his friends—many of whom he turned into enemies. He's totally paranoid. Everything and everyone becomes a target in his mind. Savannah was just that. An object he could use and abuse in whatever ways he needed."

There was a lull in their conversation as Emily sipped her soda water. "I can see why Colton would kill Savannah to stop her from testifying against him. But why harm a baby that can't do anything to harm him?"

"Didn't you hear me? In Colton's world, we're all just commodities for his use and gain. He has no conscience." Gage's cold tone raised goose bumps on Emily's arms. He stood up. "Please don't contact me again for this investigation. I don't want my brother to know you've been talking with me. And I don't want him knowing where I live. Do you understand?"

Emily rose to meet his gaze. "I can't guarantee you won't be summoned later for a formal deposition."

"For what? I've done nothing criminal. And you can be damn certain I'm not a suspect. I can provide an alibi a mile long."

"No one's saying you are."

"I don't want anything more to do with this." Gage marched off, disappearing into the lobby.

She sipped her club soda, thinking that she should have ordered it with gin. Gage's last words about his brother pricked her: *We're all just commodities.*

Except for babies. Babies were innocent, vulnerable little liabilities. They had nothing to give and everything to take. A person like Colton would gain nothing from keeping a baby alive and caring for it. Brooklyn would be the biggest burden ever for someone like Colton.

Emily's thoughts spun, doing a one-eighty as she kinked her mind to think like the depraved Colton. Through Nick's experience in China, she'd learned how humans could be treated as commodities, any piece or part bought and sold to the highest bidder.

The sale of human organs was just the tip of the iceberg. Human beings as commodities extended to the modern-day slave trade of sex and human trafficking. There were even black-market adoptions happening right here in the States.

You'll pay for this.

A baby like Brooklyn could yield a large payday on the illegal market. Colton's golden ticket to escape prison and flee the country.

CHAPTER 68

Aditson and his partner Officer Matthews took the hiker's statement and dismissed him back to the trail. It took them nearly two hours on that late Monday afternoon to carefully excavate the body so as not to disturb any vital evidence.

Meanwhile, back at the station, Skylar had looked up the property information and found the land belonged to Thomas Chauncey. He owned 110 acres of field and woods with an old farmhouse built near a private dirt road maintained by the few residents who lived along it. Taxes on the property hadn't been paid in over twenty years, so there was a lien on it, making it vulnerable. But no one had ever come forward with an interest in buying the backcountry land.

Despite the decomposition and dirt, when they uncovered the face, Aditson knew right away who it was. He stepped away from the grave to call Emily. Thankfully, he had caught her in her truck, on her way back to Ann Arbor from Detroit.

"I have news."

"I can tell from your voice it's not good."

"Raven Kane is dead."

"Oh no. Where?"

"Found her in a clandestine grave on the back of the Chauncey property."

"Colton's place?"

"No, his parents, Thomas and Ruby. I can't see the house from where we're located, but I'll be heading there after we finish up here to see if I can find anyone home."

Aditson heard Emily release a heavy sigh. "How was she killed?"

"That's your department."

"I can't believe he got her too," said Emily, making the assumption.

"I know you're tied up across the state right now. How do you want me to handle this?"

"Take her livor temp. And pictures of the body. Then bring her to the morgue. I'll get to her first thing when I get back."

"How was your meeting with Gage?"

"He endured a nightmarish childhood, but I don't think it defeated him."

"A story for another time," Aditson said, looking at the sky, which was turning a soft pink as the daylight dissolved to dusk. "I've got to get this wrapped up here."

"Of course. I was just thinking, though: Who's going to take care of Raven's pet raccoon now?" Emily said with a little laugh.

Aditson grinned. He appreciated Emily's gallows humor at times like this.

CHAPTER 69

"Fascination Street" was a metaphor. As the gray daylight darkened into night, Giggs led Nick to a downtown homeless encampment in an alley off Division Street.

"The bad man is meeting you here?" Nick asked the man.

Giggs pointed to a large park across the street. "Over there."

"When does he come by?" asked Nick.

"When I see him."

"What does he look like?"

"He wears a hood. Always sunglasses."

"Is he tall? Short? Thin? Thick?"

"Taller than me. I don't know if he's fat or not. He wears a lot of clothes."

Giggs was a short man. Nick guessed no more than five feet five. If this was six-foot-one Chauncey, he might seem like a giant to Giggs.

Nick took stock of his surroundings. A cluster of men near a fifty-gallon burning trash barrel was sizing him up.

"You're full of crap, aren't you? You brought me here to get more money out of me."

The man began to hum "Fascination Street." Did this guy know the whole song?

"Bob needs to relieve himself." The man nodded at his mangy mutt, and they took off for the park.

Nick was fairly certain Terrell Nalene wasn't about to show up. Nick was waiting for Colton Chauncey.

He watched Giggs and Bob park the cart a little ways from the barrel and then wander into a fenced-off dog run on the park's south side. Bob pranced alongside him happily. Dogs were easy to please and had no awareness of the social or economic status of their owners.

Nick scurried from the encampment and headed to the other, more forested side of the park. Picnic tables and built-in grills dotted the landscape. Nick tried to look inconspicuous as he leaned against a tree to observe any activity in the park.

He kept an eye on Giggs and Bob. They lingered in the dog run for close to half an hour. Bob proved friendlier than Giggs, happily sniffing every canine he came into contact with. Eventually, Bob and Giggs trailed back to the homeless encampment.

Nick planted himself atop a picnic table and faced the encampment. As darkness fell, he kept a lookout. More carts and characters joined, but no one appeared that resembled either Terrell Nalene or Colton Chauncey.

Nick curled atop the picnic table. He struggled to stay awake, and hunger pangs returned. He hadn't taken his antibiotics in several days. He couldn't remember where he'd put them. His face glistened with perspiration, and his midsection felt warm. A slight fever was setting in.

Nick used his phone to search for the closest take-out restaurant. Lebanese. He craved a lamb-kofta plate. He called and gave them the park as his address.

"We will only deliver to that park if you pick up the order by the restrooms."

The public restrooms were on the north side, and he calculated that it was a ten-minute walk to the other end of the park.

"I'll add twenty to the tip if you deliver to the picnic tables on the south side," he told the cashier.

"Hold on."

Nick heard the cashier's muffled voice checking in with the driver. Then: "That's fine. We'll need payment now, though."

He placed the order and gave them a credit card number, his gaze never leaving the homeless encampment.

"That'll be twenty to thirty minutes."

"Fine. I'll be here. Tell the driver to call me, and I can meet him at the curb."

While he waited and watched, another two shopping carts rolled up.

Their owners seemed to be a couple. They unpacked sleeping bags, one from each cart, and laid them on the ground side by side. In the midst of the camp, the newly arrived man poured a box of trash into a trash can fire, and the flames leaped several feet above the rim.

Several others joined them, warming their hands. Light from the flames illumined the camp, and a movement off to the side drew Nick's attention.

Nick saw a figure approaching Giggs. He was dressed in a long robe with a scarf covering his head and face. The outfit draped his body, rendering him a shapeless form.

Bob barked as he approached. Giggs turned from the trash can fire.

The figure hovered over him in a demanding posture.

Nick strained to get a better look. Just then, his phone rang in his coat pocket: the Lebanese delivery guy. He tapped ignore to shut it down and glanced back at the action in the encampment.

The robed and hooded figure stood in front of Giggs, who was now desperately fumbling for something in his trench coat pocket.

This was the pickup. Colton Chauncey!

Nick launched himself off the picnic table and sprinted across the uneven lawn of the park toward the street. He dashed over the curb only to be met head-on by blinding headlights. A car horn blasted. Nick froze, shielding his eyes from the high beams.

"Are you Bernie?" yelled the delivery driver. Nick had given a false name.

He jogged up to the driver's side. "Yeah." The delivery guy was glaring at Nick and holding out a food bag. "Thanks."

The guy curled his lips in disgust. "Guess the streets are treating you pretty good, buddy." He hit the gas and peeled away.

Nick's glance flashed back to the encampment. The hooded figure was quickly moving away from the crowd. He looked back at the trash can and saw Giggs wheeling his cart away from the camp. Bob was perched in the seat, barking.

Nick flung his glance back to the hooded figure, who was now hurrying down the alley, away from the encampment. The man shed his robe, and Nick recognized Chauncey, confirming his theory that he had been stealing Terrell Nalene's Social Security checks.

Chauncey picked up speed, sprinting across the street to disappear into another alley. He would be out of sight if Nick didn't move on him right now. Just as Nick launched off the curb, a homeless man intercepted him, his face taut with hunger.

"Can you share some of that?" the man asked Nick.

Nick shoved the bag into the man's hands. "Here. Enjoy."

When he glanced up, Chauncey was gone. Nick raced toward the alley.

CHAPTER 70

After sending Raven's body to the morgue with the ambulance team, Aditson and Officer Matthews headed to Thomas Chauncey's home. The light had long ago faded as they climbed up the long drive. An old farmhouse appeared before they were met with a strange, awe-inspiring view, even in the dark.

Rows and rows of brown sunflower stalks stood like headless soldiers. Aditson slowed the patrol car as they approached and scanned the expansive property. Flower stalks covered the entire garden and yard.

"It must be incredible when they're all in bloom," Aditson told Officer Matthews.

"I'll bet it takes weeks to plant this many flowers," Matthews responded. "They're annuals, you know. Have to be replanted every year. An incredible feat for anyone, let alone an elderly person."

Matthews searched the exterior of the home while Aditson went inside. He found no evidence that a man—the one named by the deed, Thomas—was living here. No men's boots or shoes were set by the door. Nor were there men's coats hanging in the coat closet. The bathrooms showed no signs of men's toiletries. He assumed the man's wife, Ruby Chauncey, was still living here, but no one seemed to be home. He was struck, however, by how little food was in the house. He sorted through the trash. His heart skipped a beat when he found an empty baby-formula can in the bin.

Had Brooklyn been here? Was she here now?

"Aditson, you need to see this," Officer Matthews called from the backyard.

Aditson went out the back door and saw Officer Matthews standing near a mound of dirt in the center of the yard with his flashlight pointed into a hole in the ground. A shovel was resting next to it. It struck him as odd that someone would have dug up the ground here in late fall. It wasn't planting season.

But Matthew's grim look told Aditson that this was no garden plot.

CHAPTER 71

Nick sprinted across the street and into the alley, but there was no trace of Chauncey. He darted down the alley, making a sharp right on the side avenue intersecting busier Division Street, guessing that Chauncey would want to blend into the emerging bar scene.

Nick picked up his pace, his gaze stretching ahead, and he spotted Chauncey jogging up the sidewalk into a gentrified neighborhood, where residents were returning home from work. The streets were clogged with cars, bikes, and pedestrians. Nevertheless, Nick did his best to chase him, even as his lungs were burning a hole through the center of his chest.

Up ahead, he could have sworn Chauncey made a left at the end of the block. But with his compromised lungs, Nick had to slow and could only muster a jog. Soon even this pace left him winded. Eventually, Nick's lungs forced his legs into a brisk walking pace, and he was panting like a marathoner. He zigzagged through a pop-up stadium where a folk-rock band was gathering fans. By the time he reached the end of the block and made the turn, Nick had lost his target and was gasping for air. He made his way at a fast walk another three blocks, moving into a highly concentrated residential area that boasted newly built multiuse apartments. The area was teeming with the afterwork crowd. Nick resigned himself to the fact that he had lost Chauncey. And his body was spent.

He sat down on a bench and tried to think like Colton Chauncey. The rat would want to cash that check and get out of Rock River as soon as possible. No way he would cash it in Freeport. He'd be spotted in an instant. If Nick had to guess, Chauncey would stay here in Rock River, hiding out until businesses opened tomorrow morning and he could get his money.

After he felt his pulse return to normal, Nick rose and made his way back to his truck. Even at a slow walk, he was struggling for breath. He sucked it up. Hadn't he endured much worse than this? He set his focus on returning to the river.

CHAPTER 72

Emily arrived back at the U of M, as promised, just in time to head out with the forensic student group for pizza dinner. She and Samantha Eckhardt kicked back in a booth to chat about the latest developments in IGG while twenty high school students devoured a mountain of pizzas and gallons of soda at a nearby family-style table. The U of M's forensic anthropology department was currently the only one in the country with a program to train researchers to utilize genetic genealogy in crime investigation. Emily was impressed and wondered if Flora might have a future here in four years.

The next morning, Emily went with Flora to the lab. Dr. Eckhardt assigned them to a table together.

"I don't want to interfere," Emily said, stepping back. "This is Flora's show." Her niece had partnered with Ethan, a senior from upstate who wanted to study biology at U of M next fall.

Dr. Eckhardt started the class by reviewing the previous day's experiments. After morning lectures on DNA-testing and IGG practices, each student had taken part in a demonstration on how to extract DNA from their saliva. By the end of the lab, every student had created an STR pattern of their own individual DNA.

Today the class was diving into the digital lesson: how to use genealogy databases to produce a candidate lead and make a match.

Because extracting DNA from bone matter was a time-consuming process that could take days, Dr. Eckhardt had taken it upon herself to process a genome sequencing from the DNA of Flora's found bone before the workshop began. The results had been returned just in time. Samantha presented them to Fiona and Ethan, informing them that their job today was to learn how to upload the profile to GEDmatch Pro and FamilyTreeDNA and conduct a search.

"I want you to have realistic expectations," Dr. Eckhardt told the team. "You may not leave here today with a candidate lead. The point is to become familiar with how the matching process works." She mirrored her computer on the large classroom screen and clicked through a demonstration on how to upload DNA samples.

Flora and Ethan followed along as Emily watched over their shoulders.

"Let's divide and conquer," Flora told Ethan. "I'll take GEDmatch Pro. You upload to FamilyTreeDNA."

Ethan agreed. In a few clicks, the bone's DNA profile was entered into the two databases. Dr. Eckhardt made the rounds to ensure each team was on track and had their profiles loaded correctly.

"Excellent. Now the tedious part," she told the class.

Flora and Ethan were glued to their screens. When Dr. Eckhardt called for a fifteen-minute break, Flora opted to stay at her desk.

"You sure you don't want to come outside and get some

fresh air?" asked Emily, but then she stayed back with her niece after the room had cleared.

Flora was hunched over the keyboard, fingers moving at lightning speed, eyes darting back and forth across the screen. Emily noticed an urgency in Flora that she had never seen before.

"Flora, don't you even need a bathroom break?"

The girl shook her head. "What if this were your child or sibling or best friend who had gone missing, never to be heard from again? Wouldn't you want to know as soon as possible?"

"I suppose you're right." Emily proudly watched her niece scroll through profiles, her attention locked on the screen. "I'm going to find a vending machine. You want anything?"

Flora didn't hear her even after Emily repeated herself. "I'll get you a snack and some water," she called back at her niece as she exited the lab. Flora had to be hungry. Or she would be, once she peeled herself from that computer.

Emily traveled down the hall and descended to the main classroom level. She loved the feeling of being at a university. Learning spaces held good energy for her. She found a poorly stocked vending machine near the restrooms. It took her five minutes to decide which was the better nutritional choice: Cheez-Its or Fritos. She bought both. The water bottles were out of stock, so she purchased the orange Gatorade and immediately regretted it. What was she thinking? She hated sugary beverages. Maybe Flora would drink it. She took her time and a different route meandering back to the lab, hoping she'd stumble across a better-stocked snack machine. She didn't. By the time she returned to the lab, Emily had scarfed down the Fritos and half the bottle of Gatorade. She attributed her unhealthy choices to stress.

Emily paused in front of the lab door, feeling a little sick from all the sugar. The queasy feeling intensified. Maybe she should find a bathroom. A burp surfaced, and the feeling passed. Emily grabbed the handle to open the door, struck by the sudden feeling she had gone to the wrong room. It was quiet. Too quiet.

She peeked inside to find Dr. Eckhardt and the class huddled around Flora's desk. The students were so tightly packed together that Emily couldn't see her niece. *Is she okay?* Emily hurried over and peered over the muted crowd.

Dr. Eckhardt sat beside Flora. The two of them were beaming while looking at Flora's laptop screen.

"What's going on?" Emily asked, breaking the silence.

Flora jumped at her aunt's voice and turned to find her at the back of the crowd. The brilliance of discovery filled her face. "I found out who the arm bone belongs to."

CHAPTER 73

Tuesday morning Colton drove to Ruby's. He ditched his pickup for his father's 1998 Oldsmobile sedan, abandoned in the barn. The battery was dead, and he had to siphon gas from his truck into the car, but once he did, it sputtered to life, then purred. They didn't make 'em like they used to. It was a bonus that the classic car was neither registered nor plated.

That afternoon, with Brooklyn in tow, he pulled into the parking lot of the Oak Creek salon, parking in the back near the employee entrance. Then he put his plan into action, opening the Oldsmobile trunk and placing the baby in her car seat inside.

When Colton saw the hairstylist exit the building just after five, he gave the baby a hard pinch and jumped behind a neighboring van. The baby let out a piercing wail, which stopped the young woman mid-stride. A confused look washed over her as she tried to process what she was seeing. The trunk was open, and the baby was sitting inside.

She rushed over in a panic. "Hey, what's wrong, little one?" She bent over to soothe the child. "Where's your mommy?"

The baby stopped crying, and that was when the stylist had her second revelation. "No. You can't be—"

Colton emerged from behind the van and in one swift move shoved the young woman inside the trunk with the baby and slammed it shut. It was the oldest trick in the book.

He got in the car and rolled out of the lot, pleased with himself that he had thought to keep the engine running.

CHAPTER 74

"Whose bone is it?" Emily asked. As she wedged herself through the students crowding around Flora, she noticed the arm bone sitting next to Flora's computer, encased in a clear plastic bag and labeled with the U of M anthropology department. Emily hoped this did not mean Dr. Eckhardt was taking ownership of the remains. Because the bone had been found in Freeport County, it legally belonged to the Freeport County Medical Examiner's Office.

"Looks like you might have a cold case on your hands," said Dr. Eckhardt, sending a reassuring glance to Emily. "Walk your aunt through the case," she instructed Flora.

On the screen of Flora's computer was an old black-and-white, pixelated police sketch of an African American boy in a button-up cotton shirt from the mid-twentieth century. He wore his hair sleek and short.

"His name is Danny Hale, and he disappeared on December twenty-seventh, 1953," Flora explained. "He was just ten years old."

Flora clicked on a series of links that showed the DNA

graphs from the known sample and then a comparison of them with a profile from 23andMe.

"See? They match on twenty-six loci," Flora said, pointing them out on the screen.

"The DNA match appears to be definitive," Dr. Eckhardt said.

"Incredible work, Flora. Whose DNA is it?" Emily asked.

"Henrietta Hale. She's eighty-six years old. Danny is her little brother."

"Is she still alive?" asked Emily, drawn into the excitement.

"We haven't gotten that far. She submitted the test over a year ago. So fingers crossed."

"Danny was last seen in Baldwin," Flora explained.

"If the Hales lived there, then we should start there to track down Danny's sister," said Emily.

"The family was from the South Side of Chicago," Flora corrected. "They came north that year over Christmas break to visit their grandparents."

Emily knew the tiny city of Baldwin well. It was an old village about thirty minutes' drive north of where the Hartfords lived. It was part of Freeport County but was now a nearly vacant community. In its heyday between 1900 and the 1960s, Baldwin and the little town of Idlewild nearby had been known as "the Black Eden," a vacation and entertainment mecca for African Americans who wanted to get away from prying white eyes in cities like Detroit and Chicago. Black entrepreneurs bought up the land and built hotels, cabins, and several nightclubs, like the Flamingo Club, whose shell of a building still stood, a reminder of segregation days. The club had been a world-class entertainment venue, hosting celebrities like Madam C. J. Walker, Della Reese, B. B. King, Jackie Wilson, the Four Tops, and Aretha Franklin over the decades.

Emily had always marveled that such a historical legacy existed almost unknown in the center of her rural county.

"How do you find out this personal history?" Emily looked at Dr. Eckhardt.

"Once we got Danny Hale's name, we accessed national media databases. Often there are news stories that were written about missing loved ones, which help us put together the puzzle of their disappearances and identities."

"The *Lake County Star* ran several articles." Flora clicked onto a digital copy of an old newspaper article.

"What do they say about how he disappeared?" Emily asked.

"The last time his parents saw Danny, he had been heading into the woods to go sledding with his sister. She got tired and returned home, but he wanted to keep sledding. Later that day, a storm front set in off Lake Michigan—a huge blizzard. Over twenty-four inches of snow. They kept waiting, but Danny never made it home. And they couldn't go out and search because the storm and temps were so bad."

"I assume they searched for him later," said Emily.

"For days. The whole town was out looking for him," said Flora.

"The police concluded that he froze to death and was buried under deep snow," added Dr. Eckhardt.

"They must have searched again in the spring after the snow melted," said Emily.

"They did. But again, they found nothing. It's like he disappeared in the storm."

Winters in the middle of the last century had been much harsher and longer than in the last thirty years. Snow piled up for months and did not melt until early May. By the time the snow would have receded, Danny's decomposing body could have been the target of animals that would have distributed his bones all through the woods.

"Dr. Eckhardt says we need to locate Henrietta to notify her and return the bone remnant to the family," said Flora.

"Yes. That is protocol." As Emily glanced again at the bone on the table, an unsettled feeling stirred in her.

"Flora might be the youngest person ever to solve a missing person case with genetic genealogy," said Dr. Eckhardt. "We're going to have fun writing this one up for the journals."

Emily grinned at her niece. "I think you might have a future in this."

"That'd be so flash," said Flora.

Flash?

Flora must have read Emily's confused look. "It means cool."

"Oh. Is that what the *yutes* are saying these days?" Even as Emily teased her niece, dark thoughts swirled in her mind about this boy's real demise.

Knowing the long history of the area and the unexplained nature of the boy's disappearance, and remembering their discovery of the wooden handle, Emily hated to admit that Danny's death might have been overlooked and underinvestigated by the local police and sheriff's office, which she knew did not patrol that side of the tracks with the same degree of interest or integrity they did in whiter parts of the county. Racial attitudes up north had been slow to melt, even after desegregation. Generations later, improvements were on the rise, but far from utopic.

"Nicely done. But—"

"Why does there always have to be a but?" Flora groaned.

"There could be more to Danny's story than those newspaper articles are telling us," said Emily.

"Like what?"

Emily wasn't going to get into it with an audience looking on. "Dr. Eckhardt is right. There might be a case here."

"I knew it! This kid was murdered, wasn't he? You had a look in your eye that day we found the handle," Flora said excitedly, jumping to conclusions.

"Slow your roll, Nancy Drew." Emily gave her a wink. "One step at a time."

"Isn't this exciting, class?" Dr. Eckhardt said. "Flora, I have all the information I need to move forward with an article. I'll be counting on you to help me write it."

"Really? Will my name be on it?"

"You and I will be coauthors."

Flora was beaming. "Thank you, Dr. Eckhardt."

"You may not thank me after you see how much work and editing is involved."

"It'll be a nice résumé builder," Emily added.

"Class, let's get back to work on your samples. I'll be around to help each team." She disbanded the crowd, taking Ethan with her. "Why don't you follow me and observe?"

Emily sat down next to her niece, taking the spot Ethan had occupied.

Once they were alone, Flora turned to her. "You think Danny was killed, don't you?"

"Let's not jump to any conclusions. For all we know Danny Hale may have had a medical amputation on this arm."

"What do we have to do next?"

"We start by finding his sister, making contact, and talking with her to see what else she knows."

"I'll start searching for Henrietta Hale in Chicago."

"I'll work on getting a tool ID." Emily thought of Delia and her expertise in tool analysis, among many other forensic talents. When the Chauncey investigation had settled down, she'd give her a call. She missed her old friend. If anyone understood Nick and what he'd been through, it was Delia, retired FBI field agent who'd spent most of her career in foreign attachés. Delia would have sound advice for her and perhaps for Nick—if he would listen.

CHAPTER 75

Nick stayed in his truck all night and through the next day, surveying Terrell Nalene's apartment building. He'd seen no trace of Chauncey. He was achy and hungry and had to piss, which meant leaving his post for a short time. There was no getting around nature calling. He slipped from the truck and went around the back of the building to relieve himself in the shadows. Coming back to his truck, he rummaged through his backpack and found an old granola bar. He scarfed it down, all the while keeping his eyes on the apartment building. Soon he found himself dozing off.

He woke to his phone buzzing. Darkness had fallen over the city, and a light rain had blurred his windshield. Nick flipped his phone over to read a text from Jasper616.

> Where are you? Someone's breaking in! I'm scared!

Sweat instantly beaded on Nick's skin. He pulled a hunting knife out of the glove box and strapped it to his ankle, then scooped up the gun on the passenger seat and set off.

Nick wheezed as he climbed the cement stairs to the fifth-floor apartment, wanting to hurry but knowing he'd need all his strength for what was to come. He found the door of 504B partially ajar, its frame damaged. Someone—presumably Chauncey—had forced their way in.

Nick's adrenaline surged as he drew his gun and entered the unit's living room.

He stopped to listen and heard a man muttering and a clattering of dishes coming from the kitchen, to the right beyond the living room. He couldn't see into it from where he stood but assumed it was Chauncey in there.

Where was Jasper616?

Nick inched his way across the living room. To his left was a hallway, and at its end the bathroom door was open. But the bedroom door next to it was shut. From behind it came a muffled moan.

Nick rushed as quietly as he could down the hall and tried turning the bedroom doorknob—locked. The cheap lock could easily be forced, but that likely wouldn't go unnoticed.

Colton Chauncey was the imminent threat, and Nick should deal with him first.

In that split second, as he was about to head into the kitchen, he thought about protocol. He should call for backup. But if he stepped out to do so, he'd risk Chauncey hearing him, escaping, or, worse, killing Jasper616.

No, he couldn't leave Jasper616. He had to act alone. And right away. He took off the safety and padded down the hall.

When he got to the living room, Nick realized the noises from the kitchen had stopped. It was eerily quiet, and he had the feeling he was being watched. He froze in place, his heart ramming the inside of his chest cavity. Even at a standstill, he was becoming winded. The thought flashed through his mind that his lungs might give out, and he wouldn't have the strength to save himself.

From the kitchen came a guttural roar so unnerving that it jolted Nick from his stance and caused him, in that brief second, to lower his weapon.

Before he knew it, Chauncey had launched himself at Nick, eyes glazed and pupils wide with death. He lunged at Nick with the strength of two men. Nick was overpowered as Chauncey slammed him to the floor of the living room.

Nick felt his gun slip from his grip and fly under the couch.

Chauncey seemed a man possessed as he boomed a stream of nonsensical words.

Nick tuned out. He knew what to do in these situations. Keep a calm head. Brace every muscle in resistance. And fight.

Rage and adrenaline seemed to course through Chauncey as he ramped up his attack on Nick, slamming his head into the floor over and over. Nick used every last resource available to his weakened respiratory system to pull himself out of the fight. They were equally sized in height, but Chauncey outmassed him in muscle and strength.

Nick refused to see this disadvantage and held on, stiffening his torso, neck, and head—which made it harder for Chauncey to slam him into the floor. The ratty shag carpet also offered a slightly soft surface that protected Nick's skull from fracture.

When Chauncey realized his efforts were not working, he changed tactics by wrapping his abnormally giant hands around Nick's neck. He squeezed, and Nick felt his windpipe caving.

If he didn't get out now, he'd be suffocated.

Nick had one thing Chauncey didn't: pent-up remnants of his hostile overseas nightmare that were about to find purchase. A visceral revenge surged in him. Flailing his arms, Nick tucked his legs up, curled his core, and rocked his body with all his might. The momentum gained him the leverage he needed to set Chauncey off balance. He grabbed his attacker under the armpits and flipped his body off him. The move took Chauncey by surprise, giving Nick the chance to launch himself upon him, pinning him to the floor next to the sofa.

Chauncey swept his long left arm under the sofa to search for Nick's gun. With his right hand, he grabbed Nick by the throat again and clenched.

Nick slammed his right knee over Chauncey's arm, pinning it down, at the same time reaching for the knife strapped to his ankle. Chauncey grunted, and the flames in his eyes blazed hotter. He tightened his grip on Nick's windpipe. Nick knew he had only seconds before he'd pass out. He thrust the knife into Chauncey's chest. His blood coursed out, but Chauncey did not let up. Nick stabbed at the arm that was strangling him. And still, the brute's deadly clasp choked Nick. He had only moments left. Nick's lungs spasmed in pain as he drew from every reserve. He had no other choice: He plunged the knife into Chauncey's throat.

The man let out a guttural cry, and his fingers released Nick, who heaved for breath. Chauncey's body twitched as it went into death shock, his lungs filling with his own blood and suffocating him.

Nick peeled himself off the body.

He needed to find Jasper616.

CHAPTER 76

Emily and Flora had planned to stay another night on the campus, but with Raven Kane's body waiting in the morgue, Emily had to cut the trip short. They were leaving after dinner. Flora's success had given Emily a short respite from worry over the Chauncey case. But as she waited—in the driver's seat of her Yukon, outside the U of M dormitory—for Flora to say her goodbyes to her new forensic friends, a tidal wave of dread came over her.

She tooted the horn for Flora to hurry up. One last group hug, and Flora jogged over to hop into the truck. They started their three-hour drive back to Freeport.

"So did you and your friends make plans to get together again soon?" Emily asked Flora.

When there was no answer, she glanced over at her niece and found her fast asleep. Emily recognized the exhaustion of a job well done. It was one of the most satisfying sleeps there was.

She pulled onto the entrance ramp of the highway, set the cruise control, and settled in for the ride. She had to get out of her thoughts about Raven Kane's impending postmortem.

Victim number four. Emily fiddled with her Sirius stations, flitting between news, comedy, and eighties hair rock. Nothing could take her mind off the string of potential victims still out there, fearing for their lives: Gage, Peyton, Ivan, André, Bradley the raccoon—and, obviously, Brooklyn. Five minutes later, Emily turned off the radio and drove in silence.

She couldn't keep herself from dialing Nick's cell. The call went straight to voicemail. To call again would be futile, but she did it anyway. Same result. The only way to tamp down her worry was to retrace her steps and see if she could plot a path forward.

The search for Brooklyn was foremost in her head. She shifted her jittery thoughts that direction, sorting through all she knew about baby Brooklyn. Who had seen her or been with her before she'd disappeared besides her mother? Emily went over the details about that night they'd both gone missing, and she recalled what Sadie had told her at Brown's Bakery, what Bradley had said about their plan to pick her up. Brooklyn had been with Savannah that Saturday night when Laney, her cousin, had dropped them off at Jonah's. From what Bradley said, Laney was supposed to have taken Brooklyn while Savannah hid up north. But instead, Savannah had kept Brooklyn with her. What had caused her to deviate from the plan? The night Savannah disappeared from Jonah's trailer, Laney had dropped her off at Jonah's. But she had begged her cousin to let her take Brooklyn for the night. Why so adamant? Being the protective cousin, it made sense that she felt Savannah was putting herself and her baby in danger by hanging out at Jonah's. Or did Laney have a premonition Chauncey might show up again now that his trial was near?

Where was Laney now? How had she been overlooked?

Emily dialed Skylar's cell, hoping she'd pick up after work hours.

CHAPTER 77

Colton Chauncey was supine on the living room floor, lying in an ever-widening pool of blood as Nick stooped over him, panting, trying to catch his breath. He felt the sticky moisture on his face and arms, blood from Chauncey's arterial spurting. Thoughts marathoning around his brain were so bifurcated he couldn't have spelled his own name if asked. He was brought back to the present when he heard footsteps from the hallway outside the apartment.

"What's going on in there?" a man's voice called out. "I'm calling the police!"

Nick pulled himself away from the grisly sight of dead Colton Chauncey and rushed toward the bedroom, using his remaining strength to crash through the bedroom door.

Jasper616 was tied to the bed, eyes and mouth sealed with duct tape.

"It's okay. It's me, Agent Larsen. One of the good guys."

Jasper moaned.

"I've got you. Hang on." Nick quickly untied the teenage boy and helped him to his feet. The boy looked at the bloody Nick, shell shocked.

"Are you okay?" Nick asked. "Did he hurt you?"

Jasper616 shook his head.

"What happened?"

"He busted in here. Looking for that box," Jasper616 said, struggling against tears. "Said he was gonna kill me and toss me into the river, like he did with Terrell."

"You knew all along?" Nick said softly.

Jasper nodded.

"What box are you talking about?"

"Terrell's money. He kept it here, didn't trust banks." Jasper616 began to hyperventilate.

Nick sat him on the bed. "Head between your knees and breathe."

Jasper616 took several deep inhales, and eventually his breathing evened out. He sat up and stared at Nick.

"You know where it is, don't you?" asked Nick.

"It's gone. All of it."

"How much was in there?"

"Enough."

"What'd you do with it?" Nick pressed as gently as he could under the pressure of the moment.

"My older sister. She's nineteen. After Terrell died, I found her on the streets living with her boyfriend. But he wasn't really her boyfriend—if you know what I mean."

She was a commodity. Nick understood that.

"And you gave the money to her? It's probably all been stolen by her boyfriend."

"No way. I'm not stupid, dude," Jasper616 snapped back. "I handled it. I got her out of here and got her an apartment in southern Indiana, where she's studying to be a vet assistant."

"Oh," Nick said, swallowing a heaping spoonful of pride. "Sorry I misjudged you."

"Everyone does. Why should you be any different?"

Jasper616 rose and took a few wobbly steps forward. Nick reached out to steady him. "Let's get you some water." He started to lead the teen into the living room before he remembered the dead body in the middle of the room. He stopped, but it was too late.

Jasper let out a cry. "What'd you do?"

"He was going to kill me," Nick hissed at him. "And he would have killed you too!"

Jasper backed away from Nick. "This is wicked messed up."

"You don't know what this guy's done."

"I'm out." Jasper616 dodged Nick. He snatched his backpack, which had been dropped near the front door, and ran from the apartment.

CHAPTER 78

After she dropped Flora at home shortly after 11:00 p.m., Emily went to the police station to meet up with Skylar. She had news that she didn't want to share over the phone. She found Skylar at her desk in front of her computer with a grim look.

"I started by calling Laney's family here in Freeport. Her younger sister, Celia, answered."

Emily remembered Sadie mentioning Celia was a senior at Freeport High.

"When I asked her for her sister's phone number, she broke down in sobs."

Emily's gut twisted.

"She said she hasn't heard from her since this morning. Laney's not answering her phone or texts."

"Why was she so upset? That was only like twelve hours ago."

"She and Laney are close. It isn't like them not to text and call all day long. Celia thinks something bad has happened."

Had Emily's instincts been right? She thought about how Chauncey had been at the Walmart in Oak Creek.

"Her roommate last saw her leave for work this morning. Nothing seemed out of the ordinary."

"Have you had a chance to track Laney's calls today?" Emily asked.

"Yup. I got a call record from the phone provider. The last call out from her phone was today at four forty-seven p.m. at the salon."

What had happened in six hours to Laney Browdey? "Who was the call to?"

"Laney was calling an Italian restaurant, Bella Lago, for pizza takeout."

"And did she ever pick it up?"

"Nope. According to the hostess at Bella Lago, her order's still sitting in the kitchen, wrapped and ready to go. But they charged her card."

"Please tell me there's surveillance cameras at the salon."

"Fingers crossed. The salon owner's name is Katie Gerrig. She was my next call."

"Give me the number," said Emily. The caller ID would show it was from the Freeport Police. She prayed Katie Gerrig would be awake and pick up at this late hour.

"Hello?" a groggy woman on the other end said.

"Hello, Ms. Gerrig? This is Dr. Emily Hartford. I'm with the Freeport Police Department. I'm sorry to bother you this late," Emily said.

"I'm sorry. Why are you calling me?" Katie had panic in her tone.

"We may have a potential emergency situation, and I'm trying to locate an employee of yours, Charlane Browdey?"

"You mean Laney?"

"Yes. Do you happen to know where she might be?"

"Have you tried her cell?"

"I have. Her voicemail's picking up."

"She's probably in bed. Like I was."

"Do you know what time she left work today?"

"She works till six. But her last client was a no-show. So she left a little early. Maybe around five? I don't remember exactly."

"And does your shop have security cameras?"

"Several. Inside. And all around the building."

"Do you mind if I take a look at the footage from today?"

"Now?" Katie said.

"If that's okay."

"Is Laney in trouble?"

Emily wasn't going to explain. "I can be at the salon in thirty minutes."

"Sure." Katie Gerrig hung up.

Emily turned to Skylar. "Thanks so much. You should really ask Aditson for bonus pay."

Skylar smiled. "Oh, believe me, I will."

She had no sooner said it then Aditson buzzed Emily.

> On my way to Rock River. New
> case development. Call you
> when I have more.

Emily stared at the screen. So many questions arose. Why hadn't he asked her to go with him? What was he holding back? Did it have to do with Nick? Something else shifted underfoot. She'd have to hunt down Laney alone. Nothing about that seemed safe.

"Everything okay, Dr. Hartford?" Skylar asked.

"Can you stay on duty for a bit longer?"

"I'm here if you need me."

Emily sailed out, troubled by Aditson's text but even more worried about Laney. Emily might be Laney's only lifeline. She had no idea why Chauncey would go after her, but if he stayed true to his track record, Laney's life was going to end soon.

CHAPTER 79

Nick sat on the sofa, staring at Chauncey's body.

In the distance, thunder rumbled. Wind howled through cracks in the unsealed apartment windows, and his mind shadowed with memories as dark and thick as the looming thunderclouds.

He heard a single fly buzz into the room and join the swarm around the newly decayed flesh. The sound tweaked at Nick's brain, rewinding it like a scratchy VHS tape and causing everything in front of him to morph into a nauseating blur.

Em. Em!

Nick reached for his phone and called her. It went to voicemail. He left a message, then hung up. He dialed Roe, who didn't pick up either. Nick left another message, giving him Terrell's address and nothing else. Roe would know what to do. He slid the phone into his back pocket. Glancing back at Chauncey's body, he felt constriction from his chest up to his throat. His pulse quickened, and the sharp pain in his lungs returned. Shallow inhales followed. An irrational panic overtook him. Approaching sirens could be heard.

I gotta get out of here.

Nick fled the apartment, leaving the entrance to his destruction wide open. He raced down the staircase and lunged from the exit onto the sidewalk. *Head for the river. The river is freedom!* It would take him north. Home. That was all he wanted: to go home.

Hard rain came down, blurring his path, but he pressed on, tripping over ruts in the ground and uneven sections of the cement sidewalk.

There was no stop button. As lightning flashed around him, Nick saw a skeletal form of himself on the grassy riverbank, foraging for food. He looked away and picked his way down to the river's edge as the sky above opened up and more rain flooded down, drenching every centimeter of his clothing.

Another flash. Nick saw his prison self rejoicing over a dead bird found under a bush.

Another flash. He cooked its carcass, skewered on a stick, over a firepit.

Another flash. He pinched his nose to overcome the awful smell of the burning fowl. He picked shreds of meat from its charred body, then retched it back up.

Nick pushed through the foggy memories, moving one soggy foot in front of another along the muddy bank and finding himself back in the present, fighting winds that sent small sticks and leaves flying past him.

His feet didn't stop until he heard shouts behind him.

"Agent Larsen, freeze. Hands to your sides!"

He placed his palms on the sides of his legs. But he didn't turn around.

"Belly to the ground!"

He wasn't afraid. In fact, a rush of relief flooded over him as he knelt, then flattened his belly to the earth, pressing his hands behind his head.

It was finally over. He could stop running from himself.

CHAPTER 80

Emily arrived at the salon at 11:45 p.m. and waited for Katie Gerrig. She pulled up to the back door at twelve after midnight, and Emily followed her into her small office space at the rear of the salon. Katie started her computer and clicked onto the app that held the building's security footage. She selected the time frame—between four thirty and five thirty Tuesday afternoon—and a camera that showed the parking lot from the back door of the salon. Katie scrolled through the timeline until they saw a young woman exit the building at 5:07 p.m.

"Is that her?" Emily asked excitedly.

"Yes, that's Laney."

Emily leaned in for a closer look. Laney was a petite girl with spiked dark hair. She had on jeans, wedged black boots, and a white puffer coat. Her small handbag hung across her chest, and she was looking at something on her phone. Emily hated that the girl wasn't paying more attention to her surroundings. Situational awareness was the first line of personal defense.

"I have all the girls park in the far row so we can leave space near the door for the clients," Katie explained as they watched

Laney cutting through the lot, focused on her screen. All of a sudden, her head jerked up. Something had caught her attention. She stopped in her tracks and looked around. Then she made a sharp right and headed toward a car parked three spots away from where she was standing. It was an older powder-blue Oldsmobile sedan with its trunk open. The car was facing the camera, so when Laney went around to the back, she disappeared from their view.

"What's she doing?" Katie said, baffled by the scene unfolding in front of them.

Suddenly, a man that Emily recognized as Colton Chauncey leaped out from behind a van next to the sedan.

"Oh my God!" Katie shrieked.

Emily's eyes were glued to the screen.

Moments later, Chauncey slammed the trunk closed and jumped into the driver's side.

"That man just kidnapped Laney!"

The sedan's headlights went on, and the car pulled out of its spot.

"I can't believe it." Katie's face was white with shock.

"Make sure that footage is saved with backups."

"How did you know she was in trouble?" Katie turned to Emily.

"I have to make a call," Emily told her, walking out. She slipped outside the building, not wanting Katie to overhear. When she looked at her phone, she saw Nick had left a message. How had she missed the call? Checking her phone, she realized it was on silent. She tapped the play arrow on the message.

"Hey, Em. Ah, first, I'm okay. But I needed to tell you before you hear from anywhere else. Chauncey's dead." There was a long pause. She heard a sniffle. A cough. Then the message cut off.

Emily stood at the back of the building, staring at the salon's empty parking lot and struggling to make sense of the CCTV footage she'd just seen and Nick's message.

But where was Brooklyn? And Laney?

Emily called Aditson.

"At seven minutes after five yesterday afternoon, Chauncey kidnapped Laney Browdey, Savannah's cousin," blurted Emily. "And now . . . Chauncey is dead."

"Yes. I'm at an apartment in Rock River with his body."

"How did he die?"

"That's for the ME to determine. And that ME will be you."

"What? Why? They have their own MEs."

"Agent Roe wants you to do it. The body will be shipped back up to Freeport County, where the case originated."

Emily swallowed down the news, trying to hold herself together. "Nick left me a cut-off message. Do you know where he is?"

There was a pause on the line before Aditson said, "Emily, Nick killed Chauncey."

"How do you know that?"

"He made a verbal admission. This incident is under FBI investigation, and there's a good chance it will result in legal action. The FBI is already sending out their legal defense team."

"Where's Nick right now?" Emily demanded.

"County jail. He's been arrested on homicide charges."

"No. It can't be. Surely if he did it, it was in self-defense!"

Aditson exhaled. "He fled the scene. They had to stop him at gunpoint."

Emily groaned. An autopsy of Chauncey's body would be crucial evidence for or against a self-defense plea. She braced herself mentally for what was to come. She would have to be extra meticulous. Record everything. There was no room for error.

"Where are you now?" Aditson broke into her thoughts.

"Oak Creek. At Laney's salon."

"Let's concentrate now on finding Laney and Brooklyn," Aditson said. "I'll meet you there."

Emily's hand drifted from her ear, and she hung up without knowing what she was doing. Her head throbbed at the base of her skull. She paced the parking lot, her mind whirring through the trail of victims. All of the dead—except Jonah Hampton and Hank Shepherd, who were just in the wrong place at the wrong time—had served a specific purpose for Chauncey.

Raven.

Ruby.

They were Brooklyn's caretakers. Chauncey had needed them to watch Brooklyn while he was hiding away, making his plans, and trying to get his money.

Emily stood in the parking lot, tracing Chauncey's steps from the time of Jonah's and Savannah's murders. After he took Brooklyn from Jonah's trailer, he had brought the girl to Raven, who was already on the outs with him. She must have gotten wind of his crime and decided to dump the baby at Ruby's. It was the one place she knew the baby might have a chance and be hidden from society. Chauncey took the baby from Ruby, but then he needed another caregiver. There was no one left to turn to in Chauncey's small circle. It had to be someone from Savannah's.

Laney.

Savannah and Laney were close. There was a good chance Chauncey would have seen Laney with Savannah somewhere along their path. Most likely it was at Chauncey's initial court hearings. Of course, Laney would have gone with Savannah to support her. Perhaps Chauncey took note of Laney then. It would be hard for Chauncey not to notice how much Laney cared for Brooklyn and Savannah during those courtroom moments.

Fast-forwarding, Emily recognized Chauncey's clever calculation to bait Laney at the parking lot. Laney would have been in such shock to see Brooklyn alive that it would have clouded all judgment and thoughts of safety.

However, now that Chauncey was dead, Emily couldn't be sure the two of them were still alive.

What had Chauncey done with Brooklyn and Laney?

What if he had been keeping them somewhere else while he was in Rock River? A temporary location that wasn't his home, the fishing shack, or Ruby's place. It had to be in a remote area with little to no public access. It wouldn't be a place that was new to him. He had to be assured no one would come across his captives.

Emily's train of thought was disrupted by a titanic dog bark behind her.

She spun around to see it was only a man meandering across the parking lot with his colossal Saint Bernard.

Shame on her for not heeding her own warning to pay better attention to her surroundings.

The dog barked again, fraying Emily's worn nerves. Glancing over her shoulder at the dog, she thought of Shepherd's dog, Milton.

It was only a hunch, but she reasoned there was one place Chauncey could have hidden Laney and Brooklyn. A place Colton Chauncey would have known well, because he'd spent so much time there as a kid. A place no one would ever consider looking because it had already been investigated as a crime scene.

Emily ran for her truck.

CHAPTER 81

It was 1:30 a.m. when Emily approached Lake Isabella. She parked near the trailhead and dashed off a text to Aditson before she hiked her way through the dark to Hank Shepherd's property, where there was no more cell service. The cottage was dark, and Emily's fingers began to tingle as she got closer. Perhaps it had been unwise to come alone. But it was too late now.

She saw Hank's unfinished porch project, tools lying right where he'd left them.

Emily found the door unlocked and crept in slowly. "Hello! Laney? Anyone here?" It didn't take her long to search Shepherd's tidy seven-hundred-square-foot cottage.

She walked around the back of the cottage and saw double metal doors that led to a Michigan basement—a structure sunken underground like a basement but shallow like a crawl space. They never had enough light, and they always felt damp and musty. Michigan basements creeped Emily out, but she quashed her phobia and lifted the heavy metal door.

CHAPTER 82

Laney let out a long moan from under duct tape when she saw Emily. She was crouched on the floor of the cellar, tied to a post with just enough rope that she could reach the car seat where Brooklyn was resting.

Emily rushed over to the baby, checking her all over to see if she was hurt or in pain. From what she could determine in the dim light, Brooklyn seemed unharmed. Of course, a pediatric physical would be necessary. She had to get these two to the ER right away.

Emily gently peeled the tape from Laney's mouth.

"Are you hurt?" she asked.

Laney shook her head, too traumatized for words.

"It's okay," said Emily. "You're going to be fine. I'm going to get you out of here." She found a handsaw on the workbench and sliced through the thick rope that bound Laney. Emily took Brooklyn from her car seat, hugging her snugly to her chest. She led Laney out of the cellar and into the light of day.

Laney dropped to her knees, sobbing.

"That's right. Just let it all out. You're safe now, Laney."

Emily joined her on the ground, embracing baby Brooklyn.

Safe at last.

Laney stopped crying and turned to Emily with a panicked look. "He's coming back here!"

Emily wrapped her arm around the girl. "No. He's not. Colton Chauncey's dead. He's never going to hurt anyone ever again."

CHAPTER 83

Emily drove Laney and Brooklyn straight to the emergency room at Freeport Hospital. Laney was placed in a quiet, curtained area with a nurse who never left her side. She insisted that she hadn't been hurt or assaulted and wouldn't let anyone touch her until her mom arrived.

Meanwhile, Emily stayed at Brooklyn's side in a separate, curtained-off area of the ER. The baby was swaddled in a white hospital blanket with her little sprig of an arm hooked up to an IV drip. A heart monitor beeped steadily. No major damage had been done, but she was dehydrated, had sustained some bruising, and was very hungry. The baby was downing her second bottle of formula in less than thirty minutes, with another one on the way.

"I can feed her," Emily told the nurse. "I know you have other patients to tend to."

"Are you her mother?"

"No. I'm the one who found her and brought her in. But I'm also a doctor."

The answer seemed satisfactory, and the nurse revealed more:

"Her vitals are good, and blood work should be coming back soon."

"Her grandfather and uncle will be here soon."

The nurse handed Emily the third bottle and left.

Emily stroked her index finger across the little girl's arm. At Emily's touch, Brooklyn turned to her, kicking out her legs and breaking into a broad smile.

"Hi there, little girl." Emily continued the soothing motion.

When Brooklyn grabbed her finger and held on, Emily wanted to give voice to the child's predicament. She wanted to tell her how sorry she was about her mom's death, but that Brooklyn would never have to fear her killer. "You are clearly a survivor and are so strong," Emily said.

Brooklyn's fingers relaxed their grip on Emily's. She cooed and reached for the bottle in Emily's hands. Emily brought the nipple to her lips, and the infant latched on.

"Excuse me? Where can we find Brooklyn Browdey? We were told she was admitted here."

Emily recognized the voice and poked her head past the curtain to see a young man and his father vibrating with anxious emotion. She cleared her throat. "Over here!" She smiled at the two.

Ivan and Peyton Browdey rushed over, and Emily parted the curtain. "Brooklyn is so beautiful and perfect."

Emily saw tears rimming Peyton's eyes.

"Is she all right?" Ivan stammered in a loud, nervous voice. "Did he hurt her?"

"Dad, shhh," said Peyton. "Not so loud."

Emily gently gripped Ivan's arm to reassure him. "No. She's doing great and she's going to be fine." She stepped aside and left the exam area. She made sure the curtain was folded over itself to give them the privacy they deserved. A few seconds later, she heard the sighs and cries of a family being reunited, and it pulled her heart tight in her chest. She exited the ER to compose herself in the hallway.

With Brooklyn safely in the hands of her family, Emily's thoughts shifted. She needed to contact Gage Chauncey, next of kin. Even though he had wanted nothing to do with the baby, they were legally bound to inform him of his daughter's status. Would Savannah have wanted him to be the father to her child? She probably didn't know him well enough to say. And since he was Chauncey's brother, the answer likely would have been no. Emily tapped a tissue around her damp eyes. *Nick.* She wanted to call Nick and tell him Brooklyn was safe and sound. But she guessed his phone had been confiscated in the arrest.

CHAPTER 84

"Dr. Hartford?"

Emily startled awake. Standing in front of her in the hospital waiting room, wearing a suit and tie, was Gage Chauncey. She sat up on the two-seater bench, where she had fallen asleep sometime after 3:00 a.m. She'd been too tired to drive home.

"Gage? What time is it?"

"Just after nine."

Emily shook the sleep off and stood up.

"Laney, is she here?" He had a shaky timbre to his voice.

"Yeah. But—how did you know she was here, in the hospital?" Emily had only told him on the phone that his brother had been killed and his daughter was alive and safe.

"I called Laney's mom after you and I spoke."

"You know Laney?"

"We met a few times when she was in Freeport visiting her cousin and family."

"Of course. Small world." You could always count on the good ol' Freeport gossip train to pull into the station on time.

"Is Laney okay?"

"Laney's in shock but physically unharmed. I can see if she's able to have visitors."

"No. It's okay. I'm actually here to see . . . my daughter."

"Oh. I thought you wanted nothing to do with—"

"I thought I should at least meet her."

"Right. Are you sure?"

"I'm her father," Gage said meekly. "That means something."

Emily glanced back to the curtained area where Ivan and Peyton were doting over the little girl. She sent Gage an empathetic look. "I'm not sure they're going to want you here. But we can try."

CHAPTER 85

"Will I lose my badge?" Nick asked the veteran FBI agent who had joined him in the interrogation room at the Rock River police station Wednesday morning.

"I can't answer that, Nick," said Delia Andrews. "What I do know is that you're suspended for the moment. Later, there will be an internal FBI investigation and a full psych examination, and there's a good chance it'll end up in court." She crossed her arms in front of her chest. The red-haired firecracker of a woman wore black leather pants and black leather boots with spiked heels that added four inches to her petite stature. Her cropped leather jacket showed off her muscular figure. Her domineering presence might have been more intimidating if Nick didn't know her so well. They were long acquainted with one another. Almost like a mother and son.

"It's not what it seems," Nick pleaded. "He was going to kill me."

"It looks to me like you were playing cowboy, but I'm not here to judge that. You'll be assigned legal counsel through the bureau."

"Then why are you here now?"

"Because Dutch couldn't make it."

"He's involved?"

"Trust me. You want him to be."

"How's that?"

"You're in hot water, Larsen."

"I think that the investigation will show that it was self-defense."

"Maybe so. But you went rogue."

Nick felt his throat tighten. "I stepped out of bounds some."

"And I have a feeling you'll continue to do so, if left unchecked."

He looked at her, knowing deep down that she held the key to his future.

"Will you agree to come with me?" asked Delia.

"To do what?"

"It'll take a while to get legal sorted out and determine what's to happen to you. In the meantime, there's a unique plan in place for you. If you choose to accept it."

Nick searched her, hoping she'd tell him more.

"Is that a yes?" she asked.

"Do I have a choice?"

"We always have a choice," she said firmly. "That's the first thing we're going to work on."

"And if I say no?"

Delia gave a small shrug. "It's your funeral."

"I'll go." Nick sighed, resigned.

"Good. We leave now," she said, rising from her chair.

Nick followed her to the door. "Wait. Is there any way I can see Em first?"

Delia didn't change her expression. "Sit back down. I'll see what I can do." She left the room.

CHAPTER 86

"Come with me." Emily led Gage out of the hospital waiting room and into the hallway, where they could chat in private. She wasn't sure if she believed him. His decision to exercise his parental rights seemed knee jerk to her. What was the underlying motive here?

"What's made you change your mind?" she asked him when they were alone.

"Colton is dead. My mom too. I'm free from all that now."

Emily's tone was compassionate but firm. "That's not a strong enough reason to want to be a father."

"I think that being a dad might help me shake off the past. Get a fresh start."

Emily couldn't blame him for that. Not with his family tree. "But you barely knew Savannah."

"True. But she was a nice girl who came from a good, loving family," he said. "I can build off that."

"Can you? Why not just let the baby be with the family who already knows and loves her?"

"Because she's a part of me. Whether I planned it or not."

"No one's going to hold it against you if you want to just move on. Find a nice girl. Start over with her."

"Just abandon my flesh and blood, like my father abandoned us?" He sounded hurt.

"I didn't mean it like that," Emily said. "I'm just trying to understand. And I'm sure the Browdeys will want a good answer too."

"I never told anyone this before." Turning toward Emily, Gage lowered his voice. "One time after Dad beat up Colton real good, Ma went to his room to see to him. She wanted to take him to the hospital, but that wasn't going to happen."

"How bad was it?"

"Broken bones. Internal injuries for sure. Probably several concussions. Colton was slurring his words and drooling."

"That's serious. He could have died."

"Ma was pretty beat up too. But at least she could walk."

"Where were you during all this?" Emily asked.

"Ma put me in the pantry. To hide me from our dad. I wanted to come out and . . . help." Gage cleared the lump in his throat.

"It's not your fault. You would've gotten hurt had you tried," Emily said.

Gage nodded, brushing away a stray tear.

"What did your father do after beating your brother and mother?" asked Emily, struggling to process the terrible tale.

"Dad went outside to the garden to have a smoke. Smoking always calmed him down." Gage's face paled. Emily suspected nightmarish memories had tangled his mind, because he went quiet for some time.

"Do you want to talk about what happened next?" Emily coaxed softly.

"The next thing I knew, I heard two gunshots from upstairs.

I ran up to Colton's room. He and Ruby were on the bed with the hunting rifle between them. Neither of them looked at me. I didn't see any blood, so I knew they weren't shot—" He drifted again into the nightmare.

A frost blanketed Emily, chilling her skin.

"Colton's room overlooked the garden." Gage released an exhale that welled up from the depths of his soul. "I don't think Dad knew what hit him."

"Which one of them—?"

Gage looked away, shaking his head. Emily didn't press further.

"Now that Brooklyn is here. Now that I have a child. I want to do better. To be better."

"This is about you, then?" Emily challenged. "What about what Brooklyn needs? Do you even know what you're getting into?"

"The last thing I want to do is take Brooklyn away from Savannah's family. I just want a chance to be a part of her life," said Gage. "I'm scared to death, but I need to try."

Emily felt it would be an uphill battle, but it was not hers to fight. She squeezed Gage's arm. "Okay. Then let's go see if you can meet your daughter."

CHAPTER 87

Emily prepared for her meetup with Nick on Thursday morning with freshly washed hair styled in loose waves over her shoulders. She wore a light-pink cashmere crew sweater and dark denim jeans.

Please let some of the old Nick remain, she prayed.

One of the officers had placed her in an interrogation room at the Rock River police station. She took a seat and tried to calm her jitters. When Nick was brought in, she tried to stand, but nerves kept her glued to her chair.

Nick was clean shaven, wearing aviator sunglasses and a leather jacket. He looked older than his thirty years. Under it all, he was still that handsome man she had fallen for at age fifteen. That long-ago first-love flutter conflicted with Emily's anxiety.

Nick sat, tossing glances at the walls and floor. He was broken, she could tell. He finally looked at her. "I'm sorry, Em. I know I've been . . . difficult . . ." He wrung his hands on the table. "What's wrong with me?"

Emily slipped her hand around his trembling ones.

"When it was happening—I used to think about us on the

beach, when we were teens." He stopped and drifted into himself. "I lived for days in those moments."

"You mean what happened between you and Chauncey?" she asked.

Nick's gaze wandered to hers. "No, I meant back in China."

"We never have to talk about it again if you don't want to. But I think it would help . . . with everything. Please."

Nick slipped his hand from hers. "I'm remembering more and more. I don't know how long I was in that place. They kept me sedated, and days crept into weeks. I never knew what day it was. Several times I found myself waking up screaming in pain. My chest. My side. Under my ribs. I could see that the incisions were infected."

"Who else was there?"

"There were many doctors and nurses. Never the same ones, though. Or at least I couldn't recognize them in my stupor. They never spoke to me. They took my temperature, my blood pressure, checked my wounds."

"Did you ever get up or call out for help?"

"One hand and one foot were secured to the bed at all times. Except when I needed the bathroom."

"Did you know why they were keeping you there?"

"I was aware only that I was growing weaker each day. I knew I was in a place where organs were being harvested. I guess on some level, I must have known what they wanted. But not to what extent. I was drugged up the whole time I was in there."

Maybe he had been too scared to admit to himself such horrors had been taking place in his own body. Emily kept silent, waiting for him to continue.

"One day a team of doctors examined me, then strapped a yellow plastic bracelet around my wrist, like the kind for bars or events. A guard was placed at my door."

"You were tagged for death."

"I found strength. I don't know how. I used my robe to . . ."

"You had to, Nick."

He blinked back the tears forming. The next part came out rapidly. "I took the guard's jacket and pants and his wallet and ran for the stairwell door. I threw on his clothes, which were too short, but because I had lost so much weight, they fit me. I ran down the stairs and out onto the street. I kept running several blocks until I found someone and asked them which direction to the train station."

"Where did you go?"

"To . . . the sea." Nick's expression tightened.

"The sea?" Emily repeated.

"I got on a container ship and . . ." He was shutting down again.

"And the rest is one big gap year hike across the world." Emily reassured him with a warm look.

He flashed back a quick smile. He knew he didn't have to say another word about it.

"It's a miracle you survived, Nick. Not just in China but just now. Here. But how many more times can you tempt fate?"

"What kinds of monsters treat humans that way?"

"You were going to help expose it."

"Yeah. And instead . . ."

"You still can. You're part of the evidence now."

"Never thought of it that way."

"You can still redeem this."

His gaze went through her. She didn't press further. She would never fully understand what he had gone through. Perhaps it would always be a gap between them. The question now was whether they could bridge that gap and move on.

"I just want to feel . . . like myself again," he said.

"You will." Emily searched for more reassurance to offer him during this fragile moment. But nothing told her for certain that Nick would be okay in the long run.

"My beautiful terror," he said with a smile.

Emily couldn't help but crack a slight grin at the old nickname he'd called her behind her back. She'd never minded.

"Did you tell Agent Roe about your missing lung?"

"He's seen the images. Everything's on the table. All the government agencies have been informed: Congress, World Health Organization, Interpol."

"It's gone global. Good." Emily gave a small sigh. "And now what?"

"I'm not sure what my future career will look like." Nick was holding back tears. "In the meantime, I'm going away for a while."

"Again?"

"Up north to Dutch's compound until I'm fixed. Or so says Delia."

"What are you talking about?" Emily didn't understand what Dutch had to do with all this.

"Dutch has been developing a rather unconventional PTSD reentry program for military and law enforcement. I'm not sure what to expect, but at this point I think it's the only chance I have at getting myself back to normal."

Dutch, no known last name, had chosen a covert location in northeastern Michigan to build his compound after retiring from FBI fieldwork. He worked now on contract with whatever agency hired him, using his tactical skills to unravel the toughest criminal entanglements. He had seen and done it all. And based on how he had swooped in to help with the Blakely kidnapping case, nothing would surprise her about Dutch's methods.

"I trust him," Emily said. "And you should too."

"What about us?" he asked.

"Do you want there to be an us?" Emily would not assume anything about where their relationship was headed. So much had changed in the last forty-eight hours.

"I want to try. If you do."

Emily quaked inside. "How do I know *it* won't happen again?"

"I'm not sure I could even make that promise to myself."

Emily appreciated the honest answer. "If this is going to work," she said, "I need to be let into all of you, even the dark parts."

"I'll try. Will that be enough for you?" he asked, his look desperate and pleading. Nick reached into his jacket pocket and pulled out a box that Emily had once retrieved from the FBI attaché in China. She knew what was in there. "I don't ever want to be without you," he said.

Nick pried the box open, and Emily recognized what was inside immediately. Grandma Larsen's ring. Its center stone was an oval cut, one carat. White-gold band. It embodied a legacy of lifelong sacrifice and love.

"We fought long and hard to get to this moment," Nick said.

Emily nodded. "It's been a marathon of obstacles."

"We've never been the kind of people to shy away from difficult things. Have we?"

"It's not in our blood." She smiled at him.

"Then why not run the rest of this course together?"

She had been trying to keep her mixed emotions and flickers of doubt about him at bay since Nick's return. But now they thickened, like the marine layer of fog that blanketed the Lake Michigan coastline at dawn.

Nick sank to one knee beside her. "Emily Hartford, will you marry me?" His hand was vibrating as he held out the ring.

Emily stared at the familiar piece of jewelry but kept her hands knotted in fists.

"Em, did you hear me? Will you be my wife?"

Emily pressed one fist to her chest. Fear. Longing. Apprehension. Desire. Her emotions were in a cocktail shaker. "I want to . . . but . . . whatever you need to work through has to be unattached from us . . . or the promise of us." She slid her hands under the table, placing them on her lap.

Nick's shaky hands put the ring in its box and then his jacket pocket.

She bowed her head as tears welled. She tried to pinpoint the hesitation in her spirit. Fear of being hurt again. Fear of being left. Fear of being alone. She had never let fear stop her in her investigative life. But with Nick, she didn't want any more fear or surprise. And in light of everything heaped upon them over the previous two weeks, she could not absolutely predict a successful future as husband and wife.

Eventually, she lifted her gaze to his. "Whatever happens, it will never change the fact that I love you." This was her truth and always had been.

Nick rose and took her in his arms. "Please, Em. I don't ever want to be without you again."

In his embrace, she heard his strong, clear lungs and his slightly elevated heartbeat, but this did not concern her. It was a heart's normal reaction to nerves and excitement. She wished she could reassure him that they would have a happy ending.

But she couldn't.

Not yet.

CHAPTER 88

Emily, Anna, Flora, and Fiona went to the animal rescue on Saturday morning. Emily was grateful to have her family at her side. The last time she had been this nervous was before her MCAT.

"Are we crazy for doing this?" Emily asked them.

They stood in front of the kennel that held the giant Great Dane Milton. His nose was pressed into the metal slats, trying to sniff them.

"Can you even imagine what he's been through?" said Anna.

Milton let out a soft whine and scratched at the door.

"He's a beautiful dog," Flora said.

"He's a big dog," Fiona added.

"This is a big responsibility," Emily said, more to herself than her nieces. "We never had a dog growing up."

"Neither did we," Flora said.

And Anna added with disdain for her ex, "Kyle thought they were a filthy nuisance."

"With all four of us chipping in, it'll be easy," said Fiona.

Emily adored her enthusiasm.

Fiona stuck out her hand for Milton to sniff. His long, leathery tongue licked her palm and made her giggle. "Could I ride him?" she asked.

"No," her mother told her, and the rest of them laughed.

"He'll be good protection for us," Emily justified.

"He'll be good company," said Anna, before adding, "something you could use right now."

Emily nodded to the shelter worker that they were ready to meet Milton. The worker unlocked the kennel door and led him out. The dog's head came to Emily's stomach. He was big, all right. But not overactive or jumpy.

"Do we really want something this giant meandering around the house?" Emily asked.

"There's always room for one more," Anna approved.

"Plus, we have plenty of outdoor space," Flora said.

"Think of the giant poops," Emily kidded.

"Ew!" Flora and Fiona cried.

"You can do that job, Aunt Em," said Flora.

Emily held out her hand, and Milton sniffed it, giving his approval. She petted the top of his head, and he looked up at her with gentle dark-brown eyes. His bottom slowly lowered to the floor so that he was seated in front of her.

"I think he's picked you, Aunt Em," said Fiona.

Emily was mesmerized by his stare. Flora tried to get his attention, but he wouldn't take his eyes off Em.

"She is definitely his person," Flora said.

"So what do you think?" asked the rescue worker. "Ready to make this happen?"

Milton pressed himself against Emily's side, as if he had been hers all along.

"I am," Emily said.

And they walked out together.

ACKNOWLEDGMENTS

In gratitude for and memory of Detective Richard (Dick) Miller (DOD 2025-01-08). Forever friend of our Graeser family. Beekeeper, bear hunter, biologist. Gentle spirit. Humorist. Outstanding investigator. Relentless pursuer of justice.

For their stellar research, compiled in a riveting true crime story, a thank-you to L. C. Timmerman and John H. Timmerman, the father and uncle of the real-life victim Rachel Timmerman. If you want to learn more about this real murder case, I highly recommend reading their book, *The Color of Night*.

Special thanks to *The Epoch Times* and their consistent and thorough investigative reporting on the harrowing stories of human-organ harvesting in China. Many of the articles I read in this publication and others inspired my desire to build a plotline around this emerging genocide. We need to continue to shed light on this developing story until human-organ trafficking is fully exposed and eradicated.

Thank you, *Forensic Mag*! I couldn't live without you! So many of the articles I read inform and inspire my work. Like this one: "High School Student Assists in ID of Military Man in

1951 Accident." And congrats to that student, Ethan Schwartz, reportedly the youngest person ever (at the time of writing) to help resolve a case using investigative genetic genealogy. Schwartz took part in the Ramapo College IGG boot camp. Ramapo's camp became the impetus for Flora's forensic workshop at University of Michigan. If IGG interests you, Ramapo College offers an online certificate program for adults. Learn more at https://www.ramapo.edu/igg.

I am most grateful for the people who took the time to share their expertise with me. Thank you to my professional consultants: retired medical examiner and forensic pathologist Dr. Ronald Graeser; fellow author and psychologist Joel Shulkin; and dear friend Dr. Sidney Showers. Thank you to nurse and coroner investigator Joi Wagner, who tolerates my random text questions with patience and humor. Thank you to friend and fellow literature lover Ava Maring, who regaled me with stories of her time working at the Great Wolf Lodge in Traverse City, Michigan. I am also most thankful to my friend Richard Wheater, editor of the Fremont *Times-Indicator*, who provided me with all the press coverage on the Timmerman case, as well as a copy of a handwritten letter from Marvin Gabrion to Mr. Wheater. It's a weird, rambling diatribe that makes little sense but reveals the damaged mind of a monstrous killer.

AUTHOR'S NOTE

The case in this novel was prompted by the real-life case of Marvin Gabrion. In 1996, Gabrion raped and murdered nineteen-year-old Rachel Timmerman at Oxford Lake in Newaygo County, Michigan, my "home" county in northwestern Michigan.

Gabrion left a trail of bodies. Three of his alleged victims have not been found but are clearly connected to Gabrion: his friend John Weeks; another friend, Wayne Davis; Rachel's daughter, Shannon; and Robert Allen, a veteran who Gabrion is believed to have killed to steal his Social Security checks.

Oxford Lake, where Gabrion murdered Rachel Timmerman, is in the Manistee National Forest, which is federal land. The FBI ended up getting involved in the investigation, ultimately arresting Gabrion in the state of New York, where he was committing Social Security fraud. Later the case was tried in a federal court. Gabrion was given the death penalty, the first time this happened in Michigan, which is a non-death-penalty state. *United States v. Gabrion* was therefore a landmark case.

However, at the end of his term, former President Joe Biden commuted the death penalty sentences of thirty-seven federal criminals on death row. Gabrion was one of those thirty-seven. He will remain in prison for life.

You can learn more about the Gabrion case through the book *The Color of Night: A Young Mother, and a Cold-Blooded Killer*; the Investigation Discovery show *FBI: Criminal Pursuit*; the documentary show *Unsolved Mysteries*; and the book *Cause of Death: Forensic Files of a Medical Examiner.*